BENEATH A GOLDEN VEIL

Center Point
Large Print

Also by Melanie Dobson and available from
Center Point Large Print:

Chateau of Secrets

**This Large Print Book carries the
Seal of Approval of N.A.V.H.**

BENEATH A GOLDEN VEIL

MELANIE DOBSON

CENTER POINT LARGE PRINT
THORNDIKE, MAINE

This Center Point Large Print edition is published
in the year 2017 by arrangement with
Amazon Publishing, www.apub.com.

This is a work of fiction. Names, characters,
organizations, places, events, and incidents are
either products of the author's imagination
or are used fictitiously.

The text of this Large Print edition is unabridged.
In other aspects, this book may vary
from the original edition.
Printed in the United States of America
on permanent paper.
Set in 16-point Times New Roman type.

ISBN: 978-1-68324-312-0

Library of Congress Cataloging-in-Publication Data

Names: Dobson, Melanie B., author.
Title: Beneath a golden veil / Melanie Dobson.
Description: Center Point Large Print edition. | Thorndike, Maine :
Center Point Large Print, 2017.
Identifiers: LCCN 2016056205 | ISBN 9781683243120
    (hardcover : alk. paper)
Subjects: LCSH: Large type books.
Classification: LCC PS3604.O25 B43 2017 | DDC 813/.6—dc23
LC record available at https://lccn.loc.gov/2016056205

For my husband
Jon Dobson

Thank you for holding my hand
along this journey.
My heart overflows.

Prologue

April 1844

She birthed her first baby in the early afternoon hours, a beautiful boy who cried out once and then rested peacefully in her arms.

As the midwife cleaned up, Mallie clung to her son as if he might float away into the field below her window. For the first time in her life, she had something—someone—to call her own.

He looked up at her, his hazel eyes searching her face. It was as if he knew he had someone to call his own as well.

She would be a good mama to her child for as long as the master let him stay in the house. She would feed him when he was hungry. Sew him warm clothing to wear when he was cold. Teach him to use his strength for good instead of evil.

She wiped the birthing blood off his arm with her nightgown, his skin dark against the white linen. She'd been praying for months that her baby's coloring would be a beige hue so he could work in the master's house instead of the fields. God hadn't lightened his skin, but He had answered one of her prayers. The child was a boy instead of a girl. For that, she was grateful.

A female slave was expected to do unspeakable

things in this house, things no one ever told her about as she worked for her former missus. It wasn't until after she turned thirteen that the new master called for her. Then she worked solely for him.

Her stomach turned. She couldn't abide by the thought of her child forced to appease the insatiable appetite of that man.

Mallie kissed her baby's forehead.

She glanced toward the door, waiting for the master to visit.

What would he do when he saw their baby? She prayed he wouldn't take him to the market or give him to a slave wet nurse. Mallie wanted to be devoted solely to him.

If she continued to please the master, perhaps he would let her keep their boy, at least until he was old enough to work in the fields.

If her son was sent to the fields—when he was sent—she would pray every day for him. That he would be strong. Courageous. That he would face the future with resolve instead of fear, knowing he was created to be exactly who God wanted him to be.

But she wouldn't think about leaving him now. All she would think about was loving him.

He squirmed in her arms, his lips pressing together.

Across the room, the midwife looked up from her work. The elderly Negro woman helped all the slaves birth their children—inside the plantation house and out in the slave quarters. She knew what babies needed. "Feed him," she commanded.

Mallie unbuttoned her gown, and the baby latched on to her breast. Milk flowed slowly out of her into him. Life-giving liquid to sustain. She smiled as she watched him, knowing she could care for him on her own without the master or the missus. She was his mama.

The boy ate voraciously before releasing her. Then he looked back up, into her eyes, and her heart felt as if it might burst open, joy flooding onto the wooden floor.

The midwife reached for the baby. "I have to clean him, Mallie."

"No!" She never wanted to let him go.

"We'll just be downstairs," the woman said. "I'll bring him back to you when I'm done."

Mallie kissed her son's forehead and both cheeks. His eyes were closed now, and he was content with his full belly and the world around him.

If only she could keep him in this peaceful state forever, cushioning him from the realities ahead.

The midwife slipped her hands under the baby.

"I love you," Mallie whispered to him. "With all my heart."

The midwife lifted him and held him out in front of her as if he were a bundle of sticks or straw. Mallie watched him until he was gone; then she glanced out the window at the pine branch brushing against the glass. For her entire life, she'd longed for a family. Someone she belonged to. Someone to love who would love her in return.

Her mama was gone—she'd been sold almost a decade ago. Mallie remembered the morning Mama had left for the market. She'd waited and waited by the front door for hours for her return, but the master came home alone.

She didn't know the name of her father. As far as she could remember, Mama never spoke about him. Master Jesus, Mama had said, was the only father she needed to know. A master who loved his children.

But now she had family on this earth too, and she'd do her best, in the short time she had, to instill right and wrong in her son so he'd grow up to be a gentleman.

She didn't have a name for him yet. A name meant hope, and she hadn't allowed herself to hope until after he was born. She'd given him life, and now she could give him a name as well.

Her eyes grew heavy. Her body was spent. The midwife had said she must sleep, but she wanted to wait until after her baby was beside her again, safe in her arms for the night.

In the spring breeze, the branch tapped a steady rhythm against the glass. She closed her eyes, listening for the midwife's footsteps in the corridor, for the cries of her son. Sleep beckoned to her as she waited, the weight of exhaustion pressing down. She tried to fight it for only a few more minutes, but her body rebelled against her will, worn out from the labor of bringing a child into this world.

Hours later, she awoke when the chamber door flung open. Morning light flooded through the window and across her narrow bed.

Rising on her elbows, she expected to see the midwife holding her son, ready to be fed, but the missus stood at the end of her bed instead, wearing her cornflower-blue traveling gown.

"Get dressed," she told Mallie.

Mallie looked toward the door. "Where's my baby?"

The missus didn't answer.

Mallie inched her legs to the side of the bed, trying to ignore the lingering pain. "I must feed him."

"I'm sorry," the woman said as she opened the small dresser beside the window. "The baby didn't survive the night."

Mallie fell back against the wall, her body trembling as she tried to process the missus's words.

Her baby didn't survive? No—the missus must be wrong. Her son was fine last night. Healthy and strong.

"Bring me my baby," Mallie demanded, but when she looked into the eyes of her mistress, at the pity and disdain, her words ebbed into grief.

A wail erupted from deep inside her, carving its way around her heart and up her throat, echoing across the room.

"Lower your voice, Mallie."

A whisper now. Begging. "Bring me my baby."

"I can't—"

"I want to see him."

"He was ailing," the woman said. "Abe buried him before daylight."

Mallie wrapped herself in her arms, sobs heaving from her chest. She rocked back and forth, her head banging against the wall. She never should have fallen asleep. Never should have let him go.

"We have no time for this," the missus said, pulling things out of the dresser.

She didn't understand the missus's words, didn't care what she was saying.

The woman turned toward her. "Get out of bed."

Mallie yanked the bedcover up, trying to bury herself in the quilt her mother stitched long ago. If only she could join her son in the grave. She couldn't bear to stay in this world a moment longer.

The missus took her arm. "You must get dressed. Right away."

She cried as the missus dressed her. Cried as the others watched her walk down the steps, into the black carriage.

It wasn't until hours later that she realized.

The master never came to see her at all.

PART ONE

Having heard all of this,
you may choose to look the other way,
but you can never again
say that you did not know.

—William Wilberforce,
in a speech to the
House of Commons

Chapter 1

West End
December 1853

Lantern light spilled out from the carriage post as Alden Payne climbed inside the brougham, setting his valise on the broadcloth seat. The lantern cast a veil of light from the frosty window on the carriage up to the holly berries intertwined in a bough of fir hanging limply on his sister Eliza's front door.

He should have been elated at the thought of going home early this morning, excited to see his parents and younger sister after another semester at Harvard, but his chest filled with dread instead.

As he waited for the coachman, his father's face ballooned in his mind. The intense gray eyes that could find fault in any argument, the ash-colored hair salted with white.

Alden had inherited his father's gray eyes and ash-brown hair. His father had inherited Scott's Grove, a thousand acres of tobacco in Virginia, and the obsession to enlarge this plantation.

After Alden graduated from Harvard in the spring, his father expected him to join in his work at the plantation. What was he going to say when Alden told him that he'd already made a different choice? Other plans—especially ones that differed from his father's decrees—weren't tolerated.

The Negro coachman, dressed in formal livery, climbed onto the bench above the carriage's front window, but before the carriage rolled forward, the front door to the house opened.

"Wait!" Eliza called out, tramping down the narrow carpet of light to the carriage door. She was tugging on the arm of the Negro boy who'd carried a pitcher of water up to Alden's room last night.

Alden opened the door, concerned.

Eliza stopped beside the carriage door, tying the cord of her dressing gown around her waist. "I almost forgot to give you this."

He looked at his sister's hands for some sort of package, but they were empty. "What are you giving me?"

She pushed the Negro boy forward. "It's a Christmas gift for Father."

He eyed the boy standing in the shadows. His curly black hair was trimmed short over his ears, and he was as gangly as one of the stalks in Victor's fields. Instead of studying the ground, the boy confidently met Alden's gaze.

Alden glanced back at his sister. "You're giving Father a slave?"

Eliza nodded, brushing her frizzy hair back over her shoulder. "To help him plant the tobacco."

Alden stepped down onto the packed dirt of the driveway. Eliza's husband, Victor, had inherited a farm on the outskirts of a village called West End, but Victor wasn't nearly as competent of a planter and overseer as Alden's father. It seemed to him that Victor needed the boy here to help with their hundred acres of corn.

"Are you certain?" Alden persisted, but Eliza didn't seem to hear him.

"Father will be pleased," she replied before commanding the boy to climb on top of Alden's trunk, which had been tied to the back of the carriage.

She wagged her finger at him. "Don't you move until you get to Scott's Grove."

"Yes, ma'am," the boy replied.

"And I don't want to hear of you giving my father or anyone else trouble."

Alden studied the boy perched up on the wooden trunk. Temperatures had dipped below freezing this morning, but he only wore a linen tow shirt and trousers. His feet were bare. "Does he have a coat?"

Eliza shook her head. "He doesn't need anything."

"Perhaps a blanket?"

"Discipline is all he lacks, Alden. Don't you dare coddle him."

Alden climbed back into the carriage. "Thank you for your hospitality," he said before tipping his hat toward his sister. Then he closed the door and rapped on the front glass.

The coachman prompted the horses forward, and the farmhouse slowly faded behind them, their lantern light illuminating the remnants of decayed corn stalks in Victor's fields as the carriage wheels rocked over ruts in the road.

Victor and Eliza used to spend Christmas at Scott's Grove, but they hadn't visited in the past two years. Eliza had loved the annual festivities when she was younger, and in their early years of marriage, Victor seemed to enjoy celebrating with the Payne family as well. But Alden's brother-in-law had grown more isolated as the years passed. His once immaculate farm had begun to fall into ruin. And now Eliza was acting oddly as well.

Turning, Alden looked through the window behind him at the boy clinging to the ropes around the trunk, his bare feet dangling over the side.

No slave—even the most defiant one—should be treated this way, but especially not one so young. It was at least a four-hour drive to Scott's Grove. If the child didn't freeze to death, he would surely catch pneumonia or something else from the cold air.

Eliza and Victor may not care if they lost one of their slaves, but it wouldn't happen on his watch.

After they rounded a bend, Alden wiped the fog off the front window and then knocked on the glass until the driver slowed the horses. When the carriage stopped, Alden opened the door, the wind cutting like a knife through his wool coat.

The coachman looked down over his shoulder. "Yes, Master Payne?"

"What's your name?" Alden asked.

"Thomas, sir."

"And do you happen to know the name of the boy sitting on the trunk behind me?"

"His name is Isaac."

"Very good," Alden replied, stepping down onto the road. A patch of frozen leaves crunched under his boots as he rounded the carriage.

Isaac's arms were wrapped around his chest. "Why'd you stop?"

"I want you to join me inside the carriage."

Isaac didn't move. "The missus told me to stay here."

"It's much warmer in the carriage."

When Isaac shook his head, Alden wondered how often the boy had felt Victor's whip on his back. He tried one more time. "You'll freeze up there."

"Niggas don't freeze."

Alden's heart raced. "Who told you that?"

"Master said Africa boiled my blood."

"That's not what I mean. Who said you were—" Alden stopped. "Who called you that name?"

"The missus," he said, rubbing his arms. "She don't know my real name."

Alden looked toward Thomas sitting up front in his warm livery jacket, and then back at the boy. "At Scott's Grove, you'll be known as Isaac."

"That's fine, mister." He leaned against the window, his teeth chattering. "But I still ain't gettin' in the carriage with you."

"I understand." Alden closed the door to the brougham. Then he removed his leather gloves, stuffing them into his coat pocket before he propped his foot on the axle of the back wheel and propelled himself up on the spokes. "I shall have to join you up here, then."

When Alden sat down beside him, Isaac scooted to the far side of the trunk. "It's going to be a long ride to Scott's Grove."

The boy shrugged. "I've been on longer ones."

Alden replaced his gloves and reached for the strap around the trunk. Then he called toward the front of the carriage. "Drive on, Thomas."

The brougham didn't move.

His voice rose. "I said to drive."

Thomas climbed down from the bench and marched toward the back. Instead of looking toward Alden, he addressed Isaac. "When Master Payne tells you to get into the carriage, you get into the carriage."

"But the missus—"

"Won't know a thing if none of us tell her," Thomas said, his deep voice resounding down the quiet road.

Alden leaned forward to whisper, as if Eliza could hear them from the house. "I won't say a word."

Thomas leaned against the wheel. "Neither will I."

Isaac looked at one man then the other. "I'd never tell," he finally said.

"Then it's settled." Alden inched away from the boy and grasped the side of the trunk before climbing back down the wheel. "Honorable men never break their promises."

Inside the carriage, Isaac sat as close to the window as possible, his nose pressed against the glass, his feet tucked under his thighs. Thomas snapped the reins, and the steady beat of horse hooves drummed the route toward home.

What would the other students at Harvard think about his riding south in a carriage alongside a slave? Many of them were abolitionists, but their rhetoric against the institution of slavery was born out of blind passion. They knew nothing about the practicalities of running a Southern plantation that provided the tobacco they liked to smoke. Nor were they actually doing anything to abolish it.

Talk was easy. Cheap. Both students and professors liked to rant about freedom for all men—and pontificate about the evil Southern planters —but in Alden's opinion, none of them were willing to sacrifice a thing—especially not their cigars—to help free the slaves.

The interior of the brougham was warmer than outside, but the boy beside him could still catch pneumonia. Alden reached under the seat and pulled out a blanket. "Put this around you."

Isaac glanced down at the blanket, but he didn't touch it. "I told you, my blood runs hot."

"But your skin doesn't," Alden said, holding out the blanket.

"I'm fine, mister."

"Suit yourself." Alden lowered the blanket. "Are you always this defiant?"

"Obstinate is what the missus says."

"Are you always obstinate?"

"Only when I have a mind to do what I want."

Alden leaned back against the seat. "If you get ill, you won't be able to work in my father's tobacco fields."

"I don't aim to work in your father's fields either way."

"I suppose I can't blame you for that."

The boy's chin climbed a notch. "I've got plans for my life."

Alden eyed the boy again. He looked like he was about nine years old, but he talked as if he were a young man. "When we reach Scott's Grove, you'll want to keep those plans to yourself."

Pale gray light slowly rekindled the morning as they journeyed toward the Shenandoah Valley. On the left side of the road was a grove of spindly looking trees. Isaac's gaze was fixated on the mountain range silhouetted against the horizon on the right. The courtyards up at Harvard were blanketed with fresh snow when Alden left Massachusetts two days ago, but there was no snow yet for Christmas in Virginia.

"Out of curiosity," Alden said, "what exactly are your plans?"

Isaac turned toward him, his face serious. "I'm going to California."

That made two of them, then. "And what are you planning to do there?"

"Find a field of gold."

He smiled. "I don't think it grows out there like corn."

"I'll still find it."

"Then you'll be a wealthy man."

Isaac studied him for a moment, as if trying to decide if he were going to trust him. Then he leaned forward. "What are your plans?"

The carriage hit another rut, and Alden grasped the rail on the side to steady himself. He wasn't about to share that information with this boy or anyone else, at least until after he spoke with his father. "I'm still trying to figure it out."

Isaac eyed the interior of the brougham. "Do you reckon you could drive this all the way to California?"

"I think passage on a ship would be the best option."

"Not if you get seasick."

"It's definitely a risk to consider," he said. "Are a few months of seasickness worth a field of gold?"

Isaac seemed to ponder his words. "What's Scott's Grove like?"

"It's much bigger than the Duvall farm. My father has at least a hundred slaves working the tobacco fields."

"I don't know who my father is," Isaac told him. "But my mother was a princess."

Alden's eyebrows rose. "A princess?"

"She was the most beautiful woman in all of Virginia," Isaac said. "Her father was an African king."

"So does that make you a prince?"

When Isaac nodded his head, Alden had to keep himself from smiling. Unlike his father and Eliza, he believed that slaves felt just as deeply as their owners. He didn't want to hurt this boy.

"Missus Eliza said you were going to school to learn the law."

Alden nodded. "That's correct."

"You must be right smart."

"School doesn't make a person smart," Alden said. In fact, he'd thought himself to be quite smart until he started taking classes at Harvard. Then he realized he didn't know much of anything.

"It sure don't hurt," Isaac said.

"I suppose not."

"One day, I'm going to school too."

Alden glanced out the window at a lake beside them, at the gaggle of geese that peppered its shores. Isaac reminded him of his childhood friend, a Negro boy named Benjamin. Except Alden hadn't really seen Benjamin's light-brown skin when they were children. Didn't ever think about him as a slave. Benjamin was three years younger, and Alden treated him like a brother.

They used to race through the halls of the plantation house when it was too cold to play in the forest outside. They built forts in the drawing room, played Snakes and Ladders on the floor, and when his father was gone, they bowled in the cellar with his cricket ball.

They'd been the best of friends until his father sent Benjamin out to work in the tobacco fields the day Benjamin turned twelve. That year, Alden had been sent to Richmond to attend a private school.

He'd missed his friend when he came home, but he had been too distracted by the flurry of schoolwork to think much about the differences in their positions. Their futures. It wasn't until he went to Harvard that his eyes were opened to the cruelty of an institution that seemed common-place in Virginia.

"What about your mother?" Isaac asked.

Alden looked back at him. "What about her?"

"Is she a princess?"

Alden pondered the question. "More like a queen, I suppose."

At least, that's how he saw Nora Payne. The truth was that he didn't know his mother very well. He'd been raised by Benjamin's mother, a beautiful Negro woman they both called Mammy. In his mind, Mammy was the princess.

Isaac cleared the fog off his window. "How long until we get there?"

Alden slid his timepiece out of his pocket. "Another three hours."

"And how long are we staying?"

"I'll be there for two weeks," he said. He didn't know how long his father would keep this boy.

When Isaac yawned, Alden slipped the blanket back out from under the seat and handed it over. This time, the boy didn't argue.

As Isaac slept, dread slowly trickled back over Alden. Then it began to pour. As the carriage neared the edge of his family's tobacco fields, he felt as if he were drowning.

His father would be happy he'd come home, but it wouldn't last for long. Not when he found out that his plans for the plantation were about to implode.

Alden would wait until after Christmas to say what was on his mind. Then he'd brace himself for the aftermath.

Chapter 2

Scott's Grove
December 1853

No one—not even Alden's younger sister, Rhody—rushed out to greet them when the carriage rolled down the long drive at Scott's Grove. No one saw Isaac climb back onto the top of the trunk a half mile back and wrap himself with the blanket that Alden insisted he use for the end of their journey.

Usually the fields around the plantation were humming with activity this time of year, every day of the week except the Sabbath. Jeptha—the Negro overseer—made certain slaves were clearing the stalks and burning debris as they prepared the land for next year's crop.

Alden had never seen the plantation dormant in the days before Christmas nor had he ever arrived home without his sister racing down the steps to welcome him home.

Thomas stopped the carriage and opened the door for Alden. Isaac hopped down onto the stone walkway and followed Alden up to the plantation home that was at least twice the size of his former master and mistress's house.

It was time for the noon meal, but when Alden

opened the front door, he didn't smell roasted meat or baking bread. The wide entrance hall was silent—no sounds came from either the drawing room on the right of the great hall or the dining room on the left.

"Where are your people?" Isaac asked behind him.

"I have no idea."

"Perhaps they've gone to town."

"Perhaps," he replied, but his family never went to town on Christmas Eve. Typically, the household was bustling with preparations for the holiday meal. His mother directed the house slaves to decorate for their annual party. The cook prepared a goose with sage dressing, the Christmas pudding with currants and raisins, and the eggnog from fresh cream, nutmeg, and Jamaican rum. His father usually worked on the accounts in his office, balking at the festivities until Mother forced him to come celebrate with their family and a few neighbors.

Alden dropped his valise on the floor and moved forward, expecting to find his mother and sister trimming the Christmas tree in the drawing room, but when he opened the door, no one was inside.

The fire had been tended in front of the settee, and the logs warmed the room with their steady blaze. An evergreen tree stood by a tall window, its crown brushing the dogwood blossoms and branches molded into the plaster ceiling. But its own branches were void of candles, tinsel, or the garlands made of colorful glass beads. There were no candles or ribboned boughs on the mantle either, no wrapped gifts under the tree.

It was as if he'd gotten the date wrong, like no one was expecting his return or the holiday.

The door at the back of the room from his father's office opened, and his mother walked briskly toward him, her fingers arched stiffly in front of the bodice of her brown muslin dress. Her graying hair was wrapped tightly into a bun, and her lips were pursed firmly together until she saw him.

"I'm glad you're home," she said, but her voice was void of emotion.

He leaned forward, kissing her cheek. Her skin was as cold as the wind outside the house. "What's wrong?"

She drummed her fingers together. "Benjamin has run off again."

Alden's chest clenched at her words. A long time ago, when Benjamin was about fourteen, Alden had told his friend that one day he would help him escape slavery. Alden had been sixteen at the time, but he'd never forgotten his promise. Six years had passed, and he still hadn't figured out a way to help his friend. Nor, if he was honest with himself, had he tried very hard to come up with a solution.

Merely thinking about helping Benjamin was

just as cheap as all the abolitionist rhetoric up in Cambridge.

"How many times has he run?" Alden asked.

"Twice since the summer. Your father is quite distraught."

Distraught was probably a vast understatement. His father, he speculated, was raging mad. No one defied John Payne, especially not a slave. And certainly not three times.

He was shocked that his father hadn't already sold Benjamin at the market in Charlottesville. Someone else would probably buy him and take him farther south to Mississippi or Louisiana, where it would be impossible to escape.

But then again, Benjamin had always been a good worker and was stronger than most of his father's slaves, perhaps because he had grown up with a mother who loved him, plenty of good food, and a best friend to play with outside their house.

"Where is Mammy?" he asked, overwhelmed by concern for the woman who had raised him. She was probably in her room on her knees, praying that her son would be safe, that freedom would find Benjamin before Master Payne did.

"How am I supposed to know where that foolish woman is?"

Alden cringed. "She's not a fool."

His mother walked toward the tree and brushed her hands over the barren needles. "If she'd reared her son the right way, he wouldn't be running."

How could she call Mammy a fool? The woman had poured her life into raising not only her child but also the three Payne children. He, Eliza, and Rhody had adored her, flourished in her affection. As he grew older, he admired Mammy's courage and tenacity even more when he realized she'd chosen joy even when she was enslaved.

In his heart, he admired Benjamin's courage too. His determination to leave. Perhaps his friend would find the path to the elusive underground railway that traveled north, to the abolitionists who were risking their lives to help runaways find safety in Canada.

"Stella is coming this evening with her parents, along with the Morris family," his mother said. "But if your father doesn't return by five, it will ruin our dinner plans."

"I'm certain they will understand." It was perfectly fine with him if their dinner plans were ruined. His parents had decided that he and Stella Bradford were to marry after his graduation, but neither he nor Stella had agreed to this marriage. Sitting beside her, everyone hinting and prodding about their future during the meal, was agonizing for both of them.

She pointed toward the door, the glass trinkets on her bracelet clanging. "There's soup down in the kitchen. Hattie can serve you lunch."

"Is Rhody upstairs?"

She shook her head. "Rhody went to Charlottesville with your father. Jeptha has the dogs and other slaves searching the fields and forest."

How strange it must be for his sixteen-year-old sister to hunt for a slave. And for the other slaves to hunt for a brother, knowing the punishment he would face if they found him—and the swift punishment they'd endure alongside Benjamin if they tried to hide him.

If a slave found Benjamin, Alden prayed they would ignore him. The dogs were another matter. They were trained to hunt and—

"Who's that?" his mother asked, her gaze wandering from the tree branches down to Alden's side. Isaac stepped out from behind him, his head held high.

"This is Isaac," he explained. "Eliza sent him to help in the fields."

His mother waved her hand. "He's too young to do us any good."

Isaac started to reply, but Alden placed a firm hand on his shoulder to silence him. He didn't want Isaac sold before he'd had a chance to prove his worth.

"I'm sure he's a hard worker," Alden said.

"There's nothing to him." His mother glanced out the window and then looked back. "Did Eliza send his papers?"

Alden shook his head.

"Then we can't even sell him," she fumed. "Just because she can't afford to feed another mouth—"

"I don't eat much," Isaac interjected.

Alden pressed into Isaac's shoulder as a warning, but it was too late. His mother's eyebrows pinched together, and she bent down toward him, clearly irritated that he spoke without permission. "We don't tolerate thievery here, for as long as we decide to keep you."

"Yes, ma'am."

"Nor any kind of sass."

"Missus Eliza don't tolerate no sass either."

His mother groaned. "Doesn't—Eliza doesn't tolerate any sass. Why can't your people learn to speak the English language?"

"Probably 'cause it's illegal to teach it to us."

A vine of red crept up his mother's neck and then flooded her face. Isaac was right—a slave's education was a punishable offense. If slaves could write, they might forge their own emancipation papers. If they could read, they might find out about the abolitionists fighting for their freedom up north. And if they found out they had a home waiting for them in Canada, they might encourage a larger group of slaves to run away.

But there was no arguing this with his mother. She didn't erupt with words like his father, but if Isaac angered her, she would make his life at Scott's Grove miserable.

Alden pushed the boy toward the door. "I'm going to get some stew."

She nodded grimly. "Then you must join the search."

He didn't answer, knowing he could never hunt for his friend like he was an animal. Instead, he planned to find Mammy.

His mother pointed a shaky finger toward Isaac. "Take that boy down to help Hattie. No matter what happens, we will have a meal to celebrate Christmas Eve."

Back in the corridor, he leaned against the papered wall. Isaac looked up at him, his eyes wide. "Will Benjamin get away?"

"I don't know."

"I pray he runs like the dickens."

"You best learn to keep your thoughts to yourself around here."

Isaac prodded the edge of the braided rug with his bare toe. "Master Duvall lets me speak my mind."

"What about Mrs. Duvall?"

"She usually pretends I'm not there," the boy said, inching the rug away from the floor again. "But Master Duvall says I amuse him."

"I'm sure you do, but the master of this house won't be amused."

He stood taller. "I can hold my tongue if I put my mind to it."

"Then tell that mind of yours to lasso your

tongue and don't release it again until someone in charge asks you a direct question."

Isaac nodded his head.

"Hattie rules the kitchen," Alden explained. "If you do what she says, she'll treat you well."

"Will she feed me?" Isaac asked, rolling his hand over his stomach.

"Let's hope she'll feed us both."

Alden directed him to the kitchen steps. It had been a long time since he'd been in the basement of the house. When he was a child, all his meals were served in the nursery, though every once in a while, Mammy would slip him and Benjamin down the back staircase to sample the sweet cakes or Polish tarts. Hattie pretended not to notice them.

As he grew older, he began taking his meals in the dining room with his family. Mealtimes were strict in their home, and he respected that rule along with the many others that came with managing a household of this size.

Before he stepped down toward the basement, the front door of the house banged open, and he heard boots stomping on the floor.

As the cold air swept through the corridor, he pointed Isaac downstairs. "Tell Hattie that I sent you."

Isaac stuck out his tongue. "It's lassoed."

He sighed. "You can unlasso it just this once."

Isaac muttered to himself as he walked downstairs. Alden hoped the boy would learn the many rules at Scott's Grove so he could stay.

His father stood like a returning warrior in the entryway, with both Rhody and Jeptha standing behind him. His favorite bloodhound, Moses, was at his side.

Relief flooded over Alden when he didn't see Benjamin, but the triumphant smile on his father's face—and Jeptha's grimly set jaw—expunged any hope.

His mother hurried toward them, collecting the leather cloak his father dropped onto her arm.

"We caught him," he proclaimed.

She smoothed her hand over the leather. "Very good."

"He won't run away again."

"You all must eat," his mother directed.

His father glanced toward Alden, but didn't greet him. "Rhody earned herself a fine meal. She was the one who found him hiding in the basement of the Congregational Church."

The glory in Rhody's eyes sent tremors down Alden's spine. His younger sister had warred alongside their father, and she had won.

"Does Reverend Andrews know?" his mother asked.

"I'll find out after Christmas. His wife claimed he was out visiting the sick today."

"Likely story. I've never trusted the man."

"I'll find out the truth." He retrieved his cloak

from her hands before motioning toward Alden. "Come with me, son."

Alden moved forward. "Where are we going?"

"I've decided not to eat quite yet."

"But you must be famished," his mother said.

"I need Alden's help first in the curing barn."

Chapter 3

Sacramento City
December 1853

Isabelle Labrie swept into the elegant dining room of the Golden Hotel along Sacramento City's bustling K Street. The lilac gown she wore belled out from her fitted bodice until it reached the polished wood floor. It was modeled after the latest fashions in Paris except there were no ruffles or lace around the sleeves or skirt. And she had tiny bags of birdshot stitched around the hem to keep it from yielding to the California winds that swept up the river and through this growing town.

"Good evening, monsieur," she said to Edmund Walsh, the one gentleman seated near the rosewood box grand. It was Christmas Eve, but it didn't feel like a holiday. A light rain fell outside instead of the snow she'd loved back in Baltimore, and few wanted to stop and celebrate the birth of Christ when there was a pile of gold waiting to be found in the hills.

She reached for the bottle of Madeira the steward had left on the table, filling her customer's glass.

Mr. Walsh ate dinner at her hotel almost every night—salmon in the autumn, roasted duck in the summer, oyster loaf whenever a crate of oysters arrived from San Francisco. Rumor had it that he'd once been the milliner for Queen Victoria in London. Others said he'd been a blacksmith in Buffalo.

That was the beauty of California. A person could take on any persona they wanted. Be whomever they wanted in the shadows of this strange land.

When he'd first arrived in this new state, Mr. Walsh cast his line for gold and snagged a fortune. Gold was much harder to find in California than the East Coast papers liked to report—its dust sifted through fingers like sand in an hourglass, especially at the bordellos and saloons. Many miners wealthy at sunset were penniless again by sunrise, but Mr. Walsh was one of the few who'd managed to keep his money.

"When is Mr. Kirtland returning from the fields?" he asked.

She glanced out the large window along the front of the hotel, at the gray sky and a glimpse of river two blocks away. She'd been hoping Ross would return for Christmas, but it was already Christmas Eve. In the four months he'd been gone, she'd only received one letter from him, postmarked from the diggings near Marysville, and he gave no indication as to when he would return.

But he'd wanted to marry this spring when the flowers behind her aunt's cottage were in full bloom. She'd promised that she would have an answer to his proposal when he returned.

Isabelle glanced back at her customer. "He said he'd be back before the rains."

"Any day now, then," Mr. Walsh replied, though they'd only had a few showers in the past month. Not the torrential rains that would bring in the throngs of gold miners from the fields.

She nodded. "Any day."

Mr. Walsh took a bite of the iced Venetian cake on his dessert plate, and she filled his crystal goblet again.

Liquor was banned from her establishment, and she didn't allow her patrons to smoke cigars— there were plenty of saloons along Second and Third Streets for that sort of thing—but she did serve wine to her regular clients. The finest drink shipped over from Italy and Portugal in casks called pipes. She then transferred the wine into green-tinted glass bottles before serving it to her clientele.

Ross had said good wine was essential if they

wanted to bring in those who appreciated the refinement they missed in cities like Paris and New York. The Golden was the only hotel in Sacramento that catered to the businessmen who owned local banks, shops, and shipping companies. A few of these men had sent for their wives, and these ladies basked in the opulence of her establishment as well.

Most of their guests, though, were the miners like Mr. Walsh who'd struck it rich and craved a nice dinner and clean bed when they returned from the goldfields.

Mr. Walsh lowered his glass. "That's all for me tonight."

Isabelle replaced the cork in the bottle after he left and moved back toward the cellar where she stored her wine. Her hand against the brick wall, she slowly descended the rickety steps. She didn't bother to bring a lantern with her. Light filtered down the staircase from the dining room, illuminating the mortar and fired clay.

Whenever the Sacramento River flooded, everything in this cellar was carried to the upper floors of her three-story hotel until the water decided to recede. The last time the river seeped through her front door, Ross had been here to help her. They'd worked through the night to save almost everything on the lower floors. The piano's rosewood legs had been stained and the wood floor and wainscoting in the dining room ruined, but everything else in their hotel had survived, including the gold Ross had hidden for them behind this wall.

Smiling, she thought about the man she hoped to marry. Did he miss her as much as she missed him?

Even though she'd had proposals, she hadn't sought love in Sacramento, hadn't thought she would ever marry, but Ross had been kind to her heart. Patient. And she had learned to be patient with him too—waiting for months last summer and fall as he searched for gold along the western foothills of the Sierra Nevada. The Mother Lode.

It didn't matter to her if he brought back a bagful of gold nuggets from the fields, as long as he returned.

The bell chimed overhead, and she slid the wine bottle onto the rack, then picked up her skirt to hustle back up the steps. It was probably a late delivery from one of the steamboats—or it could be a new customer for the hotel—but every time the bell chimed, she thought Ross might have returned.

She swept through the dining room, then rounded the stairs to her right and entered the front lobby. But instead of a deliveryman or Ross waiting for her, a woman stood alone by the front desk. She was wearing a floral calico dress, and her light-chestnut hair was swept up in a knot behind her neck. Isabelle guessed she was a few years older than her own twenty-three years.

The women held a carpetbag in her right hand and a soggy sunbonnet in her left. Her face was quite pretty, but her clothing smelled of seawater and coal smoke.

A wave of nausea swept over Isabelle—most of the young women who traveled alone were from France or China, their passage purchased by so-called benefactors, the men and women who operated brothels across California.

The woman looked as if she could be from Europe or the East Coast, and Isabelle prayed for her sake that she was simply looking for a husband or father who'd come ahead of her.

Isabelle stepped behind the wooden counter where she kept her roster and the ledger of accounts. "How can I help you?" she asked, folding her hands on top of the shiny mahogany surface.

The woman glanced up at the wall beside the desk at the list of eight rules that Isabelle displayed so that all her guests clearly understood that the lawlessness in this new state didn't extend into her establishment. "I'm looking for the proprietor of this hotel."

Isabelle stood a bit taller. "I'm the owner."

The woman tilted her head, her dark-blue eyes wrinkled with confusion. "I thought Ross Kirtland owned this place."

Isabelle placed both her hands on the ledger,

wondering at the familiarity of the woman's language. How did this woman know Ross? "I bought out his portion when he left for the goldfields."

"Oh." The woman leaned back against a post. "I reckon it's good that he's looking for gold."

"He goes out for a few months every year, like most of the men around here." Isabelle sat on a pine stool. "Where are you traveling from?"

"Kentucky," she said. "Boone County."

"And how exactly do you know Mr. Kirtland?"

The woman smiled. "I'm married to him."

Married to him?

The woman's words ricocheted in Isabelle's mind, clanging together like the bells on wagons running up and down K Street. And the stool—it felt as if it had disappeared from under her, as if the wine cellar had opened up, swallowing her.

"But Ross—" she began to protest before correcting herself. "Mr. Kirtland's from New York City."

Bitterness wove through the woman's laugh. "I suppose New York sounds more sophisticated than Boone County."

Isabelle clung to a thread of hope. It was all a misunderstanding. "The Mr. Kirtland who owned this hotel was definitely from New York."

The woman shrugged. "My Ross always liked to make up a good story."

Had it really all been a story? The hotel Ross

said he'd owned in New York. The parents who were deceased. The sister who sent him letters at least once a month.

"Perhaps there are two men in California with the same name," Isabelle said, trying to explain this more to herself than to the woman across from her. Ross had fervently declared his love for her, said they would marry this spring. He never would have done that if he had a wife back east.

The woman leaned across the desk toward her, a locket dangling around her neck. She opened the clasp, and inside was a miniature daguerreotype of her and Ross. His handsome face was resolute.

"This was taken on our wedding day," the woman said.

Isabelle didn't reply.

"Is this the man who owned the hotel?"

Isabelle swallowed hard, her face warm again. "It is."

She dropped the carpetbag onto the floor. "Then I've found him at last."

Isabelle stared at her in shock. How could Ross have done this to her? To both of them?

After closing her locket, the woman collapsed on a cane chair near the front door. There was a hole in the toe of her boot, and her skirt was stained. "The whole room is rocking," she declared.

Isabelle wanted to run upstairs and hide, but instead she went into the kitchen and mixed the woman a drink with bicarbonate of soda, crushed sugar, and a dose of quinine to help calm her stomach and ward off disease.

"What is your name?" Isabelle asked, her voice shaky when she returned.

"Fanny. Fanny Kirtland."

The name of the letter writer, the woman Ross had declared to be his sister.

Isabelle tried to steady her voice. "How long have you and Ross been married?"

"Four years, though he left for California about two months after we married to make a home for us out here," she explained. "He said he would send for me, but he never did so I decided to come on my own and surprise him."

Isabelle forced a smile. "I'm certain he will be surprised."

Fanny looked at the Irish lace over the front window, then up at the lime and pink medallions above the chandelier.

"Is Ross's house nearby?" she asked.

Isabelle shook her head. "He lived in the back rooms of the hotel when he owned it."

"I suppose I shall have to stay in those rooms, then."

Isabelle hesitated. She had been living in those rooms since Ross left the city.

"Ross can pay my bill when he returns."

Isabelle wanted to turn the woman away, tell her to take the steamboat back to San Francisco and catch a clipper returning to the East Coast, but she would never turn a woman onto the streets of Sacramento City alone. Hers was the only establishment in town fit for a lady.

"I could help here until Ross returns," Fanny said, and Isabelle could hear the desperation in her voice.

"Do you know how to bake?"

"No—but I can learn."

"I need help with cleaning too and changing beds. We use real linens at this hotel."

Fanny crinkled her nose for a moment, but then composed herself. "I can make beds."

"Very good," Isabelle replied. "I suppose you can stay here and work until your husband returns."

"When he returns with his gold, we'll be able to live wherever we want."

Isabelle leaned forward to pat the woman's bare hand.

Chapter 4

Scott's Grove
December 1853

The stench of decaying leaves seeped between the walls of the curing barn and out into the yard. Alden hesitated by the door, afraid of what he would find inside. His father hadn't spoken to him during their walk to the barn, hadn't asked about his journey or his last term of school. Silence was one of the many weapons in his arsenal, and often it felt more destructive than his words.

Moses waited patiently beside Alden as Master Payne stepped into the door of the barn and returned with another of his weapons, a long black whip, the strips of leather coiled at his side. "It's time for you to grow up, Alden."

His heart beat faster as he eyed the whip. "I've already grown up."

"You've been pandering too long."

Bitterness boiled in Alden's throat, his heart slamming against his chest. His father had no idea what he had been doing, and he didn't care to know. "I've been studying law, not pandering to anyone."

His father held out the whip, but Alden didn't take it. "Where is Benjamin?" he asked.

"By the pillory."

Alden followed his father and Moses into the barn, between the wooden racks and ropes that held the tobacco as it dried each summer and fall. Light slipped through the cracks in the walls, falling on scraps of dried leaves and straw that cluttered the dirt floor.

The wooden pillory was located at the other end of the barn, positioned by the back entrance so their slaves could see them whenever they entered the barn. Usually Jeptha flogged the slaves who'd tried to run, but his father was seething in his anger—it seemed at both Benjamin and Alden.

Was it because he and Benjamin had once been friends? Or because Alden had been determined to finish law school? Or perhaps his father finally realized that Alden hated the institution called slavery.

Benjamin's head wasn't in the pillory, but his legs were shackled to it, his face bloodied, back bare. At one time, his friend's gaze had been filled with mischievousness—laughter—but all Alden saw now was rage, like the anger that boiled in his father.

What would his fellow students do if they saw Benjamin here in chains? The abolitionists would be livid at the injustice of it. It might even incite them to give up their cigars.

Moses growled as John spoke to Benjamin. "Apparently Jeptha and I haven't given you enough incentive to stay on the plantation," he said, his voice steely and cool. "This time you won't forget to stay where God meant for you to be."

Benjamin jerked against the shackles around his ankles. "You don't speak on behalf of God, John Payne."

He leaned toward the young man. "Master Payne."

Benjamin stilled, his gaze strong. "Only master I have is Master Jesus."

Alden's father unwound the whip, cracked it toward the pillory. Alden flinched as the sound echoed through the barn. He remembered the lashes on his own backside when he'd been a child, after he'd convinced Benjamin to go swimming in Morris Creek. The bruises had lasted for weeks.

His father held the handle out toward him again. "You must step into your role, son."

Alden looked at the whip as if it were a black snake, one of the deadly moccasins that hid along the banks of the creek. And courage swelled inside him. A moccasin only killed those who didn't respect its territory. Those who weren't paying attention.

He met Benjamin's gaze, and his old friend glared back at him, as if he thought Alden wanted to keep him in chains too.

Alden glanced back up at his father. "He only wants freedom, like all of us."

"Freedom to do what?" his father asked, his voice rising.

"Get an education or run a plantation or maybe have a family." Alden looked back at his friend. "What do you want, Benjamin?"

"Don't say a word," his father commanded, so bent on punishment that he refused to acknowledge Benjamin's personhood. Or perhaps he couldn't allow himself to acknowledge that Benjamin had the capacity to learn and lead and love. The realization might destroy him.

He threw the whip at Alden's feet. "Flog him."

Alden could no longer stand on that shaky middle ground, betwixt and between. The line was invisible, but it had been traced into the dirt and straw. He had to choose now, between his past and his future, between what he believed to be right and wrong.

Benjamin strained against the shackles again, continuing to struggle even when the fight was hopeless.

Alden buried his hands in his coat pockets. "I won't flog anyone."

"You will do it."

"I can't flog him," Alden said. "Benjamin's like a brother to me."

"He is not your brother!"

Why didn't his father understand? If he'd grown up with a Negro boy as his best friend, he wouldn't be able to whip him either.

His father reached down, snatching it from the ground. "You are a coward."

And he was right. He was a coward—not because he wouldn't punish Benjamin but because he was afraid to stand up to his father. He hated slavery, hated the man holding the whip for promulgating it, hated himself for not doing anything to stop men like Benjamin from getting hurt.

His father took off his hat and hung it on the side of the pillory. Then he draped his coat beside it. Grabbing Benjamin by the arm, he tried to force him to stand up. Benjamin fell back against the wooden post. His body had already been beaten, and even in the dim light, Alden could see the bruises spreading across his back.

The whip cracked, snapping over Benjamin's arms. Across his legs.

A dragon roared inside Alden, an erupting fire. He may be a coward, but he couldn't allow his father to whip his injured friend, especially when his only crime was to pursue freedom for his life. He'd tried to honor his parents the best he could, but in this, he couldn't turn aside.

Alden stepped between the men.

"Get out of the way," his father demanded, waving his hand.

"If you are going to whip him, you must whip me too."

His father lifted the whip again, fury blazing

51

across his face. Most of the thongs hit the sleeve of Alden's coat, but one hit his face, the pain searing his skin.

His father dropped the whip, and dust curled around his feet. "Now see what you've done."

Alden covered his cheek with the back of his hand, not daring to reply. He hoped what he had done was protect Benjamin from a flogging he didn't deserve.

His father pointed him toward the door. "Go back to the house."

"Not without you," Alden said. "Mother is expecting us to celebrate Christmas Eve as a family."

His father swore; then he kicked the whip away from Benjamin before plucking his cloak and hat from the pillory. He and Moses marched back toward the door, leaving Benjamin shackled on the floor.

Alden lingered for another moment. Benjamin didn't speak, but it seemed his anger at Alden had subsided. Benjamin gave him the slightest nod, the same look that had passed between them a hundred times when they were kids, especially when Alden was called away from their play-time to join the adults while Benjamin was allowed to stay upstairs, surrounded by their toys. He'd been jealous of him back then.

"Your mother is waiting," his father called from the other end of the barn.

"I'll come back for you," Alden promised Benjamin before following his father to the house.

"What happened to your face?" Rhody asked as Alden stepped into the dining room for the Christmas Eve dinner.

"I got hit by a whip."

His sister laughed, thinking he was making a joke.

Stella Bradford was already seated on his left, wrapped in green velvet, with lace on her sleeves, and Rhody sat across the table from her. His father was at the head of the table, his mother at its foot. Beside his father were Stella's parents, and Mr. and Mrs. Morris, who owned the moccasin-infested creek, sat on the opposite end.

It appeared that his mother had distracted herself by decorating this afternoon. Strips of silky white were draped from the chandelier to each corner of the ceiling, and a silver candelabrum with white candles stood as the table's centerpiece. In front of each place setting was a spray of red flowers, displayed in a slender glass vase beside the goblets of sherry.

"How was your journey?" Stella asked.

"Tolerable," he replied. "It was snowing when I took the train through New York."

"How I wish we would get snow this year." Stella swirled the sherry in her goblet. "It makes everything look so magical."

His father's chair scraped against the wood as he stood and began to pray over the meal, an elaborate show of thanksgiving. Alden glanced around the table at all the heads bowed in prayer. How could his parents and Rhody enjoy this meal knowing that Benjamin was shackled out in the barn? That he was hurting and hungry?

His gaze landed on Thomas, who was waiting along the wallpapered wall with a silver platter in his gloved hands. His mother must have instructed Victor and Eliza's coachman to assist the other house slaves with dinner, but he didn't see Isaac.

In all the confusion, he'd forgotten about the boy who didn't seem to realize he was a slave. Poor Isaac. He might be dreaming about California, but there would be no future for him outside Virginia. No schooling and no freedom even to speak his mind. His tongue would have to be lassoed for a lifetime.

After his father finished praying, Thomas stepped forward to place a fricandeau of veal on each plate. Even though the smell was intoxicating, Alden's appetite had waned.

His mother lifted her fork. "It's your favorite, Alden."

"I fear my tastes have changed."

"Oh, Alden." Rhody laughed. "Don't be so disagreeable."

Part of him wished he could block out Benjamin's face and his agony, like the rest of them. He was tired of feeling so helpless. Trapped.

Tonight, both he and Benjamin would break free.

"Did you find your slave?" Mr. Morris asked.

His father nodded. "Rhody found him for me."

"It wasn't hard," she replied. "He left tracks across the church foyer."

John took another bite of the braised veal. "Rhody's better than any of my hound dogs."

A proud smile slid across his sister's face again, her youth evident in the ribbons that Mammy had woven through her blonde hair, but she was growing more mature each time he came home. And more like the man who'd reared her.

"Father taught me well."

Alden shook his head. Even if his sister hadn't spent hours listening to the lectures of abolitionists, how had her heart grown so cold? Alden was six years older than Rhody, but Benjamin was only four years her senior. Rhody and Benjamin had played together for years, from the time she'd been old enough to stumble over the wooden blocks in the nursery.

Rhody sipped gingerly on her sherry before changing the subject. "I heard Robert Kelly just returned from California."

Mr. Morris leaned forward, an extra layer of flesh bulging above his collar. "Did he find his gold?"

Rhody dabbed her napkin on her lips. "Claims

he brought enough home to save their plantation."

"At least he's doing something to help his father," John said, pushing away his plate.

Alden ignored the slight.

"The *Daily Dispatch* said millions of dollars' worth of gold are buried out there."

"Then I wonder why he came home," Alden said.

Rhody glanced over at him. "I'd go to California if I could."

His mother set down her spoon. "There are no ladies out west."

"And no slaves," Stella said. "At least that's what Robert said."

"Now, Stella—" Mrs. Bradford started, but his mother's curiosity had already been piqued.

"You've seen Mr. Kelly?"

Stella blushed. "I suppose I have."

"We all visited him," Mrs. Bradford explained. "As a family."

As the others talked about California, an idea began to sprout in Alden's mind. He'd been offered an apprenticeship with Judah Fallow, an attorney who'd left Boston for San Francisco more than a year ago. But what if he didn't go alone? What if Benjamin went with him? If there really were no slaves in California, they could partner together as free men.

Stella elbowed him. "You're awfully quiet."

"I'm just thinking."

She smiled at him, the pink in her cheeks glowing in the candlelight. "About the future?"

His mother smiled as she took another bite of veal. "One more season and then Alden will be home for good."

Chapter 5

Sacramento City
December 1853

Isabelle rinsed her face in the basin of cold water and slathered her face and arms with a milky cucumber-and-lemon cream. Then she climbed between the clean sheets of a bed located on the hotel's third floor.

She'd given Fanny the two rooms she'd been occupying next to the dining room—they reminded her too much of Ross to stay there anyway. The feather mattress should help the woman's rocking world settle, though the truth of what Ross had done might set it churning again.

The people of Sacramento were too preoccupied to celebrate Christmas Eve, but back in Baltimore, she and Aunt Emeline would have strewn an evergreen tree with popcorn and bows. Then Uncle William would read from the old family Bible about the journey of a woman who'd birthed a remarkable baby in her youth.

A baby who ended up saving the world.

Fanny didn't seem to realize it was Christmas Eve. Or perhaps she didn't care. After her long journey, all Fanny wanted was to bathe, eat, sleep—and find her husband.

Isabelle couldn't begin to comprehend what would happen when Ross did return.

His face flashed into her mind, his dark-blond hair parted neatly in the middle, the beard he trimmed faithfully even when most men in California no longer bothered with the cost or hassle of doing so. She'd stopped trusting men a long time ago, but he had won her trust with his confidence and because of his compassion toward her aunt.

She'd thought she had found a man who would be faithful to her, a man she could trust, but it was all a façade. A California mirage. He hadn't left behind a sister in New York or a fine hotel. According to Fanny, he'd never owned or even managed any other sort of establishment. Fanny's father had hired Ross to work on his stud farm, though he hadn't worked there long. Ross and Fanny were married six months after he came to their farm, long enough to earn the rest of the money he needed to travel west.

He had been as unqualified as she and Aunt Emeline when it came to hotel management. Perhaps even more so. At least Uncle William and Aunt Emeline had operated the mercantile in

Baltimore. Her aunt had kept the accounts for that business and helped Uncle William purchase supplies for their shop, especially items for their female clientele. Then she'd taught Isabelle how to operate the business in the hours after school.

Isabelle had trusted Ross when he'd said he loved her. That he wanted to spend his life with her. But all along, he'd been hiding the fact that he was already married.

Her hand brushed over her right shoulder; then she tucked it back under the covers. She had secrets of her own—no one except Emeline knew about her past, and even her aunt didn't know the entire story. She'd intended to tell Ross everything before she married him and let him decide if he wanted to proceed.

Even if California was a sanctuary, a place for people to hide from their pasts, it wasn't right to keep secrets from the man—or woman—you intended to marry. Especially if your secret was that you happened to already have a wife!

How could she have been so wrong about Ross?

As she lay on the guest bed, the mattress stuffed with dried grass, she felt no ill will toward Fanny —it wasn't her fault that Ross had played them both for fools. She should have questioned the many letters from his sister, his relentless pursuit of wealth when she wanted security through the steady business of their hotel, his lack of communication from the diggings even after he'd asked her to become his wife.

She had no intention of telling Fanny the complete truth about her and Ross's relationship. First of all, she was mortified that she had considered marrying another woman's husband. And second, she wasn't certain how Fanny would react when she found out what Ross had done.

Better to wait until Ross returned. He'd caused this mess—he should be honest about his deception.

She clasped her hands together, holding them against her chest. Was her heart forever scarred from loving a man? Perhaps she would never be able to marry.

Starlight edged through the curtains on the window, offering an escape into the peaceful world of sleep, but still her eyes wouldn't rest. Hours ago, she'd been excited to see Ross, counting down the months until they married. What would she say when he returned now?

Another thought crept slowly into her mind, startling her.

Perhaps Ross hadn't really been planning to marry her at all. He'd made good use of their partnership over the years, of the money that Aunt Emeline had invested into their work. Perhaps he'd been mining as well in the city, except he'd been trying to extract gold from the pockets of her and Aunt Emeline to supplement what he found in the diggings.

In hindsight, Ross hadn't volunteered to compensate her or her aunt when he'd decided to head east to the goldfields. Aunt Emeline had asked a local attorney to draw up papers that clarified their agreement, and Ross signed them without comment.

Isabelle had stored the papers downstairs, not bothering to read what she'd thought to be inconsequential, but the terms on that contract would be critical now. Slipping out of her bed, she reached for her silk robe and lantern before moving down the steps, into the lobby.

The front door was already locked, the curtains over the picture window closed. Even if all her guests were asleep, she still took the precaution of locking the door to the dining room as well.

Behind the counter, she pushed aside the chair from her desk and folded back the rug. When she pulled up on a latch between the planks, a wooden panel lifted up toward her. Then she climbed down the rungs of a wooden ladder, the lantern in her hand illuminating the small room between her building and the bank next door.

Both buildings had been built after the 1850 flood. The previous owner had installed this space between the walls of his two buildings to store gold as well as to hide on occasion from those angry at him and his questionable business practices. There was no back door to this building, so after hiding, he would escape through a hatch he'd built into the back wall, slipping into a small courtyard along the alleyway.

Eventually the people of Sacramento drummed the man out of town, but as far as she knew, they'd never discovered his hiding place. When Aunt Emeline bought the hotel, she'd asked Ross to bolt up the entrance into the building next door.

Isabelle's light skimmed across the dirt floor, stopping when it reached the metal lockbox. She slipped off the silver chain from her neck and removed the key. Inside was her collection of gold, profits from hotel guests and dining room customers alike.

She also kept her most important papers hidden inside.

Rifling through the documents, she found the one that Ross had signed before he left. The wording in the contract left little room for dispute.

Ross was paid fairly for his co-ownership of the Golden Hotel, making Aunt Emeline the sole owner of their enterprise. In order to resume his co-ownership, he agreed to pay her aunt back the same amount he'd taken to finance his quest for gold. If he didn't have the money to reinvest on his return, he and Emeline would discuss new terms, but her aunt was not obligated to partner with him again.

The document was signed by Aunt Emeline, Ross, and their attorney.

Isabelle read the terms one more time and locked it back in the box. After this, she and Aunt Emeline couldn't go back into partnership with Ross, but what if he earned enough money to resume his ownership? She supposed they would have to sell him the hotel.

Sighing, Isabelle climbed back up the ladder and replaced the panel and rug. Then she returned to her room and lit a candle to celebrate this Christmas Eve on her own.

Chapter 6

Scott's Grove
December 1853

Alden sat on the edge of his bed, fully clothed in his cord breeches and traveling cloak, his valise resting on the floor beside him as he listened to the clock outside his room strike the hour of midnight. Except for the grandfather clock, the house was silent now, had been for the past hour, but still he waited. He didn't want anyone to disrupt his plans.

In the hours after dinner, while his family and their guests drank themselves into a stupor, he binged on black coffee. And his mind churned. The house staff had been up late cleaning after the party, but once they were asleep, he planned to sneak down and fetch the keys locked in his father's desk.

The skill of lock picking was something he and Benjamin acquired a long time ago, motivated by the Belgian chocolates his father kept hidden in his office. They'd been careful as children—only taking one piece of chocolate for each of them before locking the drawer again. Tonight he'd be even more careful as he used a hairpin to retrieve the key that imprisoned Benjamin. And if he couldn't find the key, he and Benjamin would figure out how to pick the lock on his shackles.

Standing up, he moved quietly toward his door and listened one more time before opening it. There were no sounds in the hallway. No padding of feet up the steps or rustling of skirts. If one of the slaves did see him, he doubted they would inform Master Payne, but he didn't want anyone else to be indicted in what the local and national government considered a crime.

The federal government had passed the Fugitive Slave Act more than three years ago, a supposed compromise between the Northern and Southern states. The northern part of the country used to be a safe haven for runaway slaves, but now anyone caught helping runaways was either given a steep fine or imprisoned. Or when the law looked the other way, some people were feathered and tarred for loving their neighbors.

His father hadn't yet given him the money to finance his last term in school, but his train ticket north was in the valise, and he had enough money to buy a ticket for Benjamin as well. As long as the conductor believed Benjamin to be a slave, traveling as his manservant, he should be able to transport him as far as Boston.

Patrick, his roommate at Harvard, was an abolitionist. Surely, he would have the contacts to help Benjamin find refuge up in Canada until they traveled out to California.

His own plans to finish school would be dashed—his father would never forgive him for this offense—but his conscience would be intact. And Benjamin's life would be saved. Then he would work to secure tickets for both of them on one of the steamers going toward San Francisco. He could complete his education under Judah's tutelage.

Slowly he stepped into the hallway, a candle in one hand, his bag clutched at his side. This decision sealed the fates of both him and Benjamin. After this, he could never return to Scott's Grove.

He turned to close his door, but before it shut, a scream pierced through the darkness, echoing down the papered walls in the corridor. In an instant, he tossed his travel bag back into his room, followed by his cloak; then he rushed down the corridor toward his father's chamber.

Someone yelled again—a man's voice—and he heard crying. A woman weeping behind his father's door.

"You should care what happened to him," the woman shouted.

Ice glazed over Alden's skin. It wasn't his mother in the chamber. It was Mammy, screaming at her master.

"You killed my son, and you don't even care . . ." her words trailed off in a sob.

Alden collapsed back against the wall, stunned at her accusation. Then rage bubbled up inside him, and his head felt as if it might explode.

He knew his father was outraged, that he might try to maim Benjamin in some way to ensure he'd never run again, but Alden never imagined him killing one of their slaves.

Across the corridor, his mother opened the door and peeked out at Alden in the candlelight. In that brief moment, he saw something unfamiliar in her eyes. A trace of vulnerability. Shame.

Perhaps she saw something new in his eyes too. Without a word, she slammed her door shut, as if the wood barrier could block out the reality of what her husband had done. And block out the fury—the accusations—of her son.

Mammy's wails grew louder. "How could you kill him?"

"He wouldn't stop running away," his father replied.

"You should have let him run," she said, her voice trembling. "All he wanted was to be like Alden . . . and you."

"If I'd let him go, the others would have followed him."

"You are a proud man, John Payne, and the Lord above despises pride."

"You spoiled him ever since he was a child," his father said, as if Mammy had somehow wronged him. "He was useless as a slave."

"Indeed." She paused. "Benjamin was too much like his father."

A sound—a slap—resounded into the hallway, and when Mammy cried out, Alden reached for the doorknob, throwing the door open. Mammy cowered near the window, her dark eyes swollen. The red mark on her cheek matched Alden's, and he felt as if he might be sick all over his father's woven rug.

His father towered over Mammy, his face stark white like one of the marble statues at Harvard. Lifeless and resolute. He pointed Alden back toward the door. "Leave my room."

"You—" His voice trembled with shock as he stared at the man who'd sired him. "You killed Benjamin."

"Get out, Alden."

Weariness swept over him, his soul reflecting the look on Mammy's face. He was tired. Tired of his father's demands and the expectations placed on his shoulders. Tired of watching other people being treated worse than his father's dog. Tired of hands that folded in prayer over a meal before striking the backs of people who had harvested and prepared it.

Mammy wouldn't suffer anymore at his father's hand.

Alden reached out toward her. "She's coming with me."

"This isn't your business," his father said, stepping closer to him.

Alden's voice escalated. "You killed Benjamin, and now you want to hurt her?"

"I own them."

"No, Father," Alden said, his tongue burning in anger. "It seems that slavery actually owns you."

His father lifted his hand again to strike, and Alden closed his eyes, waiting for the pain. He wanted to feel what Benjamin and Mammy had felt, suffer alongside them.

But instead of hitting Alden, he lowered his hand. "Leave my room."

"Not without Mammy."

His father swore. "Both of you leave my sight."

Mammy slipped out in front of Alden, and as he turned to follow, he heard his father mutter, "Nigger-lover."

The vile words echoed in his mind as he clenched his fists. He wanted to flog the man, then strap him to the back of the carriage and make him ride all the way back to the Duvalls' farm in the freezing night air.

Alden dug a grave for Benjamin's body long past midnight, in the small Negro plot by the trees. As they buried him in the icy chill of moonlight, he and Mammy grieved together the loss of her son.

After Mammy returned to the house, Alden paced the rows of tobacco plants alone. In an hour or so, Mammy would be expected to help dress his mother and sister for Christmas morning, her tears dried, but Alden wouldn't join them in the festivities. He had a week left before he was supposed to return to school—perhaps he would lock himself in his room until it was time to leave. Then he would never return.

The decision was quite clear to him now. This plantation and all of its property was the pride of his father. Alden would never return to oversee the man's kingdom.

He plucked a dried leaf off the tobacco plant—Virginia's own version of gold—and crushed it between his fingers, the pieces falling on the clumps of dirt below. If only he had whipped Benjamin like his father commanded. He would have saved his friend's life.

Or if he had left the house earlier last night, right after dinner while everyone was drinking and singing in the drawing room, he could have retrieved the keys and helped Benjamin escape.

He knew his father intended to harm Benjamin, but he never thought his father would kill him.

At this moment, he didn't know his father at all.

Bitter tears fell from his eyes. When had his father's heart grown so hard? How could he not understand Mammy's grief at losing her son?

He sat on the cold ground beside the smokehouse, his mind in turmoil. He'd promised Benjamin that he would help him escape, both when they were younger and yesterday in the barn. He'd told young Isaac that an honorable man keeps his promises, but his own honor had shattered that very night. Promises—years of good intentions—couldn't save someone's life.

He wasn't any better than the other students who only talked about abolition. He had failed to save even one slave. Failed at being an honorable man.

His friend was with his eternal master now, and Alden hoped he was finally running north, south, east, and west—whatever direction he liked. The image of Benjamin running free, his arms spread wide, made him smile.

Benjamin no longer had to run away from the pain. And Alden could no longer stay here and either inflict pain or watch other slaves suffer at his father's hand.

The glitter of gold didn't drive Alden like it did many who went to California, but the promise of freedom was as enticing as any type of gold, especially now. He would finish his degree at Harvard, and then somehow he would make his way to the land where he could carve out his own future instead of stepping into the one that would shackle him here as a slaveholder for the rest of his life.

Chapter 7

West End
December 1853

Victor Duvall rang the silver handbell by his bed for the second time. It was 7:15, but Isaac still didn't come.

Insolent boy.

Every morning Isaac brought his morning coffee and a copy of the *Alexandria Gazette*, precisely at seven, but he wasn't here today— nor had he come yesterday. Victor had to walk all the way down to the kitchen in his dressing gown to collect his coffee and paper.

No thirty-year-old self-respecting farmer and gentleman should be collecting anything. Or getting dressed on Christmas morning by himself to attend services in town.

Yesterday, he'd searched the entire house for the boy. When he finally asked Eliza about Isaac's whereabouts, she'd said he went with another slave into Alexandria to buy gifts for Christmas. He had scolded his wife for letting Isaac go. Victor was the master of this house, and no one had asked him if the boy was allowed to leave their farmhouse. When it came to matters about Isaac, they all knew permission came directly from him.

Either way, no one would have sent a slave into town on Christmas Day.

He lifted the bell over his shoulder, and its trill shook the glass panes on his window. Still Isaac didn't walk through the door.

The boy needed more discipline. And more duties so he would appreciate the little that was required of him here. If Isaac wasn't careful, Victor just might send him out into the cornfield to labor with the eight other slaves his father had passed along to him a decade ago.

He flung back the covers and stepped into the hallway, clutching the leather strap of the bell in his hand. "Isaac!" he shouted from the banister, ringing his bell again.

At the other end of the corridor, the door to the servants' staircase crept open, and he turned to reprimand Isaac for being late. He wouldn't whip him this time for his delay, as long as he apologized properly.

But instead of Isaac emerging into the corridor, it was Hannah, the old Negro woman he'd bought at the market last year to work in the kitchen. She hobbled forward, her gaze on the floor.

"Where is Isaac?" he demanded.

Her face turned to the door behind her, the room where Eliza slept. Most mornings his wife stayed in bed until late, sometimes not emerging until the lunch hour. He always locked himself into his study before she rose, and unless he needed to go into town, he remained there until the dinner hour required that he join her for a meal.

This morning was different, though. Eliza would be up soon to dress for church.

He bent toward Hannah. "Look at me."

As she lifted her chin, her eyes shifted right and then left, refusing to meet his gaze.

He stepped closer to her, towering over her by more than a foot. "Where did Isaac go?"

"Miss Eliza—" she whispered, her gaze falling back to the carpet.

Anger surged inside him. "What did Eliza do this time?"

The woman shook her head. "She done put that boy on the back of the carriage when Master Alden left, in the terrible cold."

The bell flew from his hand, banging against the wall like a crack of thunder, falling to the floor. "Why didn't you tell me yesterday?"

"I figured it weren't my place."

"It's always your place when Eliza's lost her sense."

"Please don't tell her I said anything," Hannah begged.

Victor stomped right around her, his gaze focused on Eliza's door. His wife thwarted every attempt he made to achieve happiness, as if his pleasure gave her great pain and his pain brought her joy.

Eliza was sitting up on her throne of pillows. Her mossy-brown hair, frayed from years of ironing, was tangled at the base of her nightcap, and the entire room stunk of stale rum. Her face, pockmarked with acne scars, was covered in a white paste. "What was that dreadful noise?"

He clenched his fists together, the nails digging into his palms, in an attempt to control his anger. He'd only hit Eliza once since they'd been married. Afterward, she'd threatened him, saying if he ever hit her again, she would go straight back to Scott's Grove and tell her father that he'd hurt her. Then she would stay at her parents' home, and any chance of him inheriting even a portion of the Payne estate would be gone.

The only reason he'd married Eliza was her family's plantation—and because his father, Arthur the Honorable, had threatened that if Victor didn't marry a respectable woman before he died, he would give the Duvall house and farm to charity.

The only reason Eliza had married him was because no one else would have her, and she didn't take well to the title of old maid. She preferred overseeing the two floors of the Duvall farmhouse to listening to her younger sister prattle at home. Rhody, he was quite certain, would have no problem finding a husband.

He crossed his arms. "Isaac didn't go into Alexandria yesterday."

"Of course not." She laughed. "I gave him to my father."

"You can't give away my slave."

"It was a Christmas gift."

"A gift I never authorized."

She reached for a jar of hand cream on her nightstand and dabbed it onto her thick palms, rubbing them together. "He's incompetent," she said as she leaned back against her cushions. "And we had no use for incompetency here."

Victor stepped closer. "He was our only house-boy."

She shrugged, his rage seeming to have no effect on her. "I suppose, but you never treated him like a servant. You treated him like he's your son."

"He is my son."

Eliza glared at him. After twelve years of marriage, she hadn't been able to give him a single child, and she despised any reference to the reality that Isaac was his only flesh and blood.

He pressed his fists together again. "I swear, if you killed him—"

"Then he can go be with his mama."

"You don't know that his mother is dead."

"Seems likely," Eliza replied, leaning back on her pillows. "To think that girl chose to run away instead of live with you."

He raised his fist, but he didn't strike her. Instead, he shouted for Hannah. Seconds later, the woman rushed into their room.

"Get Thomas for me," he commanded.

Before Hannah replied, Eliza spoke. "Thomas took Alden and Isaac to Scott's Grove."

"How are we supposed to get to church?"

"You know how to drive the runabout just fine."

He sat on the bed beside his wife. "I'm going to get Isaac back."

She reached for the jar of cream again. "My father won't be very pleased if you ask him to return your generous gift."

His face steamed. "I'll tell him that you deceived me."

"And I'll tell him that you coddle a slave boy."

He leaned close. "Perhaps I don't care what your father thinks."

"Oh, Victor." She sunk down into her pillows again, smirking. "Of course you don't."

Chapter 8

Scott's Grove
December 1853

The sun rose over the frost on the tobacco fields, but the warmth didn't penetrate Alden's room. His family might be able to ignore what happened to Benjamin, but he could not.

With his door cracked open, he could hear Rhody outside, calling for Mammy.

Mammy should be grieving, but instead she'd have to suppress her grief as she buttoned, ironed, and powdered his sister into a proper young lady. For two decades now, Mammy had worked tirelessly for his family, raising the three Payne children and then serving the women, yet they didn't give her a day off to mourn her loss.

His mother entered his room, dressed in a Sunday gown that shimmered red and gold. In her hands was a wheat-colored carpetbag. She quickly scrutinized his nightclothes. "Why aren't you dressed?"

He leaned back against the bedpost, raking his fingers through his messy hair. "I'm not going to church."

"But it's Christmas."

He bowed toward her, forearms resting on his

knees. "Do you remember the Christmas before I turned ten?"

She shook her head.

"It was so warm that Benjamin and I rose early to swim in the pond. Benjamin was only seven, and yet he'd figured out how to make a diving stage from the racks in the curing barn."

His mother's eyes narrowed. "I thought you stole the racks."

"I couldn't tell Father that Benjamin did it. By then, I'd figured out that Benjamin would be whipped with the switch if he did something wrong while my punishment was usually to skip a meal."

She shifted her feet. "That was a long time ago . . ."

His gaze traveled back toward the window to the oak and hickory trees in the forest beyond his father's field. "I knew we were different, but I didn't really know why until I was much older. In my early years, I just saw him as a boy like me."

"He's not anything like you, Alden," she said stiffly.

"But he was. Not his skin color, but he was smart—much smarter than me—and so clever. Then he lost everything when he was sent out to the fields."

She closed the door and sat on the bed beside him, the carpetbag in her lap. "Your compassion is admirable, but you can't change the way of the South on your own. Nor should you. Your father may be firm, but he also provides food and clothing and shelter for our men and women. He cares for them much better than some of our neighbors do their slaves."

His stomach churned. "You should have seen Benjamin's body—"

She waved her gloved hand above the bag. "I don't want to hear about it."

"His treatment was much more than firm, Mother. It was cruel."

"You didn't know Benjamin in his later years. His rebellion was stirring up all the slaves. Your father had to make an example of him to stop the others from running away."

He leaned toward her. "Perhaps it will stop others from running now, but it will also make them angry. You should be worried about what they might do."

She glanced over at the closed door. "After last night, your father doesn't want you to return to Harvard."

"I suspected he might not."

"He says you're learning all the wrong things."

"I'm learning to think for myself."

Fear flashed across her face, replaced swiftly by the resolve in her gaze as she opened the carpetbag, displaying the banknotes inside. "This is enough to pay for your final semester."

He looked down at the money. "Does he know you're giving me this?"

She clasped it shut again. "You will leave with Eliza's driver tomorrow before breakfast. I will explain after you're gone."

For a moment, he felt like Isaac, being shipped off in the carriage in the early morning hours, except he believed his mother was doing this for his well-being. And perhaps to protect him from her husband's wrath.

"No matter what your father says, he is proud that you're going to be a Harvard graduate." She stepped back toward the door. "Use your education for good, Alden."

"I will." He stood and kissed her cheek. "Thank you."

A half hour later, he watched the horses pull his family's carriage away from the house. Then he cleared out the dresser in his room swiftly, unceremoniously dumping his possessions into his steamer trunk. The money for school went into his leather valise.

He wouldn't wait until his family returned to celebrate the holiday with dinner and gifts. He'd leave now, and perhaps he could take Mammy with him instead of Benjamin.

While the other house slaves prepared for the festivities, Mammy sat by the kitchen hearth in the basement, staring down at a plate of grits and boiled chitterlings. He had always thought

Mammy was beautiful, like the African princesses in the adventure stories she used to tell him and Benjamin, but her loss, and the years of her service to the Payne family, had pared away most of her outer beauty. She probably hadn't lived more than thirty-five years, but she looked to be at least fifty.

He filled two cups with black coffee and handed one to her as he sat beside her on the hearth. Even though her body was frail, he knew she remained strong inside—and beautiful.

"Benjamin was a good boy," she said, stirring the grits with her fork. "Could have gone off to the university with you."

"Yes, he could have."

"Made something big of himself."

He twisted the cup in his hands. "What my father did was wrong."

"John Payne never thinks about anyone except himself."

A loyal son would have corrected her, might even have sent her out to the pillory for her impertinence, but unlike his father, he wanted to protect instead of harm her.

He set his cup on the wooden counter. "I want you to come north with me."

She shook her head. "Your father won't emancipate any of his slaves."

"It won't matter up in Canada."

"Even a half-wit slave hunter would suspect

something if I crossed over that Mason-Dixon Line with you. Then he'd bring me back, and Master Payne would kill me, like he did Benjamin." She pressed her spoon into the grits and grease from the chitterlings puddled over it. "I want him to sell me, Alden. I don't care where I go as long as I don't have to be here."

He threw his remaining coffee into the fire. "It's not fair, Mammy."

"Please call me Naomi," she said. "It's the name my mother gave me."

All these years, he'd never even known her name. "Thank you for being a mother to me."

"I wish I could tell you that I did it from the kindness of my heart, but I cared for you the best I could alongside my own son. You've grown into a good man, Alden Payne. A strong one. If you come back here after school, I fear it will all be taken away." She met his gaze with a new boldness. "You need to leave this plantation and| never look back. Go someplace where you can use that brilliant mind God gave you and your passion to help other people."

Isaac peeked around the stairwell, staring at both of them before he focused on Alden. Then he pointed toward his mouth. "My tongue won't stay lassoed."

Alden sighed. "Say what you want."

"I'll never look back."

He stared at the boy. "What?"

"If you take me with you, my eyes will stay on the road. I won't even steal a glance behind us."

Alden was considering his words when Naomi spoke again, her voice laden with grief. "Take him instead of me. So he won't suffer the same fate as Benjamin."

Looking back at her, he reached out, taking her calloused hand into his. "Benjamin was like a brother to me."

"Oh, Alden." Tears filled her eyes before she spoke again. "Benjamin wasn't just like a brother to you. He was your brother."

Her words stung more than the whip his father had lashed across his face. The scales blinding his eyes dropped, everything falling into place. Benjamin's skin may have been dark, but he was smart and confident and bold—just like the man who'd fathered him.

"Does my mother know?" Alden asked.

When she nodded her head, his stomach roiled. "And Benjamin?"

"I told him when he was twelve."

"Isaac," he said, turning toward the boy. "Please find Thomas."

"Yes, sir."

"Tell him to prepare the carriage."

He and Isaac would leave Scott's Grove straightaway. And he would never return.

Chapter 9

Sacramento City
December 1853

Gray fog clung like plaster to the sky as Isabelle plodded up the knoll to her aunt's cottage—a prefabricated house, painted white and then trimmed with green in Baltimore before being shipped in pieces around Cape Horn.

She'd splurged and bought two hen eggs along with fresh cream to make eggnog for her aunt. In one hand, she held the pitcher of Aunt Emeline's favorite drink. In her other was a satchel with her Christmas gift. The Methodist church had celebrated with a service this morning, but Aunt Emeline had been too ill to attend. She'd stayed home with Sing Ye, a young Chinese woman who tended to her care.

When Isabelle arrived, her aunt was sitting up against a heap of pillows on her bed, her yellow quilt folded back over her nightdress. Outside the window was a fenced garden blooming with pansies and calendulas, thriving in the warmth of California's winter.

Even on gray days, her aunt's home always felt cheery. A respite in a constantly changing city. A safe haven for the women Aunt Emeline loved.

Isabelle scooted a chair to the bedside. "How are you feeling today?"

Aunt Emeline smiled. Her lips were cracked, but her eyes glowed with kindness. "I'm happy that both my girls are here."

Sing Ye picked up the porcelain basin on the side table. "You are just as lovely as your aunt."

"Thank you," Isabelle replied. "I think you are quite lovely as well."

She shook her head shyly. "Not in China."

"Here in California, you are beautiful."

Sing Ye turned softly on feet that were too large to be considered pretty in her homeland, but Isabelle still thought they were small. Everything about Sing Ye seemed delicate, yet she had shown more strength than any woman Isabelle had ever known.

A year ago, Sing Ye had arrived on a steamer in San Francisco while Aunt Emeline was in the city commissioning a seamstress to make new curtains for the hotel. Most of the Chinese girls shipped to San Francisco were swept away by their so-called benefactors into the underworld of slave brothels and secret organizations called tongs. These women became known in Chinese as *baak haak chai*. One hundred men's wife.

But Aunt Emeline had rescued Sing Ye, paying for her passage before someone with sordid intentions bought her. Then she brought her back to live in Sacramento as a daughter instead of a slave.

"Nicolas Barr has proposed marriage to Sing Ye."

Isabelle smiled. "That's wonderful news."

"He will take good care of her."

Nicolas worked down at the wharf, and he seemed to be an honorable young man, a hard worker from Germany who had been spellbound by Sing Ye since they met months ago at church. Then he began visiting her at Aunt Emeline's house every Sunday afternoon.

Isabelle hoped for Sing Ye's sake that Nicolas was exactly who he purported to be.

Aunt Emeline clasped her hands together. "Now both my girls will be getting married."

Isabelle's smile fell. "Actually—"

"It's exactly what I wanted before I leave this world."

Isabelle leaned forward, kissing her wrinkled forehead. "You're not leaving us anytime soon."

"Oh, child." Aunt Emeline reached forward with one of her hands to grasp Isabelle's arm. "When God calls, I must go home."

Isabelle wanted to keep her aunt here for many more years—she was the only family Isabelle had left—but Emeline's heart longed to sweep through the gates of heaven that awaited her, to greet her Savior with William at her side.

"My only regret," Aunt Emeline began, leaning

back against the pillows, "is that I didn't rescue hundreds of more girls like her."

"You and Uncle William helped so many." Isabelle wrapped her fingers over her aunt's hand, blinking back the tears in her eyes. "I wish I could help women trapped in slavery too."

Aunt Emeline's gaze wandered toward the gray light in the window. "I suppose both of us must be faithful in caring for whomever God sends our way, like Queen Esther when God asked her to save her people."

"You have been a faithful servant, Auntie. In many ways."

Aunt Emeline began to cough, the hollow rasping of a woman whose body refused to heal, the coal smoke and stench of sewer in this city inflaming her lungs.

Isabelle helped her sit up, gently patting her back, but the cough persisted. "I'm going for the doctor," Isabelle finally said.

"No." Aunt Emeline shook her head. "I'm not ill, Isabelle. Just old."

"He can still give you something for that cough."

Her aunt pointed at the parade of blue and brown glass bottles lined up on the windowsill. "Nothing works anymore."

Isabelle held up her pitcher. "I brought you eggnog."

She poured the drink, and her aunt took several

sips before smiling. "It reminds me of home."

"Do you miss Uncle William?"

"Every day."

Isabelle opened her satchel. "I have a gift for you."

She took out the package, wrapped in white tissue paper and decorated with a red ribbon and piece of lace.

"It's beautiful," Aunt Emeline said.

"But you haven't even opened it."

"I think it's too pretty to open."

Isabelle peeled back the paper for her and lifted out the watercolor painting she'd found of her aunt's beloved home of Marseille. The sails flapping in the breeze along the port. The cliffs along the coast. The basilica called Notre-Dame de la Garde with its bell tower on the hill.

Aunt Emeline clutched the picture to her chest, tears in her eyes. It was where she'd spent her childhood, where she'd met and married her William more than forty years ago.

Slowly she lowered the picture, looking over at the cypress writing desk by the door. It was the only extravagant piece in the cottage, one purchased from a Brazilian man who'd brought it on a ship when he traveled north. When he arrived in Sacramento, he realized he needed money more than furniture. Aunt Emeline, she guessed, had given him even more than the piece was worth so he'd have the funds to start over.

Her aunt pointed toward the desk. "I have a gift for you too."

But even as she spoke, her eyes began to close.

Isabelle leaned forward. "I'll open it next time."

Aunt Emeline nodded. "Have you received any news from Ross?"

"Not yet." She'd do just about anything to help her aunt recover, including shield her from the realities of what Ross had done.

"He'll be home soon," Aunt Emeline said, her voice growing weaker. "Then we'll have a wedding for you too."

She kissed Emeline's soft cheek as her aunt drifted to sleep.

In her heart, she wanted a love like the one shared by her uncle and aunt: two people who'd longed to be together, who trusted one another even when they were apart.

There would be no marriage for her, but perhaps it was for the best. Her uncle and aunt had partnered together to rescue exploited women and children. Helping them find freedom. Ross had been a good business partner, but she suspected he wouldn't feel the same about helping those in Sacramento City who needed a friend, especially if it threatened his business.

She glanced back out the window again, the glass a dull canvas splattered with vagrant droplets of rain. There was no clarity on it. No beauty. The water clung to it as if it feared falling, as if the clinging was much better than the unknown.

She didn't know what would happen to her either in the months ahead, but she knew well that she couldn't cling to the past. She would hold on to her aunt's hand, content in the comfort of her prayers as she stepped into the unknown.

Smiling, she rose to her feet. She needn't concern herself with Ross's perspective any longer. Like Aunt Emeline, she could be faithful to help whomever God sent her way.

Chapter 10

Scott's Grove
December 1853

Isaac was true to his word. He didn't even glance over his shoulder as Thomas drove the horses swiftly away from Scott's Grove. Instead of returning to the Duvall home, Alden had asked Thomas to transport them directly to Alexandria.

His mother would be angry that he'd left without saying good-bye—and his father would think him foolish—but as long as they didn't suspect that he took a slave with him, they wouldn't send someone in pursuit. Hopefully, Isaac would be in Canada before anyone realized he was gone.

Taking Isaac north was much different than trying to steal Mammy—Naomi—away. If they were stopped on the boat or train, he'd claim Isaac was his manservant. If a slave hunter insisted on seeing papers, he would claim his own ineptness, his foolish youth, as the reason for forgetting them.

He doubted anyone would stop them, though. It was a common sight in New York and Boston to see a male Southerner traveling with a manservant or a woman accompanied by her personal maid.

The brougham swept down the lane carved between his father's prized fields. And his stomach churned again with revulsion over what his father had done to the woman Alden had loved like a mother.

He'd been so naïve. Stupid. He was twenty-three years old, and he'd never really stopped to think who had sired Benjamin. He and Benjamin had never talked about their fathers, and he'd always assumed that his nursemaid had a husband in the fields. Or at another plantation.

Last night's argument between his father and Naomi, and the shame in his mother's eyes as she cowered inside her room, haunted him. Now he understood Benjamin's resolve, the righteousness in his anger. Naomi's wounds of both body and heart, forced to have sex with a man she hated. And why his mother remained so placid in her own humiliation and fears.

No matter how much he wanted to understand, he couldn't comprehend what his father had done. Perhaps that was why his father was so angry at Benjamin. Reflected in the eyes of a slave was his own sin.

Alden pressed his fingers against his temples. Did his father's stomach ever churn over how he punished the men and women in his care?

Perhaps his father felt compassion years ago, but his heart had turned into stone over the years, the power consuming him. How else could someone with life pulsing through his veins kill his own son and then strike the woman he'd abused, threatening to sell her after she gave everything to him?

And all these years his mother had known.

Anger swelled within him again. Then sympathy. Compassion and rage.

Now he understood why his mother's heart had grown as cold as his father's, why she'd displayed no despair over what her husband had done last night. The hatred must have consumed her too.

This was why Naomi told him to leave Scott's Grove. No matter how much he protested, he wouldn't be able to change his father's mind. In the end, he would be an advocate of the evil.

The carriage hit another rock, and he reached for the rail as the wheels jogged back and forth.

Why hadn't someone told him the truth? He'd

always wanted a brother, and he'd had one—a half brother who could have thrived at Harvard if given a chance.

He glanced at the boy sitting resolutely across from him, as if he knew the gravity of what they were doing, and he realized the oak-brown shade of Isaac's skin was similar to Benjamin's.

Could this be Victor's son? Victor and Eliza had no children, and unfortunately it was acceptable in their society for slave owners, like his father, to sire a slave child—another boy to work in the fields or sell at an auction.

If Victor was Isaac's father, what had happened to his mother?

He shifted on the hard seat. He may never have answers to his questions—it was all so convoluted. And he would never return to the Duvall farm to ask. Benjamin's future might have been stolen from him, but he prayed there might be some redemption for this boy. Isaac was smart too. Courageous. If a Negro family adopted him in Canada, he could go to school, and then he could work as a freedman up north.

Isaac reached for the folded copy of the *New York Times* beside Alden's valise. Then he seemed to scan the top headlines.

Startled, Alden leaned forward. "You can read?"

Isaac nodded proudly. "Master Duvall hired someone to teach me so I could read him the paper before he gets out of bed."

"I hope Victor also told you to keep your skill a secret."

Isaac shrugged, apparently unconcerned as he continued to scan the first page. Then he turned to the second page. "Looky here," he said, flicking the paper. "There's an article about Solomon Northup."

Alden had followed that case closely up at Harvard. "What does it say?"

Isaac read the first few lines. Then he groaned before summarizing. "No one's going to be punished for kidnapping the man."

Alden reached for the newspaper and perused the rest of the story. Isaac was right. While he—and most of his fellow law students—had hoped this case would prompt change in their legal system in regard to slavery, the justice system bowed again to the wealthy slaveholders.

Thankfully, Northup had been rescued and sent back home, but because of his skin color, he wasn't allowed to testify against those who had kidnapped him or against the man who'd whipped him and forced him to work as a slave for twelve years.

Isaac pressed his nose against the cold glass. "Look at that."

Alden blinked, taking in his surroundings again. Outside the brougham were giant snowflakes, sticking to the window, salting the ground. The evergreen trees in the distance looked like cones of iced cream.

It was a miserable day for Stella to get her snow.

"Where are we going?" Isaac asked.

He wanted to say they were headed toward freedom, like Solomon Northup after his years in bondage. But he feared what Isaac might say in his enthusiasm. Much better that he found out about his newfound freedom once he was safely in Canada.

"Eventually we'll arrive in Boston."

Isaac pumped up his chest. "I know all about Boston."

"From the newspaper?"

The boy shook his head. "From reading *The Scarlet Letter* to Master Duvall. Poor little Pearl."

Alden glanced back over at him. "Who's Pearl?"

"Hester's baby."

"From *The Scarlet Letter*?"

Isaac confirmed with a nod. "Of course, good things happen to Pearl in the end."

"Of course," Alden said, though he hadn't read the novel. If only every story had a happy ending.

Five hours after they left Scott's Grove, Thomas drove the carriage into Alexandria. The streets were mostly quiet on this Christmas Day. He could see people inside some of the homes, sitting as families around their tables.

As they neared the waterfront, they passed a fenced yard with about twenty black men and women pacing inside. None of them looked over at the carriage.

"What is that?" Isaac asked, pointing at the snow-covered yard.

"It's a slave pen."

Isaac eyed the brick building next to it. "They live there?"

"No. They're waiting to be sold."

Isaac contemplated that information. "Who'll buy them?"

"Probably a tobacco or cotton planter. They need thousands of slaves to work in their fields."

"Missus Eliza once said she was going to sell me."

"I'm glad she didn't."

"Master Duvall wouldn't let her."

"It seems like you are a hard worker, Isaac."

"A man fortunate enough to find work is a man fortunate enough to eat."

Alden smiled. "I believe that's true."

Though if he were honest with himself, he hadn't spent much time working for what he was given. Other people had done the hard work for him. Even when he and his father had joined the field slaves, picking and curing their tobacco harvest, their tasks were easy compared to the others. He was anxious to begin working alongside Judah Fallow in San Francisco to finally earn his keep.

The carriage stopped at the Potomac riverfront, and he saw two steamers waiting at the wharf, including the *George Washington*, the ship that would take them up to New York. No one was working along the boardwalk today. They'd have to wait until tomorrow for the next leg of their journey.

At a nearby hotel, the porter helped Thomas transfer Alden's trunk into a vacant room on the second floor—a simple place with two narrow beds, a dresser, and a window that overlooked a row of shops.

"Thank you, Thomas," Alden said as they walked back downstairs.

"I'm just doing my job."

Alden stopped by the carriage. "Would you like to travel north with us?"

Thomas shook his head. "Master Duvall's already going to be furious when he discovers Isaac is missing."

"Do you think I'm doing the right thing?"

Thomas climbed up onto the driver's seat. "It's not for me to say."

"If you came with us, I'd find passage up to Canada for you too."

He held up the reins. "I appreciate it, Master Payne, but I'm too old to start over and too tired to run."

Alden nodded. Thomas may not be legally free, but in this case, he was free to choose his own future. "When Mr. Duvall and Mr. Payne ask about us, just tell them the truth."

"Can't see that I have a reason to lie," Thomas

said with a tip of his hat. "I don't know anything."

The snow continued to fall outside the hotel window, covering the cobblestones on the street. Alden's stomach rumbled. Even though Isaac didn't complain, Alden knew he must be hungry as well.

Alden reached for his cloak. "Stay in the room while I'm gone."

Isaac sat on the bed closest to the window. "Can I read while you're away?"

"You can read all you want in the room, but whenever we go out, you must act like my slave."

Isaac looked confused. "I am your slave."

"I mean—" Alden stopped himself.

"Missus Eliza gave me to you," Isaac said, as if Alden might have forgotten. "And I ain't goin' anywhere unless you sell me to someone else."

"I'm not going to sell you," Alden assured him.

Isaac leaned back against the headboard, looking quite pleased.

As Alden stepped out onto the cold street, he prayed no one on the ship tomorrow would suspect what he had done.

He would protect Isaac with his life if he must, for Benjamin and Naomi's sake.

Chapter 11

West End
December 1853

Thomas returned to the Duvall farm more than a week earlier than expected, saying he'd already taken Alden to the wharf in town. Victor didn't care a lick about Alden, but he'd been stewing since yesterday over what Eliza had done. He already hated his wife, but she'd propelled his hatred to an entirely new level.

Victor had insisted the coachman turn right back around, transporting him to Scott's Grove in the dark. Thomas said the two carriage horses needed rest before they started another journey, and none of the other horses on the farm were strong enough for the journey.

Victor began to reprimand him for his impertinence—and his laziness—until he saw the animals collapsed on the straw in their stalls. And he saw snow piling up on the ground outside.

There was no sense finding themselves stranded on the road, no matter how much he wanted to leave. Isaac would be safe enough with the Paynes, though John would put him right to work. Perhaps, after Victor rescued him, the boy would have a greater appreciation for his life here. A few days of hoeing or cleaning out the barns would be a good reminder of his comforts back in West End.

He spent the first hours of the night packing. Then he settled into his bed, but sleep evaded him. Every time he tried to close his eyes, all he could see were Mallie's eyes looking back, haunting him.

Leaning over on his pillows, Victor lit a candle and tugged on the brass knob of the writing desk drawer. He shoved aside *David Copperfield*—a ridiculous story that he and Isaac hadn't yet finished—and a copy of a brilliant new novel, *Moby-Dick*. They'd read the book about the whale twice.

Under the books and smattering of letters was a portrait he'd painted of Mallie after his father died, the image wrapped in a cream-colored silk. Eliza didn't know he had kept it. At one time, he'd had to keep it hidden, but Eliza never came to his room anymore.

He lifted Mallie's portrait from the silk and examined her face in the candlelight, the amber-colored eyes and slender nose and smooth skin free of any blemish. So very beautiful in those months before Isaac was born.

Mallie had been everything to him. A perfect rose among inferior weeds. A diamond buried in Virginia's red clay, waiting for someone like him to cut and polish and refine her beauty. He'd never known a fairer woman. Nor one so challenging.

His mother and then the Honorable Arthur Duvall protected her while they were alive, as if Victor meant to harm her. He had wanted nothing more than to love Mallie, to keep her as his own.

Arthur the Honorable couldn't stop him from beyond the grave.

Still, Mallie had resisted him, but in the end, she'd had no choice but to succumb. He hadn't wanted to be so harsh. He knew what was best for her—for both of them. He'd only wanted them to be together.

He held her portrait up to his chest.

Thou saw'st the locked lovers when leaping from their flaming ship; heart to heart they sank beneath the exulting wave; true to each other, when heaven seemed false to them.

He and Mallie were supposed to be true to one another—like Melville wrote—heart to heart. No matter what trials they faced in this life. They were never supposed to separate.

Anger ripped through him, like it always did when he thought about Mallie. The portrait shook in his hands.

Where had she gone? And after he had loved her so deeply, why had she abandoned him? Since he was fifteen, he'd known that she was supposed to be his—and then she left him. The loss tore him up on the inside.

He'd searched everywhere for her that spring and then summer, traveling to the slave markets and even up to Boston and Philadelphia after Congress passed the Fugitive Slave Act. It was illegal now for the Yankees to harbor runaways, and he'd hoped that he might find her hiding among the freed slaves. With this law, she would have had no choice but to return to Virginia with him. He didn't care a whit what Eliza thought.

His search had availed him nothing, though. It seemed the woman he'd loved more than any-thing had disappeared.

One day, Mallie would return to him. He'd find her—and she would pay for leaving him—but she'd change her mind. One day, she would love him as he loved her.

Closing his eyes, he savored the thought of reclaiming her as his slave. Once he found her, she would never leave him again.

He wrapped the portrait back up in the silk and secured it in his leather portfolio, along with his art supplies and the important documents he carried with him wherever he went.

Isaac hadn't left him as Mallie had done. Nor would he ever leave this house again without Victor at his side.

After Isaac's birth, Victor had swept in and personally found a colored nursemaid to care for him without Eliza's interference—at first for collateral and then because he grew fond of the boy. As long as the boy treated him with respect, he would have a comfortable home here. John Payne would have to find another slave to help in the fields.

When the clock struck the six o'clock hour, he rose from his bed and dressed quickly. He'd planned to go alone to Scott's Grove, but Eliza was waiting for him downstairs. She climbed into the carriage behind him without a word and didn't budge.

Instead of protesting, he decided that it was exactly as it should be—she could explain to her father why she gave him Isaac: because she was obsessively, insufferably jealous of a nine-year-old slave boy.

John would understand why Victor wanted him back. He was equally protective of the slaves in his care.

They arrived at Scott's Grove before noon and found Nora Payne in the drawing room by herself, beside the unlit pine tree. When she turned and saw Eliza, her stoic lips turned upward into a sad smile.

"My dear," Nora said, hurrying toward her daughter. "Why are you here?"

Eliza didn't return her smile. "Victor insisted that we visit."

Then Nora squeezed his neck much too hard.

"You are a good son," she said, soaking the shoulder of his waistcoat with an enormous amount of tears.

When she released him, he searched the room for Isaac, as if the boy might be hiding behind a high-backed sofa or the long drapery around the windows.

"John's in Charlottesville," Nora said. "He should return soon."

"Do you know where Isaac is?" Victor asked, stepping away from her before her tears ruined his clothing.

Nora looked over at him, confused. "Who is Isaac?"

Eliza snorted. "His personal page."

"Why would your servant be here?"

Victor motioned toward his wife, but didn't look her way. "Eliza sent him with Alden."

Nora pressed her eyes closed for a moment, then reopened them. "There was a boy who arrived with Alden, but I don't know where he went. Alden left us yesterday while we were in church."

Tears began to pour again.

"Yes, yes," Victor replied with a wave of his hand. "Thomas said he took Alden to Alexandria."

"He was supposed to celebrate Christmas with his family."

Victor stared at the woman, perplexed. Is that why she was crying? Because her son left early? Women were absurd. Alden was a grown man, yet Nora treated him like he were a child. His brother-in-law was a radical. An idealist. Victor wished he would stay up in Cambridge permanently instead of returning to Scott's Grove.

He moved back to the door. "Perhaps Isaac is with the other house slaves."

Nora returned to the sofa. "I suppose."

"I'll go search for him."

The two women began babbling nonsense. About the snow, the journey, Eliza's plans to stay here until the New Year.

Eliza hadn't discussed her plans with him, but Scott's Grove would be as good of a place as any to spend a week or two this winter. A welcome relief, really, from the doldrums of the farm. He and Isaac could begin reading the whale book again, and he could amuse himself with the other books in John's library.

Downstairs, he asked a woman stirring the kitchen fire about Isaac, but she gave him a blank look which made him deem her either deaf or daft. The upstairs servants said they'd seen a new boy, but they didn't know where he went.

Victor searched the bedchambers. John's office.

"Isaac," he called out into the small library, but still the boy didn't answer. Had his father-in-law already sent Isaac out to the fields?

When he couldn't find Isaac in the house, he found his coachman in the stables, grooming a horse. "Thomas, have you seen Isaac?"

The man kept brushing. "Yes, sir."

Confound it. He should have asked Thomas hours ago. "Where is he?"

Thomas looked up, confusion in his eyes. "I took him and Master Alden to Alexandria yesterday."

Victor kicked a stool. "Why didn't you tell me?"

"I did tell you."

Victor clenched his fists. "You just told me about Alden."

"I didn't think you'd care about the slave."

Victor took a step toward him. "Why did he go with Alden?"

Thomas shrugged. "Perhaps Master Alden needed a boy to help him at school."

He didn't care one whit what Alden needed. Isaac was his; no one else could claim him. "Does John Payne know?"

"I'm just the driver, sir. No one ever tells me what the master knows or doesn't know."

Victor pointed at the horse. "Get them ready."

"They're too tired for another journey."

His eyes narrowed. "You ever felt the whip on your back, Thomas?"

"Yes, sir."

"I'll whip you and your horses if you don't have me on the way to Alexandria in the next hour."

Turning, he stomped back toward the house, trailing snow behind him as he tramped across the wooden floor in the hall. When he marched into the drawing room, Nora excused herself.

Eliza leaned back on the sofa, sipping a glass of brandy. "Where's your slave?"

He towered over her. "Did you tell Alden to take him to Cambridge?"

"I did not, but it's a brilliant thought."

"What if Alden decides to sell him?"

She took another sip. "Good riddance, for all of us. That boy's not fit for any kind of decent work."

"You're right. He's much too smart to be a slave."

"Oh, Victor," she said, setting her glass onto a table. "Just because you fathered him does not mean he's smart. In fact, quite the opposite."

He fought to ignore her words. "I'm going to retrieve him."

Eliza's smile fell. "You'll do nothing of the sort."

"The boy reminds you too much of Mallie, doesn't he?"

She shook her head. "You don't know anything about me."

"But you know exactly how I felt about Mallie."

Her laugh was bitter. "And we know how she felt about you. Left you the first opportunity she had to run." Standing, she walked toward the decorated tree and fingered the needles. "Perhaps that's what Isaac is doing too. Running away from you."

If only he could put his hands around that long

neck, choke the life out of her. If the judge knew what it was like to live with this woman, he'd let him go without consequence. "I'll find Isaac and bring him back."

She stepped toward him, her voice hard. "If you go after him, I swear I'll leave you."

"Then that seals my decision." Eliza may threaten, but she would never leave him. According to the law in Virginia, a divorced woman couldn't own a single item of her husband's property. Eliza had a firm appreciation for prestige and the finer things a plantation and their slaves could offer.

"This is ludicrous," she said.

"What's ludicrous?" John was standing in the doorway, his top hat in his hands.

Victor stepped toward him. "Alden took one of my slaves north with him."

When John swore, Victor sneered at Eliza. He knew the man would understand.

"If you don't go now," John said, "you'll never see your slave again."

The chill from the hall swept over Victor. "Will he sell Isaac?"

"No. He'll probably set him free."

Eliza laughed again as he stomped back out of the room. He would find Alden and Isaac. And he would bring Isaac back home with him for good.

Chapter 12

Sacramento City
December 1853

The front door of the Golden Hotel flew open, shaking the paintings when it banged against the wall. Isabelle looked up from the ledger as a Negro boy dressed in torn breeches and a stained linen shirt rushed into the lobby.

The boy scanned the small room, and Isabelle recognized the look on his face. It was one of terror.

Outside the door, on the walk crowded with miners and businessmen, she heard a man yell, "Micah!"

She'd told Aunt Emeline that she wanted to be faithful to help whomever God sent her way. Perhaps God had directed this boy right to her. Perhaps now was the time to continue what her uncle and aunt started long ago.

"Hurry," she said, beckoning the boy behind the counter and toward the elevated desk where she sat. Then she pushed aside her chair and lifted the panel to her hiding space.

The laws of this new state might support slave owners' rights, but no matter what the government said, she could never send a boy back into slavery—if this boy was a slave.

She would have to evaluate his status later. For now, she had to be faithful to what God required of her.

The boy hesitated, staring down into the dark space. Outside the window stood a fleshy man dressed in a gray sack coat. His head ticked back and forth between his shoulders, like a clock keeping time.

The boy rubbed his hands together. "Master Bridges is gonna kill me."

"You'll be safe in here," she assured him. "If you move quickly."

He glanced back at the window and then climbed down into the dark room. Isabelle replaced the rug and sat back on her chair to continue recording expenses in her ledger.

While California was officially a free state, slaveholders who were just passing through didn't relinquish the ownership of any slaves traveling with them. Some slave owners spent months in the goldfields, claiming they weren't going to stay permanently, and the law seemed to be on their side. She'd seen advertisements of slaves even being sold in San Francisco, and now other blacks —freed men and women— were in danger of being kidnapped and sold too.

It didn't matter to her whether or not this boy hidden below her was legally free. In her mind, no person should be bought or sold.

The front bell chimed as Mr. Bridges stepped

into her hotel. In his fingers, he clutched a cheap cigar, the stench overpowering the scent of lemon verbena in the lobby.

"Micah!" he shouted. His head continued its strange ticktock rhythm, looking back and forth as if she weren't even there.

Her heart pounding, Isabelle looked up casually from her accounts, pointing with the wooden handle of her pen at the list of rules hung beside the counter. "Rule number six," she stated. "There is no smoking inside this establishment."

Mr. Bridges held up the cigar and made a grand sweep with it, trailing the smoke through the room before he spoke again. "Where's the proprietor of this place?"

She closed the ledger, tapping the sole of her patent boot on the rug. "How can I assist you, monsieur?"

"I want to speak with the person in charge."

"I am the person in charge."

His eyes narrowed in on her. "You own this hotel?"

"I'm the manager." She dipped the nib of her pen into the inkwell. "Would you like to reserve a room for the evening?"

He shook his head. "I'm looking for my slave. Someone said they saw a colored boy run in here."

"What does he look like?" she asked, leaning back in her chair.

His eyes narrowed, searching her face as if

111

trying to determine if she was being obstinate or if she was just inept. "The same as any other darky, only shorter."

A retort rose in her throat, but she swallowed it. In this situation, honey would be a more effective deterrent than rebuke.

She rose slowly, directing the man away from the hiding space. "Come with me," she said as she walked through the entrance into the restaurant. "I will enlist my staff to search for him."

Mr. Bridges followed her through the open doorway into the vacant dining room and reluctantly sat at a table near the kitchen. Then he took a draw on his cigar and puffed out the smoke in her face.

She waved her hand in front of her face, resisting the urge to gag. She would have required any other man to extinguish his cigar, but she would appease Mr. Bridges this afternoon, for Micah's sake.

"Stephan," she called. When her dark-skinned steward came up from the cellar, she waved him toward her. "This gentleman is looking for a Negro boy."

Mr. Bridges ignored him. "Micah's a slave," he reminded her. "Eleven or twelve years old and darn good at hiding."

"He said that Micah came into the hotel," she told Stephan, nodding toward the steps. "Could you please search the rooms upstairs?"

112

"You're sending him to search for Micah?" the man asked incredulously, as if Stephan wasn't standing right there—as if her steward were incapable of looking for a missing person because his skin was a shade darker than the man across from her. Her blood felt as if it might boil over, but she maintained her composure on the outside, for Micah's sake. Stephan's face remained aloof as well.

"He is quite capable," she explained. "Stephan will search the top floors of the hotel, and I will look on the bottom."

Mr. Bridges returned to his feet. "I will search with you."

She shook her head. "Only guests and my employees are allowed upstairs."

Stephan moved toward the steps, and Fanny appeared in the kitchen doorway, flour sprinkled on her apron. She'd spent her day helping Janette, the hotel cook, prepare for their evening meal.

"Could you please bring this gentleman some of the raspberry tarts you baked?" Isabelle asked.

"Of course," Fanny replied. "Should I bring coffee too?"

"No—I will retrieve some wine from downstairs."

Fanny's eyebrows arched, but she didn't say anything about Isabelle indulging the man.

Thankfully, Mr. Bridges didn't seem to realize her insincerity. "Micah's a wily boy," he said, his eyes skimming the room.

"If he's in the hotel, I'm certain Stephan or I will find him."

Mr. Bridges took a step toward the cellar door. "I will look downstairs."

Isabelle moved to stop him. "Where are you from?" she asked, blocking the entrance.

"Texas."

"I don't know what it's like in Texas, but I don't tolerate trespassing here—and the sheriff is on my side."

When Fanny brought out the tarts, the man settled back into the chair. At least he was deterred for the moment.

Excusing herself, Isabelle stepped down into the cellar. Mr. Bridges wouldn't be able to see Micah if he came down here, but it was possible he could hear him between the walls.

Isabelle slowly retrieved Mr. Walsh's Madeira from her limited collection of fine wines, regretting that she had to waste some of it on this man fuming in her dining room. But better to distract him than let him tear up her hotel. Once he left, she'd help Micah escape, but it would be better for all of them if Mr. Bridges's senses were dulled before he continued his search.

When she emerged back into the dining room, she shook her head, trying to appear disappointed by her news. "There's no one hiding downstairs."

The man shifted in his seat, but his eyes were focused on his goblet as she filled it with the dark, sweet wine. He didn't bother to sniff it, guzzling it instead. Then she refilled his glass.

After drinking three glasses of wine, he looked over at the wooden staircase that linked her dining room with the second floor. "Where is your man?"

"He's very thorough in his work," she explained. "I'm certain he's still searching."

"He best find Micah, or I'm going to enlist your sheriff to help me."

She walked to the bottom of the tall staircase and glanced up. Stephan was waiting for her signal at the top.

When he walked back down into the dining room, Stephan spoke to her. "There's no one upstairs except the guests in rooms 2 and 8."

Mr. Bridges leaped up, knocking over his fourth glass of wine. The brown liquid spilled across the white tablecloth. "He's lying."

Isabelle crossed her arms. "Neither my steward nor I can produce a child who clearly isn't here."

He backed away. "I'll return with your sheriff."

She smiled. "Rodney is always welcome."

Mr. Bridges stomped out of the dining room, and as she watched him pass by the window, Stephan moved up beside her. They were alone in the room, but still she whispered. "Micah's safe, but if that dreadful man brings back a dog, he'll find him."

"I know where to take him," Stephan said.

She looked back at her steward, a man who'd

worked hard for her during the past year. He hadn't volunteered much of his story, but she knew it hadn't always been easy. The lobe was missing below his right ear, and he walked with a limp.

"Will he be safe?" she asked.

"Much safer than here."

Isabelle glanced back out the window. "Let's move quickly, then."

The sun had fallen below the horizon, the coal lamps emitting their orange glow along K Street. Taking her cap and black cloak from behind the reception counter, she slipped outside into the fading twilight. The walkway was still crowded with workers leaving the wharf and shop owners finishing the day. She slipped around the side of the building and into the alley behind it, then waited a few moments to see if anyone followed her.

When no one emerged, she stepped into the tiny courtyard between her building and the one next door. Then she rolled an empty barrel to the side and swung down the hatch behind it. After bundling up the hem of her dress in one hand, she crawled back through the passage.

A faint ray of light stole through a crack between the buildings, and when the passage opened into a narrow room, she saw the boy sitting on the dirt floor, his legs drawn up to his chest. Near him was her metal lockbox.

"I'm Isabelle," she said, sitting between him and her gold. "You must come with me."

He shook his head. "I ain't going back."

"I don't blame you," she said. While they needed to hurry, she knew that fear could immobilize a person—what scared someone could end up destroying them simply because they were too afraid to act. "Mr. Bridges says you're from Texas."

"He's from Texas, but that ain't my home."

"I'd like to help you find a real home."

He eyed the entrance into the passage. "He'll catch me if I leave here."

"I fear he'll catch you if you stay." She scooted back toward the passage. "I have a friend who can take you to a safe place."

"How do you know it's safe?"

"I suppose I can't promise, but it's much better than if you stay here."

She retrieved three gold coins from the lockbox and pressed them into his palm for the journey ahead. Then she crawled back through the passage, not knowing if Micah was following her until she climbed out into the courtyard. Thankfully, he emerged seconds later, closing the small door as she dusted off her skirt and pinned her escaping curls back into place.

Stephan stepped around the side of the building. "Here's my friend," she said, introducing Micah.

When the boy hesitated again, Stephan leaned

down beside him. "There's no telling what your master might do if we don't hurry."

"I'm afraid," Micah told him.

Stephan pointed to his earlobe. "My master clipped off my ear the first time I ran away."

Both Isabelle and the boy shuddered.

"I won't tell you what he did the second time."

With that, Micah agreed to leave. Isabelle draped the black cloak over his shoulders and covered his hair with her cap. She didn't ask where they were going, but as the sky grew darker, she prayed they would be safe.

Two customers were waiting for her when she returned to the lobby, and she seated them in the dining room. Fanny stepped out of the kitchen, her flour-doused apron replaced with a pastel green one.

"Stephan had to fetch something for me," Isabelle told her.

Fanny reached for a menu. "I'll take their order."

She didn't know how long Stephan would be gone, and in that moment, she was grateful that Fanny was there to help.

Back in the lobby, she waited for the return of Mr. Bridges. Ross would say she was crazy to risk everything for a slave boy—a stranger they didn't know and shouldn't believe. He wasn't proslavery, just probusiness. And now she realized, pro-Ross. It seemed he had no problem using people to get exactly what he wanted—the money for his passage to California, the ownership of a hotel, the gold he thought would make him rich.

The doorbell chimed, and she took a deep breath as the inevitable arrived. Mr. Bridges stomped back into her hotel, along with the sheriff. Thankfully, they didn't bring a blood-ound.

"Evenin', Miss Labrie," the sheriff said, removing his fedora.

She welcomed him with a smile. "Good evening, Rodney."

Rodney nodded toward the man stewing beside him, still clutching a cigar. "Mr. Bridges here is looking for his slave."

Isabelle stepped back around the counter. "I thought slavery was illegal in this state."

"The federal government sees it differently."

"Either way," she said, motioning to the man beside him, "I already explained to Mr. Bridges that I don't know where his slave is. If he's allowed to bring a slave into California, then he should be responsible for his whereabouts."

Rodney glanced toward the restaurant. "He said you wouldn't let him look through your hotel."

"Mr. Bridges is a stranger to me and one who refused to obey my basic rules." She pointed again to the sign beside the counter, toward the clearly stated rule against smoking.

"I will search with him," Rodney said.

"Do you have a warrant?"

Rodney's eyes narrowed. "Do I need one?"

"Stephan and I searched every floor and found nothing, but Mr. Bridges is welcome to search as long as you stay with him." She pointed toward the man's hand. "And as long as he leaves his cigar outside."

When Mr. Bridges continued clinging to the cigar, irritation flooded Rodney's face. The sheriff had only been in Sacramento City for a few months. He was a fair man under the obligation to keep law and order in a town that didn't value either. He didn't have time for insolence.

Mr. Bridges held up his cigar. "There's no law in California against smoking."

"Miss Labrie is entitled to enforce the rules of her establishment."

"And I'm entitled to my cigar."

Rodney shoved his hat back on his head. "If your cigar is more important than your slave, so be it. I've got plenty of other things to do."

Mr. Bridges eyed him for a moment, as if he wasn't sure whether the sheriff was serious. He must have determined that Rodney was in earnest because he stepped back outside, returning seconds later empty handed. She didn't know what he did with the cigar. Hopefully he didn't hide it some-place that would set the town on fire.

Rodney removed his hat again, and the two men

stepped through the archway at the right of the room, into the restaurant. Then she heard them walking up the stairs, heard the scraping of furniture on the floor overhead, the stomping of their boots.

There were eighteen people staying in the Golden right now. Hopefully they wouldn't harass any of the guests as they looked for Micah.

Any other time, she would have protested a search—for the sake of her guests—but she didn't want Rodney to think she was hiding anything from him. And the longer it took them to look through her establishment, the more time Stephan had to hide the boy. Perhaps it would take Mr. Bridges a few hours before he relented.

Outside her window, the sky was completely black now. The walkways were still filled with men, most of them heading to the saloons or gambling halls two streets over. Some were just in Sacramento City for a few days or weeks. Others had stayed long enough to become citizens of the town. She knew almost everyone who'd decided to call this place home.

As she waited for Rodney and Mr. Bridges, she escorted customers back into the dining room and checked two miners into vacant rooms. They'd spent months, the men said, in a wet tent in the Mother Lode. They quickly agreed to her list of rules—payment due before they occupied a room, extinguishing all lanterns before they left, no spitting on the floor, no gambling, at least one bath per week at the local bathhouse, no hard liquor, no prostitution, and no smoking cigars anywhere inside the hotel. They paid twenty dollars each to reserve a room for a week, and with the keys at her side, she took the miners upstairs.

When she stepped back into the corridor, she looked for Mr. Bridges and Rodney, but she didn't see either man. Perhaps they were up on the third floor now.

Each time she escorted another customer into the dining room, Fanny flashed her a panicked look, but even if she felt overwhelmed, Fanny was handling the flood of customers perfectly fine on her own.

Isabelle was sitting at her desk, writing an order for more wine, when the sheriff and Mr. Bridges appeared back in the lobby. Rodney looked annoyed, Mr. Bridges livid.

Mr. Bridges leaned onto the counter. "Where did he go?"

She flashed Rodney a look, eyebrows raised as if the man in front of her might be crazy. "I don't know what you're talking about."

"Where's my slave?"

"Did you search the entire hotel?" she asked, equally annoyed at his interruption.

Rodney stepped up to the counter, drumming his fingers on the wood. "Two people claim they saw a colored boy run into your lobby. They never saw him leave."

She glanced around the lobby. "I'm not hiding a boy here."

"You said that your steward helped you search."

Isabelle pasted a smile on her face, much less welcoming this time. "He looked upstairs."

"I'd like to speak to him," Rodney said.

Isabelle's confidence began to falter. "I don't know if he's available."

"Miss Labrie"—Rodney's smile was condescending—"I'm certain you can open up his availability."

As far as she knew, the sheriff didn't drink, at least not while he was on duty. She'd have to think of another way to distract him until Stephan returned.

She stood slowly before stepping around the counter. "I'll retrieve him from the kitchen."

"There's no need," Stephan said from the doorway. "How can I help you?"

Mr. Bridges took a cigar from his cloak pocket along with a box of matches. He lit the cigar as Rodney turned to speak with Stephan. "I'm told you helped search for a runaway slave this afternoon."

"Yes, sir."

"And did you locate him?"

"I did not."

Rodney moved closer to him, studying his black waistcoat and trousers along with the linen draped over his arm. "Did you go out this evening, Stephan?"

"The dining room is full, sir. I've been quite busy serving Miss Labrie's clientele."

Rodney paused. "If I find out you left the hotel, I'll take it before the judge."

Stephan nodded calmly, though Isabelle knew he must be terrified inside. A colored person wasn't allowed to testify before a judge, even if there was a crime. Her steward may have achieved freedom to work and live in California, but his tongue wasn't free here, at least not in a court-room.

"You won't find out anything different," Stephan assured him.

Rodney tilted his hat toward her. "Good evening, Miss Labrie."

"But . . . ," Mr. Bridges protested.

Rodney glared at him and the cigar in his hand. "It seems to me, sir, that you need to keep as good account of your slaves as you do your cigars."

Chapter 13

Boston
December 1853

Plumes of snow piled up outside Crandall Livery & Stables in Boston, creating white pilasters along the building's gray walls. Wind spiraled a troupe of new flakes as they fell to the ground, adding their company to the growing columns.

Alden stomped his feet inside the open doorway of the livery. If the snow didn't stop soon, all of Park Square would be buried in a white shroud before dark.

The boat from Alexandria had taken him and Isaac to New York, then the train had transported them the remaining way to the depot here in Boston two days ago, but the accumulating snow had canceled the service of his typical coach over to Cambridge indefinitely.

Fellow boat and then train passengers had watched him and Isaac for their entire journey, as if they were traveling performers about to entertain. Some of the people around them were curious. Others seemed hostile at his apparent ownership of a young slave.

When someone appeared too intrigued with their arrangement, he would demand that Isaac fetch his bag or something to eat. The boy did the work swiftly, usually with a smile. And no one had asked for his papers yet.

Still Alden feared that someone would guess that he was trying to secure Isaac's freedom. Or that his father would find out that he'd taken a slave. After what his father had done to Benjamin, Alden could only imagine what he would do if he found them.

While Isaac read a new novel in the hotel room, Alden had set out to rent a rig for the last six miles of their journey. After Isaac was on his way to Canada, Alden would return the rented horses and carriage.

Horses neighed on both sides of the stables, and Alden's boots sunk into the wet straw as he strode down the alley between the stalls. The livery opened up into a storage arena that held four wagons and two carriages. The only man he saw was attending to a horse inside one of the stalls, across from the wagon storage.

The man removed his foot from a stool. "How can I help you?" he asked, transferring a brush between his hands.

"I want to rent a horse and runabout," Alden replied, pointing toward the carriages. He'd hire a coach to deliver his trunk to Harvard after the snow melted.

The man looked him up and down, at his black woolen cloak and felt derby hat. "You know how to drive a runabout?"

"Of course I do."

The man returned to brushing the horse's coat. "I should be able to rent you something by Friday."

"I can't wait that long."

The man shrugged. "I can't afford to lose one of my horses in a blizzard."

"It's not far to Harvard."

The man looked at him like he was crazy. In Virginia, an enslaved coachman would drive him, no matter the weather, but he had no power over this man.

"Are you Crandall?" Alden asked, pointing back toward the wooden sign hanging over the open doorway.

The man nodded. "Lowell Crandall."

"What if I hired you to drive me?"

Lowell pressed the brush bristles into his palm, nodding toward the gusting snow that veiled the bank building across the street. "I'm not going to get stranded in this weather."

"I'll pay you twice your usual fee."

"Twice of anything's not worth my life or the lives of my stock."

When Alden looked back at the snow again, he blinked. Then his heart seemed to stop. He thought his father might come to Harvard after him, but it wasn't his father standing outside the livery door. It was his brother-in-law.

He glanced at the alley and then toward the carriages. The only exit was the one where Victor seemed to be standing guard. Alden slipped into the stall where he'd found Lowell.

The man eyed the door, and when he turned back toward Alden, his eyes narrowed. "I think there's more to your story."

Alden kept his back against the stall's low wall. "There's always more to a story."

"You in trouble with the law?"

He shook his head. "I'm in trouble with my family."

"Ah," Lowell said. "I've spent a lifetime in trouble with mine."

When Alden glanced over the wall, he saw Victor walking toward them.

"I would appreciate your confidence," Alden said.

"I'll determine that in due course," Lowell replied. "In the meantime, this here is Daisy Sue. You two can get to know each other while I talk to this family member of yours."

Alden sank down onto the wooden stool, the stench of horse manure stinging his nose. Thankfully, Daisy Sue ignored him, keeping her distance across the stall. As he waited, Alden silently begged God to convince the owner of the livery to conceal the truth.

"How can I help you?" he heard Lowell ask Victor.

"I want to rent a carriage and driver," Victor said.

"I don't hire out drivers," Lowell told him. "Check down by the train depot."

"No one there will drive in this snow."

Through the cracks in the wood, Alden watched Lowell and Victor. As the men talked, he wrestled with his own thoughts.

If Victor was Isaac's father, should he return the boy to him? A boy should be with his father, especially if Victor treated him well. But Eliza clearly wasn't enamored with him. She was willing to give him away, and he feared his sister wouldn't hesitate to sell him.

"Where are you going?" the livery owner asked Victor.

"Harvard."

"You work there?"

"No. I'm on my way to get my slave back."

"Your slave?" Lowell asked, his tone tightening like a jack-in-the-box about to spring.

He nodded. "Someone kidnapped him."

"Why would someone take your slave to Harvard?"

"My brother-in-law is planning to free him," Victor said, as if he were indicting Alden in the worst possible crime.

"Are you certain?"

"Absolutely," Victor replied. "I'm going to find my slave and make sure my brother-in-law is flogged for stealing him."

"How about the slave?"

"Perhaps I'll have him flogged too."

The image of his own father flashed into Alden's mind, the whip in his hand ready to lash Benjamin, and he shuddered. He would return a son to his father, but not a slave to his master. He had to keep Isaac away from Victor, even if he had to escort the boy up to Canada on his own.

"I have a friend named Jameson who runs a livery ten blocks north of here, next to Park Street Church," Lowell directed. "He rents out coaches for hire, and his horses are much better in the snow than mine."

Victor stepped toward the door. "I'll find him before dark."

"I'm always glad to help someone of a like mind."

"I thought Boston was chock-full of abolition-ists."

"Only a few of them around here."

Alden stayed in the stall several more minutes until he was certain Victor was gone. "What's ten blocks north?" Alden asked when he stepped back into the alley.

Lowell smiled. "The burying ground."

Alden laughed.

"He'll never even make it there tonight in this snow," Lowell said. "You aim to keep that boy as a slave?"

Alden shook his head. "I'm trying to find him a way up to Canada."

The man eyed the snow again. "Perhaps I will drive you to Harvard myself."

"I'm afraid I'm going to have to change my plans." Again. Victor may not be able to get transportation today, but he wouldn't be far behind Alden and Isaac on the route to Cambridge.

"There aren't many places you can go by foot or carriage in this weather," Lowell said. "Certainly not up to Canada."

The banknotes his mother had given him for tuition were back in the room. She may have meant for him to finish his schooling, but she'd also told him to use his education for good.

"How about a ship to California?" he asked.

The man eyed him for a moment. "We've got two kinds of ships that leave from our harbor. The slow boat goes all the way down around Cape Horn, ending up four or five months later in San Francisco if the weather's decent. Seven months if Mother Nature's fighting you."

"What about the faster route?"

"Those ships stop at the Isthmus of Panama, and you have to cross over that neck of land to catch a ship on the other side."

"Any idea how much the passage would cost?" Alden asked.

"About two hundred dollars per person to go around the Horn. More like three hundred dollars to cross over the isthmus."

His heart sank. Even if he wanted to take Isaac

131

to California, he didn't have enough money for both of them to travel.

Lowell lowered his voice. "My brother commands a clipper ship called *Pharos* that leaves in the morning for California. Won't matter if it's sunny or snowing."

"I don't have enough money for the boy and me to both sail."

Lowell tugged on his jacket sleeves. "If you are willing to work, I might be able to get you passage."

"We're willing to work as hard as we can."

"Meet me down at Lewis Wharf before daybreak," Lowell said. "And pack light."

"Thank you."

He didn't have to ask Isaac about this new journey. It seemed the boy was going to achieve his dream of going to California after all.

Chapter 14

Harvard College
January 1854

Victor rattled the iron gates that led into Harvard Yard until the gatekeeper stepped up to speak with him. The man was clearly exasperated, his long sigh more like a groan. "You again."

"Of course it's me," Victor said. "I'm not going to stop until you let me speak to my brother."

"It's not for me to say whether or not you can go to his room."

Victor wanted to slap the man silly, preferably with something like a frying pan. They'd had this conversation repeatedly during the two weeks the students and professors were away on holiday—and in the week since they'd been back—but the guard refused to listen to him.

"I can't obtain permission if you won't let me inside."

"Maybe you'll change your mind and send your brother a message. Or at least give me his name."

An icy raindrop splashed on Victor's face, and he flicked it away. "I want to surprise him."

"It's my job to snuff out surprises." The guard's eyes narrowed. "And people who try to climb the fence."

"If you'd unlock it, I wouldn't need to climb."

The man stepped away without another word. Victor rattled the gate again, shouting for him to come back, but the guard ignored him.

His arms crossed over his coat, he stepped under the nearby tree where he'd spent much of the last three weeks waiting for Alden to walk through the gate. He'd failed in his repeated attempts to climb the fence, and he'd failed to even catch a glimpse of Alden and Isaac.

The sunlight faded as he watched the gate, and rain began to pour from the sky, veiling the iron slabs before him with a hazy gray. Isaac was behind the gate, protected by this imbecile who refused to let Victor pass. Perhaps Alden had even told the man to keep him locked out.

But they wouldn't keep him out forever. Eventually he'd find a way to get in.

He stood up a little straighter under the tree, a new idea forming in his mind. He could go straight to the police chief of this little town and tell him that Alden Payne was harboring a runaway. Then he'd smirk at the keeper when the chief demanded he unlock the gates. Perhaps he'd tell the chief that the gatekeeper was collaborating with Alden to steal his slave.

He stepped away from the tree, intent on finding the station until he heard the clamoring of a dozen voices, laughing and shouting as if they had more drink than sense running through their brains.

Victor smiled when he saw the large group of students dressed in long coats and bowler hats round the corner. Perhaps he wouldn't need the police chief after all.

The students didn't seem to notice him as he elbowed his way into the middle of the herd, the rain dousing all of them. And the keeper didn't notice Victor either as he unlocked the gate. He seemed anxious to get the rowdies off the streets, back inside his fence.

The men floundered into the muddy yard, and Victor laughed along with them as they wobbled in unison toward the dormitory.

Once they were inside, Victor asked one of the men where Alden Payne's room was.

"Third floor," he directed sluggishly. "But Alden's not there."

"Where is he?"

The man leaned against the paneled wall. "He—"

Victor watched with disgust as the man slid down the wall, landing with a thud on the polished floor.

Victor stepped over the man and rushed upstairs. Another student directed him to Alden's door, and he found it unlocked so he walked inside.

There was a student working at the desk, reading by an oil lamp. His pulse began to race until the man turned around. The drunkard was right. Alden wasn't here.

"I'm looking for Alden Payne," he said, angry that his brother-in-law had eluded him.

"He's gone."

"Gone for the night?" Victor pressed.

"No. He didn't return to school after Christmas."

Victor balled up his fists in his coat pockets. Had Alden really taken Isaac away to free him? Self-righteous fool. He had no idea how well Victor cared for him. Isaac wouldn't be treated that well in Canada or anywhere else.

If Alden took him north, Victor would search all of Canada if he must to find him.

The man glanced at the open door. "We're not permitted visitors here after dark."

135

"I'm his brother," he said as he closed the door behind him. "The family was concerned when he didn't send word that he'd arrived safely back to school."

The student studied him. "Alden doesn't have any brothers."

"Brother-in-law," Victor said, frustrated at having to explain needless details. "I married his oldest sister."

"My name's Patrick. Alden and I have been roommates for almost three years."

"Then you must be concerned as well."

"Not exactly."

Alden wanted to shake the man's shoulders until the information he was withholding dumped out of him. "His parents will be heartbroken if I can't tell them where he's gone."

Patrick rose from his chair and moved to a desk on the opposite side of the room.

"A letter came for Alden over the holiday." He picked up an envelope and handed it to Victor. "Your family will want to read it."

Victor looked down and saw that it had already been opened. "What does it say?"

"It's from Judah Fallow. He said he's relocating his practice to Sacramento City."

"Who's Judah Fallow?"

Patrick paused again, and Victor felt as if he might explode.

"Who's Judah?" he repeated.

"He was an attorney here in Boston until a year ago," Patrick finally explained. "When he left for California, he offered Alden an apprenticeship."

Victor stared down at the envelope before looking back up. "You think Alden went to California?"

Patrick nodded slowly. "I'm certain he did, but the dean doesn't know."

"How can you be so certain?"

He glanced at the door and lowered his voice. "I saw him the week after Christmas, walking toward the wharf in Boston with a black boy."

"Go on," Victor urged.

Patrick collapsed back down into his chair. "My curiosity got the best of me, and I followed them to the gangplank of a ship preparing to leave for California."

"Blast," Victor muttered. Of course, Alden had to complicate what should have been a simple search. "Why haven't you told the school?"

Patrick blanched. "Alden's always been a stellar student. I didn't want to ruin his reputation."

"I suppose you'll be at the top of your class now?"

"Close to it," he admitted. "I just assumed that Alden's family knew where he went. I wasn't trying to keep it secret from them."

"I'll tell his parents."

Patrick opened the door. "You best leave now, or we'll both be in trouble."

Coward, Victor thought as he clutched the envelope in his hands.

"How exactly did you get inside the front gates?" Patrick asked.

Victor shrugged. "I walked through."

And he walked right back out. The keeper tried to catch him, but he slipped away smoothly, blending into the darkness.

Chapter 15

Sacramento City
January 1854

"Mr. Bridges paid us a visit while you were out this morning," Fanny said as she emerged from her rooms, an apron strung over her arm. "He still hasn't found his slave."

Isabelle nodded as she picked out a freshly cut pansy from her bucket, delivered from Sutter Floral Gardens, and arranged it on a table in the dining room. Mr. Bridges had returned multiple times, but she hadn't allowed him to search again. Even though Micah was gone, she didn't want someone who owned slaves in her establishment.

Rodney had called twice as well in the past few weeks. They were seemingly friendly visits, but she suspected he was keeping his eye on her and her establishment. He hadn't asked directly about

Micah again, but he'd inquired about Stephan's past. She told him the truth—that she didn't know where Stephan had lived before California, but he was an honest and reliable steward who served this hotel well.

She'd been up until late last night, praying again that Micah was safely hidden away. She may never know what happened to the boy, but she had tried to be faithful in helping him escape slavery.

"Poor Mr. Bridges," Fanny said with a sigh. "My daddy always said to never trust a slave. They'll run if given half a chance."

Isabelle pinched the stem of a flower between her fingers. How could a free woman—one who had traveled fifteen thousand miles to find her husband—judge someone who desired the same freedom? Ignorance and hypocrisy were both revolting to her, but keeping one's views about slavery private was a fine line to walk. She couldn't help anyone trapped as a slave if she divulged her own thoughts about abolition.

Fanny tied the apron strings around her back. Still exhausted from her long journey, she'd spent most of her morning resting in the back room. She probably wouldn't survive a single day working as a slave.

"How many Negroes did you have on your farm?" Isabelle asked, focusing her attention back on the flowers to finish her last arrangement.

"Only two, but I've heard plenty of stories. Did your family ever own slaves?"

Isabelle turned the vase a half inch. "We lived in a small house in Baltimore."

"I always wanted to visit Baltimore. Are your parents still there?"

"No," she said, stepping back to scrutinize the bouquet.

"Pink or red roses would look better on your tables."

Isabelle shook her head. "I never buy roses."

Fanny sat in a chair, eyeing her curiously. "Did your parents come out west with you?"

"My aunt and I came together," Isabelle said, trying to steer the discussion away from her parents. Fanny would learn in time that most people in California didn't like to talk much about who or what they left behind. They came here either to escape from their pasts or because they had grand visions of remaking themselves into someone new—much more successful and wealthier than they'd been at home.

Fanny crinkled her nose. "Why would you come out here without a man?"

"My uncle decided to venture west in 1849, soon after President Polk announced there was an abundance of gold in the hills. He came across the isthmus, but when he sent for us, he said Panama was no place for a lady, so we went around Cape Horn."

By the time they arrived here, Uncle William was gone. He'd died of cholera after the 1850 flood.

"It took me six months to get around the Horn," Fanny said. "Not including almost a month in New York waiting for a boat."

"It felt like an eternity, didn't it?"

Fanny nodded. "We hit a storm somewhere off the coast of Chile, and I thought I was going to die. I tried to keep my mind focused on seeing Ross when I arrived, but alas, no husband of mine."

When the front bell chimed, Fanny looked over her shoulder with expectation, like Isabelle used to do, but still there was no Ross. Stephan stepped into the room, carrying a stack of letters from the post office. He handed them to Isabelle before moving toward the kitchen—some of the letters were probably for her, confirmations of orders placed or bills for their supplies. Others she would distribute to her guests.

Fanny eyed the stack of mail in her hand. "Does Ross ever write to you?"

"Occasionally," she said, weighing her words before she spoke again. "He inquires about the condition of the hotel in his absence."

"When did you last hear from him?"

Isabelle clutched the mail closer to her side. "About a month ago."

Fanny sighed.

"I'm sure he'll be back soon."

"Were you and he—" Fanny stumbled over her words. "Were you close?"

Isabelle evaded the question. "He was a good partner to my aunt and me. And a good friend."

"I worried about him a lot, being out here alone."

"I think any wife would worry about her husband."

Fanny nodded toward the white swinging door into the kitchen, hinged onto the back wall. "Do you need me to help tonight?"

"Please," Isabelle said as she glanced around the dining room. The violet blooms brightened the white tablecloths, but each place still needed silver along with the fine blue-and-white transferware she'd received recently from England. Soon she needed to send Stephan to San Francisco to order new cloths for the tables as well.

"Before you go to the kitchen, could you help Stephan finish setting the tables?"

Fanny hesitated, eying the kitchen door again. "I've never worked with a Negro before."

Isabelle set her empty bucket down on the floor. "He's a freedman."

"Still—"

"Things are much different here in California than in Kentucky," Isabelle tried to explain. "You'll have to get used to working alongside freedmen and women."

"It makes no sense to me." Fanny picked at the

edge of her apron. "How can one black man be free and another be a slave?"

Isabelle sighed. "Californians are still trying to figure that out."

With her apron neatly covering her calico dress, Fanny hastened toward the kitchen. She wasn't the first person who'd balked at working with Stephan, as if she were somehow better than the man because of her skin color. As Aunt Emeline liked to say, "God created every person equal. It was man who ascribed worth."

People may be equal in God's eyes, but they were often afraid of what they didn't understand. The entire hierarchy of freedom was absurd, founded on fear and greed and a pompous sense of self-regard.

Isabelle picked up the bucket in her free hand and began walking toward the lobby. From the Garden of Eden until today, man and woman alike tried to usurp power from the God who made them. Slavery, in her opinion, was the apex of power. One man controlling another.

After she stepped up to her desk, Stephan walked into the room. He closed the door between the lobby and dining room, then moved over to the counter.

"I saw a friend on the way to the post office," he whispered.

Her eyebrows slipped up. "Yes?"

"I wanted you to know"—he hesitated, glancing

back at the door before he spoke again—"that your package is gone."

She sighed with relief. "Do you happen to know its particular destination?"

"The Colony of Vancouver Island," he said. "It's on a steamer from San Francisco with twenty others. They should arrive in about three days."

She'd read in the paper that the British were welcoming Negroes onto the island to help populate the country, like they'd opened their borders to the runaway slaves back east. Micah and the others would be safe there. "Very good."

Stephan placed his elbows on the polished counter, studying her for a moment. "Why did you help him?"

The answer was too complicated to explain now so she chose one of her many reasons. "Because I believe all people should be free."

He smiled, the kindness radiating across his face. "You are a good woman, Miss Isabelle."

"No better than any other."

"Much better than any I've ever worked for."

She brushed a lock of stray hair back over her ear. "You let me know if anyone bothers you, Stephan."

"I can take care of myself."

"Then let me know if I can help someone else."

When he left, she fanned the stack of letters out on her desk. In the middle was one postmarked from Marysville, the town close to where Ross had mailed his last letter to her.

Her joy at Stephan's news plummeted as she picked up her letter opener and slowly slit the envelope.

She moved closer to the coal stove, warming herself as she unfolded the sheet of paper. Ross's script looked hurried, and there was a copper-colored smudge on the right-hand corner as if he'd written it while sifting the dirt for gold.

Dearest Isabelle,
I'm still digging on the fields near Marysville. I won't say much in the letter, in case someone intercepts this, but you will be quite pleased with my findings here.

There isn't much to report outside my digging—I eat beans and dried pork every day, sleep when I can, and if I'm lucky, dream about you at night. We've only had mild bouts of rain this month, and my tent stays quite dry. I will continue digging until the weather won't let me continue, reaping a harvest for our future.

In your capable hands, I'm certain the hotel is running quite well. While I'm grateful for the placid weather, I eagerly await the rains so I can return to you.

With what I've earned here, I will buy you a wedding gift that will last a lifetime. Just think—in a few short months, we will be husband and wife.

Yours forever,
Ross

She crumpled the letter in her hands. Ross may not have much to report from the diggings, but she had plenty to tell him. In person.

"Isabelle?" she heard Fanny call out from the dining room.

She quickly opened the door to the stove and tossed Ross's everlasting love into the fire.

PART TWO

The weary sun hath sunk to sleep
Beyond the great Pacific's wave,
While here I stand and idly weep
That I have been to gold a slave!

—E. Curtiss Hine,
"Lament of the Gold Digger"

Chapter 16

Sacramento City
February 1854

The faint aroma of orange blossoms billowed in the steam as Isabelle poured Fanny a cup of tea. Then she reached for the bundle of newspapers from December, two months past.

A carton filled with copies of the *New York Herald* arrived at the hotel each month, a luxury for her guests who wanted to stay abreast of news outside California. She devoured every word before passing them along to the people who stayed in her hotel. Sacramento City was a safe haven for her—a place she intended to live for the rest of her life—but she still liked to know what was happening around the world.

Isabelle chose the oldest paper from the stack—December 20—to read this morning and handed it across the table to Fanny as a gust of wind shook the windows of the dining room.

Fanny added a lump of sugar to her cup before reading a headline out loud: "Gold Seekers Flood into California."

Isabelle laughed at the words, glancing out the window. The rainy street was already crowded with men headed to work along the riverfront. "That's not news around here."

Fanny glanced up. "People on the East Coast have no idea about the chaos happening on this side of the world."

Isabelle sipped the sweetened oolong tea she'd purchased from a Chinese shop. "At least it's starting to be civilized."

"I haven't seen any sort of refinement outside the walls of the hotel," Fanny said. "And certainly no gentlemen."

Fanny began to read the story about the influx of men—and a much smaller population of women —into the new state. Six years had passed since James Marshall found that first nugget of gold in the American River. Since then, more than three hundred thousand people had migrated to California.

The next story was about a New York man who'd found a lump of gold and quartz at French Ravine that was worth ten thousand dollars. He bought a hacienda near San Francisco but lost both his home and his money to roulette.

Fanny handed Isabelle the newspaper, and she read the columns about society, cooking, and fashion.

In Ross's absence, the two women had settled into a morning routine after serving the guests their breakfasts, typically reading the paper or a few pages from a book out loud while they shared a pot of tea. Fanny always added sugar. Isabelle stirred a spoonful of clover honey into hers.

"Do you ever think about going out to the diggings?" Fanny asked when Isabelle finished reading the story.

Isabelle shook her head. "I'd much rather stay in the city."

"If Ross doesn't come soon, I'm going to look for him."

Isabelle glanced out at the river of muddy rain flowing down the street. The storms began a month ago, and droves of gold seekers had arrived back in town to wait out the weather, but she hadn't heard anything else from Ross.

"Was your uncle planning to dig for gold when he first came here?" Fanny asked.

"No," Isabelle replied. "He sold his shop in Baltimore and used the money to start a mercantile for miners."

"That was awfully smart of him."

Isabelle folded up the paper. "He was a keen businessman."

"You and your aunt could start up another mercantile."

She took a long sip of her tea. "I much prefer running a hotel."

"But what will you do when Ross returns?" Fanny asked, shifting on her seat.

Isabelle lowered her cup. She'd kept hoping Ross would return like he'd promised, so he could discuss the future with his wife.

"What do you mean?" Isabelle asked gingerly.

151

"Where will you go?"

"I'm not going anywhere. The proprietor of the hotel needs to live here."

Fanny's eyes grew wide. "I thought Ross would take over the Golden again when he returns."

Isabelle poured the remaining tea into her cup. It had become clearer as the weeks passed that Fanny envisioned herself the owner and proprietor of this hotel one day, alongside Ross. While Isabelle enjoyed the daily company of another woman, Fanny had begun acting much less like someone working for room and board and more like a paying guest at her leisure.

Isabelle sipped the tea. "I guess we'll be able to resolve all this very soon."

"But I don't want you to have to leave."

"Considering that my aunt owns this place, you don't have to worry about that."

Fanny fidgeted again in her chair. "I can't help but wonder—"

Isabelle braced herself. "What is it?"

"Were you and Ross ever . . ." Fanny took a deep breath. "Doesn't it seem strange for a married man and an unmarried woman to partner together in a business venture?"

"Are you talking about my aunt's partnership or are you talking about me?"

Fanny glanced down at her cup before meeting her gaze again. "Were you and Ross ever more than business partners?"

Fanny had attempted to ask this question several times now, and each time Isabelle had been able to evade answering. Ross should be the one talking to his wife about the choices he made after he left for California, not her. The numbness in her heart and mind had dissipated, and she was furious at him for making her clean up his mess.

As she contemplated her response, Isabelle looked out at the storm once more. This time, she saw Sing Ye stumbling along the boardwalk, holding an umbrella out in front of her like a warrior preparing to fight the rain.

Another welcome interruption to prolong this conversation.

"Excuse me," she said to Fanny, standing up. Sing Ye rarely came to the hotel, and she never came this early in the morning.

Isabelle hurried across to the lobby.

Sing Ye shook off her umbrella outside the door and left it under the awning. When she stepped into the room, her hands trembled as she brushed the water off the jade-colored silk on her *tangzhuang* jacket, splattering the rug.

She and Nicolas had married two weeks ago, but Nicolas agreed that Sing Ye should continue helping Aunt Emeline during her final days. Isabelle visited her aunt every evening for at least an hour after dinner so that Sing Ye could spend time with her new husband. When she had visited last night, Aunt Emeline never woke from her sleep.

Isabelle stepped toward her. "What happened?"

"She was in pain for most of the night," Sing Ye said. "Now she's asking for you."

"Did you send for the doctor?"

"Yes, but the messenger said he can't come until this afternoon."

Isabelle reached for her merino cloak. "Let's go talk to him together."

Chapter 17

Boston
February 1854

It seemed to Victor as if everyone in Boston were waiting for a ship to California. The line for the passage office snaked down the wharf and curled into an alleyway that stank of rotting fish and cheap liquor. Crates draped with mooring ropes and fishing nets were stacked along the wooden pier, and the snow had been replaced by broken lobster and crab shells that littered the ground.

He'd been waiting more than a week for the ticket office to open. The proprietor at his hotel said to arrive early to secure passage, so he had, finding his way to the office while the oil lanterns were still burning. The proprietor never said anything about the hundreds—perhaps thousands —of people wanting passage on the same ship.

Seven hours he'd stood in line now, clutching the leather portfolio with his papers and half of the coins he'd retrieved before he came north. Now that he knew where Alden was taking Isaac, it was such a waste to be stuck here. Waiting.

He hated to wait.

A fishing trawler crept toward the crowded wharf, searching for an available berth among the ships and boats loading and unloading.

A clipper called *Pharos*, he'd discovered, had indeed set off for San Francisco on December 30, traveling around Cape Horn. Alden and Isaac may be ahead of him, but the man at his hotel said he knew of a much faster way to get to California. And he knew of a ship sailing to Panama tomorrow.

Even though he was more than a month behind the *Pharos*, taking the journey across Panama would still get him to California before Alden.

The line shifted ahead, and then he had to wait again.

Alden may have outsmarted him for the moment, but Victor would find him in Sacramento. Then he would retrieve Isaac, and they would sail immediately back to the East Coast.

When he returned home, he would be the hero of the Payne family and Alden the fool.

Perhaps, with the absence of Alden, John would reward Victor with the plantation. He'd rule over Scott's Grove soon, his only son at his side.

Chapter 18

Pacific Ocean, Near Cape Horn
February 1854

Land had been spotted on the starboard side of the clipper, and it was a good thing. After two months traveling south, the *Pharos*'s crew was running short on supplies. They'd planned to stop in Rio de Janeiro to restock, but a storm kept them from making port.

The last remaining food supplies consisted of beans, salt jerk, a keg of beer, two pigs for slaughter, and three barrels of fresh water. It was not enough to last more than a day or two for the 117 passengers on board. If they didn't get supplies soon, Captain Baxter Crandall was going to have a mutiny on his hands.

Lowell's brother hadn't made any promises for Alden and Isaac's passage agreement beyond feeding them and providing a berth to sleep below deck. And requiring that they work from sunup until long after it went down.

Alden had worked harder in these past two months than he'd ever worked in his life. He and Isaac had washed mounds of dishes. Mopped the decks. Caulked the ship's seams with oakum. They'd also tried rigging the masts, but the captain kept Alden and Isaac mainly in the kitchen now, saying they made lousy sailors. Only another two months or so left. Then they would be in California, free to work as they liked.

The stack of tin plates beside him rattled with the ship. He picked up a plate and washed it in a bucket of saltwater. No soap. Then he stacked it on the opposite side to air dry.

In the first few weeks of their journey, he'd scraped food off most of the dishes, tossing the bigger pieces to the pigs and throwing the crumbs overboard to the dolphins that had served as the ship's companions as they sailed down the Atlantic. These days, there wasn't a morsel left to feed the dolphins, pigs, or even the rats that kept him company in the galley. Every passenger cleared his or her plate and most of them asked for more. Unlike Alden and Isaac, the passengers had paid for the finest cuisine.

Captain Crandall said they'd be having pork chops tonight for dinner. After that, it would be salt jerk and beans until they were able to restock the hold with provisions.

The *Pharos* had rounded the tip of South America a few days ago, the waves crashing up against their ship with such force that he'd thought they would surely capsize. Captain Crandall required that all the men, even those who'd paid for fancy staterooms, help the crew bail. The captain was master on a ship, judge and king, but he didn't have to put any of his passengers in chains. For an hour, their ship had been trapped in a black squall as the men threw bucket after bucket of water back into the sea, skirting dangerously around the cluster of jagged rocks that made up Cape Horn. The sea tossed them around like a tobacco leaf in the wind until it finally dumped them back out to finish their journey.

Now it was directly north to San Francisco, stopping only for supplies in Valparaiso, Chile— hopefully before the beans and water ran out.

Persila, a pretty black woman, entered the galley. She was a few years older than Alden and dressed in a simple cotton wrapper with a handkerchief tucked back over her ears, hiding her hair. She grabbed a wooden bucket and filled it with murky water from the barrel.

"The captain wants me to scrub the aft deck again, but it seems like Mother Nature gave it a good enough scrubbing already."

Alden nodded. Captain Crandall liked to keep them busy, as if a moment of rest might provoke a rebellion.

Persila leaned back against a crate. "Where'd Isaac go?"

"He took Mrs. Dawson a bowl of beans."

Isaac carried a tray twice a day to a female passenger in one of the stateroom berths. They didn't have a doctor on board, but a man from Erie was the son of a doctor. He thought Mrs. Dawson had cholera, so the captain gave the job of feeding her to Isaac. When Alden protested, the man said he would leave them at Valparaiso if the boy didn't cooperate. They could try their luck against dengue and yellow fever.

Isaac, however, didn't protest. He said he liked the woman in room 4 well enough. And she enjoyed listening to him read.

"You don't treat Isaac like a slave," Persila said.

Alden shrugged.

"What happened to his mama?"

He dipped another plate into the saltwater and added it to the stack. "I don't know."

"That's sad, isn't it?" she asked, speaking more to herself. "Every boy should have a good mama."

"Do you have any children?"

"I had a child once," she said sadly. "A long time ago."

"I bet you were a good mother."

She wiped her sleeve across her face. "He was a good son."

She lifted the mop and bucket, but as she moved toward the door, a man with a sunburned nose and thinning black hair stepped into the kitchen, stopping her. "The missus wants her tea."

She showed him the bucket. "Captain Crandall told me to mop the deck."

"You can do that, after you make Missus Webb tea."

"Yes, sir."

The man glanced over at Alden before looking back at her. "There's no time for socializing."

Alden wanted to say they had endless amounts of time on this boat, but he held his tongue. Mr. Webb couldn't whip him, but his snide comments might earn Persila a flogging.

She set the mop back against the wall. "I'll start the tea."

The man gave a sharp nod, then ducked out of the room.

Alden glanced up at the bare shelves. "Where will you find tea?"

"Missus Webb brought plenty in her trunk with her, along with sugar."

"I thought Mr. Webb hired you out."

She nodded. "My work is paying for most of his passage, but he still wants me to attend to him and his wife."

Alden turned to stir a pot of beans on the stove while Persila began heating a kettle of water.

He clung to the hope that Isaac and Persila would be free once they got to California. He still hadn't mentioned freedom to Isaac, afraid that someone on the *Pharos*—a slave owner like Mr. Webb—might do something to hinder his plan. Much better to wait until Isaac was firmly on free soil to talk about the boy's future.

"What are your plans when you get to San Francisco?" he asked the woman.

"I'll do whatever Master Webb tells me to do, I suppose."

"But California is a free state."

She glanced back over at him. "Where did you hear that?"

"From a friend."

"Master Webb said there ain't gonna be no freedom for me there."

The door opened again, and the captain barged into the galley, staring at Persila. "Why aren't you mopping the deck?"

"Master Webb told me to make tea."

"I'm the only master you have on this boat." Captain Crandall took the kettle off the stove and set it back on the shelf. "I've paid good money for you and your work, and I expect you to answer only to me."

Persila's shoulders sank. "Yes, sir."

Alden stepped forward. "I can mop the deck."

"I told you to do the dishes."

Alden stood taller. "I can do both."

Captain Crandall scrutinized him for a moment. "Fine."

Persila reached for the teapot again, but the

161

captain slapped her hand. "You and Payne can mop the deck together. If your master has a problem, tell him to discuss it with me."

The captain waited until Persila left with her mop and bucket before he turned back to Alden. "If you know what's good for you, you'll stop pandering to slaves."

Alden braced himself. That was the same word his father had used back in the curing barn. He wanted to fight both this man and Mr. Webb, but he could almost hear his dean's words ringing in his ears: *Passion is most powerful when bridled by restraint.*

Passion only sparked a fire. If you wanted to keep it burning, you needed to feed the smoldering flames.

"I'm not pandering," he finally said. "I'm trying to protect her."

"Little good it will do you, here or in California," Captain Crandall said before stomping out of the galley, the dishes rattling again.

The ship swayed to his left, and Alden swayed with it. Unlike in the rest of their country, slaves were supposed to be free in California, but what if things had changed in the past months?

It was too late for him and Isaac to change course now. Others gambled on finding gold out west. He supposed he was gambling on finding freedom.

After he finished drying the dishes, he reached for a second mop and climbed up the steps to Mrs. Dawson's room. Isaac answered his knock, slipping out into the corridor.

Alden held up his mop. "I'm going to the top deck."

"Missus Dawson just fell asleep," he said, carefully closing the door. "It took an hour of reading."

"Is she well?"

"Tolerable. She's tired of the beans."

"I'm afraid we all are."

"I'll help you mop," Isaac said, as if it were a game.

"You go rest for a bit downstairs."

"I've been resting, Master Payne. I need to earn my keep."

"What do you think about borrowing Persila's mop, then?"

Isaac nodded.

There were only two mops in the galley. Perhaps the captain would let Persila make her missus tea if Isaac joined him in the labor.

The sun beat down on Alden's back as he wet his mop. Off the leeward side, a school of bluefish escorted them through the water, and when Isaac joined him on deck, the boy leaned over the railing as if he might jump overboard to swim with the fish. Like Benjamin and his diving stage.

Isaac didn't need to find a field of gold in

California. He needed to play the games that Alden and Benjamin once played. He needed an education so he could use his mind and not have to hide behind ignorance any longer. A place to read and grow and change the ignorance of others. Perhaps a black family would adopt him into their home in San Francisco so he could have a mother and father to care for his needs.

As he and Isaac mopped together, Alden prayed this new state would remain true to moral law, offering freedom to all men, women, and children. Black and white.

Chapter 19

Sacramento City
February 1854

Isabelle leaned back against the pillows on the feather bed, holding Aunt Emeline in her arms as if she were a baby. She didn't want to let her aunt go, afraid she might slip away for good.

Sing Ye said that Emeline had awakened during the night, asking for her, but her aunt had fallen back asleep before Isabelle arrived that morning. And she'd yet to awaken again.

After much pleading, the doctor had come to the cottage, but he didn't stay long. After listening to the whisper of Aunt Emeline's heartbeat with his wooden stethoscope, he spooned a bitter syrup of black tea and morphine between her lips. Then he left Isabelle the bottle.

The morphine relieved her pain, and while Isabelle was grateful for her relief, there were so many more things she wanted to say. It was long past noon now. Even though Sing Ye had tried to coax her into the next room to eat, Isabelle refused to leave until she thanked her aunt one last time.

Stephan would oversee dinner tonight at the hotel and any needs of their clientele while she was gone. Fanny would loathe answering to Stephan, but her steward knew how to care for their guests. And he was completely reliable.

On the painted wall at the end of the bed was the picture she'd given Aunt Emeline for Christmas—the one of the port at Marseille. Beside it was a portrait of Uncle William and Aunt Emeline together in her flower garden on the outskirts of Baltimore, years before Isabelle met them. Uncle William had a thick mustache that masked most of his lips, but his smile flooded up into his eyes. Aunt Emeline's hair had been rolled tightly into curls on both sides of her head, a sprig of flowers pinned in the middle. A lace collar draped wide over her shoulders, and her smile was as infectious as her husband's.

Uncle William had been an ardent abolitionist, using his mercantile as a meeting place for like-minded people. Aunt Emeline had cared well for

165

the people who spent a night or two hiding out in their home.

They had both done so much for her—educating and supporting her, bringing her to California with them. She'd never known what a family was until they adopted her into theirs.

Her heart ached.

She couldn't envision what her life would be like with her aunt gone. Couldn't fathom the future without her. Aunt Emeline was her anchor. Her lighthouse in the storms. Her savior.

Almost a decade ago, when the doctors thought Isabelle would die, Aunt Emeline had nursed her back to health. Then she'd risked everything for Isabelle, just as she had done when she purchased Sing Ye from the steamer in San Francisco.

If only she could rescue her aunt now.

This morning, Isabelle asked the doctor if she could bring Aunt Emeline to the hospital, but he'd said she was too ill for the journey across the city. And she would surely be more comfortable spending her final hours at home.

Isabelle wanted to fight him—the man didn't know for certain that these were Aunt Emeline's last hours—but she'd finally concurred after the doctor said Isabelle would be a greater help to her aunt by easing her pain instead of trying to cure a body beyond repair.

Tears trickled down Isabelle's cheeks, and she

wiped them off with the sleeve of her blouse. She knew her aunt was sick, but she'd fought so hard against the realization that Aunt Emeline might really leave her, like Uncle William had done. That Isabelle would be alone once again.

The room was plenty warm from the fireplace that Sing Ye kept burning in the next room, but Isabelle still shivered.

She hated being alone.

The hours passed, and Isabelle dozed off, her head back against the pillows. The sky was dark when she woke again, a lantern glowing on a small table near the windowsill.

Aunt Emeline began to stir. Then she opened her eyes.

A smile graced her lips when she saw Isabelle. "Child," she said softly. "Why are you holding me?"

Isabelle looked down at her, returning her smile. "Because years ago, you used to hold me."

Carefully she scooted to the edge of the bed, laying her aunt gently on top of the quilt and cushioning her fragile body with pillows and blankets.

Aunt Emeline's soft gaze lingered on her. "You were always such a good girl, Isabelle."

"I didn't want you to stop loving me."

"Oh, honey." Aunt Emeline took her hand. "I would never have stopped loving you."

When she started coughing, Isabelle reached

for the syrup on the nightstand. "You need more medicine."

Aunt Emeline shook her head, the wisps of white hair sweeping across her face. Isabelle brushed them away.

"I don't want to sleep now. I want to talk."

"What do you want to talk about?" Isabelle asked.

"I heard a woman showed up at the hotel a few months ago, asking for Ross."

Isabelle's chest clenched, her fingers curling tightly around the glass bottle. "Who told you that?"

"It doesn't matter," Aunt Emeline said. "Is he really married to someone else?"

"I'm afraid it's true, though he hasn't come back yet from the fields to confirm it."

Aunt Emeline looked over at the picture of her husband before she continued. "Why didn't you tell me?"

Isabelle placed the medicine bottle back on the stand. "I didn't want you to worry."

"I pray, child. Not worry."

Her aunt seemed fully coherent now. Alive. Perhaps the doctor was wrong. Perhaps all she needed was this medicine and some rest to recover from whatever it was that ailed her.

"I want you to find a man you can trust, Isabelle. Someone who will cherish you for a lifetime, like my William did with me."

Isabelle's eyes wet with tears again. "I'm afraid there was only one William Labrie."

"There is a man out there who will fit perfectly with you. A man who will think you are much more valuable than any nugget of gold."

Isabelle leaned over and kissed her forehead. "I can't bear to lose you."

"This is only a temporary good-bye. Not forever."

Isabelle hated good-byes, no matter how temporary.

"After I'm gone," her aunt continued, her voice stronger now, "I'm giving this house to Nicolas and Sing Ye."

"Of course."

"Everything else I have is yours."

Isabelle shook her head. "You've already given me enough."

"Judah Fallow has all my legal papers," Aunt Emeline said. "I've transferred the hotel into your name, and you will be an honored guest in the cottage with Nicolas and Sing Ye whenever you want to come."

"Thank you," she said. "For everything."

"I still need to give you your Christmas gift." Aunt Emeline tried to push herself up with her elbows. "I should have given it to you a long time ago."

"Where is it?" Isabelle asked, gently placing her hand on her aunt's shoulder to stop her from rising any farther.

Aunt Emeline pointed her finger toward the cypress writing desk. "In the second drawer."

She pulled out the deep drawer and found a quill and inkwell inside. "What am I looking for?"

"A box." Aunt Emeline glanced at the inkwell in Isabelle's hands before pointing toward another drawer. "Try the third one."

There were gloves and other sundries inside, but she didn't see a box.

"Keep pulling."

Isabelle tugged harder, and the drawer slid out of the desk. It was much shorter in length than the drawer above it.

"Feel the back," Aunt Emeline instructed.

There was a clasp against the wood at the end, and when Isabelle turned it, the panel folded out toward her. Reaching inside, she pulled out a small chest.

Her aunt sighed, sinking back into her pillows. "I knew it was there."

Isabelle returned to the bed and examined the box. There was nothing exceptional about it—an olivewood trinket box with a lock, about a foot long and six inches wide. The top was inlaid with a painting of a red rose and a chapel on the edge of steep sea cliffs. A rendition of Aunt Emeline's beloved Marseille.

"What's inside?" Isabelle asked.

Aunt Emeline smiled again. "My greatest gift to you."

But she didn't want gold or jewels or whatever

the chest contained. She wanted her aunt to stay with her.

Aunt Emeline placed her hand on the lid of it. "I made it for Rose."

"Who's Rose?"

But her aunt didn't answer the question. "The key is in the top drawer. For years, I wore it around my neck."

Isabelle remembered well that key. She'd worn the lockbox key on her necklace, just like Aunt Emeline. "Thank you."

"One day, you'll find a man who will love you for exactly who you are." Aunt Emeline brushed her hand over the olivewood again. "Then you can be proud of this."

"I will treasure whatever it is."

"Sing me that song, Isabelle," she said, her voice fading. "The one you used to sing when you couldn't sleep at night."

She'd been terrified all those years ago. Of the darkness and the light. Of being with someone else and being alone.

But she hadn't sung in a long time.

"The one about going to Jesus," Aunt Emeline prompted.

Isabelle took a deep breath, and for her aunt, she began to sing.

My Lord, He calls me, He calls me by the thunder

The trumpet sounds within my soul
I ain't got long to stay here

"Such a beautiful song," Aunt Emeline whispered, her eyes closed. "He's waiting, isn't He?"

Isabelle's eyes flooded with tears. "Yes, He is."

"Keep singing," her aunt said, clutching her hand.

Steal away, steal away, steal away to Jesus
Steal away, steal away home
I ain't got long to stay here

Aunt Emeline's hand dropped back down onto the yellow quilt, and all Isabelle heard was the steady drum of the rain beating on the roof. She sang the last stanza of the spiritual softly, the trumpet sounding in her own soul.

The Lord wasn't calling her away yet, but it was time for Aunt Emeline to go home.

Chapter 20

Panama
April 1854

The parrots on the isthmus were driving Victor mad. Their screeching grew louder as the hollowed-out logs—*bungoes*—floated up the Chagres River. Tormenting him.

Parrots screeched, and the monkeys chattered

like a rabble of women, following their bungo through the jungle as twelve of the ship's passengers skirted around rapids and branches and the hulls of boats abandoned in the water. Another bungo followed them with their luggage.

Patience, he tried to tell himself. Soon they would be on another ship, cruising toward California. In just a few weeks, he would be in Sacramento City.

Three days ago, the ship from Boston had anchored far off the shore of this godforsaken wilderness. He and the other passengers had climbed down a rope ladder into a skiff that brought them to a muddy village, where they'd secured transportation across the sixty miles of isthmus.

Though a bungo was hardly a decent source of transportation. If he could carry his belongings, he'd walk through the jungle instead of creeping up the river in a log.

The first day of their river journey, the passengers around him had talked endlessly about the spectacular greens in the foliage, of the colors on the birds that flew down the river before them, but the fascination was long over for all of them. They'd been promised a two-day journey by river, but the crew didn't seem in any hurry to rush their trip.

Two half-naked natives—one in front of the boat and one behind him—dragged, towed, and sometimes appeared to row their passengers around the curves in the narrow canal. Mosquitos swarmed around Victor's head, biting his neck. The sun burned his hands.

He'd purchased a ridiculous-looking hat called a Panama to keep the sun off his head, but the rays found every other spot of bare skin and scorched it. The makeshift canopy over them, made of dried leaves, did nothing to keep the sun off him either.

He'd packed swiftly back home for a trip in the snow, not for a journey across this stifling country. If he were back at his plantation, he'd strip down to his trousers like the natives. Then roll his pants up to his knees.

Yesterday he'd tried to cool off by dipping his hand into the river, but one of the crew slapped him with a long pole. Victor had started to rebuke the man until he pointed at an ugly creature sunning itself on a rock, its beady eyes watching their boat.

A crocodile.

The sole woman passenger shrieked, but Victor just stared back at the animal. Until then, he'd only seen pictures of crocodiles, and none that he remembered did justice to this creature. Thorns peaked across its armored back, and its checkered gray scales blended into the rock. Sharp teeth were curved like a dozen sickles outside its mouth and bent into a strange sort of smile.

Victor had smiled back and then dipped his fingers into the water again.

An hour later, the boat floated out from the muddy banks and noisy canopy of the jungle. The land beside the river flattened as they drifted beside a field of sugarcane, the shoots emerging from the morass. He could almost taste the sweetness of sugar in his mouth.

Tonight they were supposed to arrive in Panama City, where there were restaurants and American hotels. After three nights sleeping on a hammock, covered in scratchy mosquito netting, he would rent a decent bed. Then he would eat pork loin, perhaps, or some sort of mutton. A nice cream or pie for dessert.

He turned to talk to the man sitting on the bench behind him. Levi Brooks, the agent of a bank in San Francisco, had made this trip three times already to escort shipments of gold to New York. "Are we almost to Panama City?" Victor asked.

Levi chuckled. "Hardly."

Victor stiffened. He hated people laughing at him. "When will we arrive?"

"In another day or two, we'll get to the trail," Levi said.

Victor disliked the man, but he needed more information. "What sort of trail?"

"Didn't they give you a travel pamphlet when you booked passage?"

"Of course." He'd packed it into the leather portfolio now clutched in his lap. "But I thought this river went all the way across the isthmus."

175

"We have to take an old mule trail over the Continental Divide before we go down into Panama City. You can rent a mule, but I don't recommend it. Too many of them fall off the cliffs and . . ." He stopped.

"I'm not afraid of a mule trail," Victor said.

"That's good. Most people get skittish when they see it."

The faster he could get down the trail, out of this dreadful place, the better.

The rower pointed out a cluster of primitive huts on the side of the river, each one sewn together with dried grass and bamboo, the roofs thatched with palm leaves. Perched on one was a black vulture. "We stop here."

Levi called out to the man. "We paid to travel six miles today."

The native shrugged. "Someone else paid us more to return to the last village."

"But we had an agreement—"

"We will send someone for you."

The native directed the bungo closer to the bank, and they had no choice but to disembark. The men rolled up their trousers and waded through the mud. One of the natives carried the woman passenger and then all the luggage to shore.

Victor turned toward Levi. "Can we walk to the trail?"

"You can try, but I doubt you'll make it." Levi

176

set his bag on the grass. "We'll hire another bungo in the morning."

The aroma of fish stew seeped out from a hut as one of the villagers came forward, welcoming them. They would host the visitors here—and feed them—for a preposterous fee. Victor rented a hammock inside a hut and then sat down under a palm tree by himself, a temporary relief from the infliction of sun.

Once he got to Sacramento, he would book a room in a nice hotel. One that would cater to a gentleman. The natives here might not have an appreciation for Americans, but California would be civilized. No more sleeping in huts or traveling through the jungle. No more eating half-cooked fish or beans.

He pulled out a sketchpad from his bag and began to draw a picture of Isaac so he could show people when he arrived in Sacramento. He outlined the boy's face and shaded in part of his skin. Then he pulled out the picture he'd drawn of Mallie long ago. Isaac had his mother's eyes. Her smile. Isaac's nose was easy to draw. He saw it staring back at him whenever he looked in a mirror.

When he finished the picture, he began sketching Mallie again. Instead of posing at his house, he drew her on the steps of Scott's Grove, her silk-clad arm draped over the banister.

He glanced back and forth between the portraits

of Isaac and Mallie as the sun began to set, at the two people who meant everything to him. The two people who were supposed to love him back. And his blood began to boil again.

Isaac would never run away from him. Alden—like Eliza—must have forced him to leave. Kidnapped him from Scott's Grove. Or maybe he'd tricked him into going west. Alden probably lied, telling Isaac that he'd take him home to Victor before forcing him onto a ship. Isaac was probably crying for Victor right now.

A scorpion crawled over the sandy ground as the afternoon darkened. It was moving toward the sugarcane field.

He would find Isaac, no matter how long it took to get to California. Then he'd make Alden pay for stealing his boy.

Chapter 21

San Francisco
May 1854

The *Pharos* and its worn passengers passed through the Golden Gate on the twenty-sixth of May. Fog draped over the cliffs, reminding Alden of the mythological sirens that lured sailors forward with their sultry voices, enticing them straight into the treacherous rocks.

He leaned against the railing as if it would help Captain Crandall navigate between the rocks on their way into the harbor. They'd left Boston with 117 passengers on board and were landing with two less—both men who'd died of scurvy.

The ship had made record time with the winds propelling them north. And the people crowded on the deck were anxious to set their feet on firm land. Once their stomachs had been satisfied with the provisions from Valparaiso, it seemed that none of the passengers could talk about anything except gold. As if every one of them would find a pot of it in this strange new land.

As if gold were the answer to all their problems.

Alden's work on their boat had given him plenty of time to think, though he couldn't really formulate a plan until he found Judah's office. Later, he would find a family to care for Isaac.

Someone slid up beside him, leaning against the rail. He thought it was Isaac at first, but it was Mrs. Dawson. The petite woman had made a remarkable recovery in the past week, as though the promise of land ahead was the remedy for whatever had ailed her. Isaac continued reading to her each afternoon, but she joined the other passengers in the dining saloon for her meals.

They drifted past a shipwreck partially masked in the fog, the abandoned hull rising and falling with the waves, grating against the rocky islet that ended its voyage.

Mrs. Dawson nodded toward the wreck. "Do you think the passengers made it to shore?"

"It's hard to tell," he said, though he didn't know how a smaller boat could help passengers stranded against that stone wall, especially if it was during a storm. Swimming between the outcroppings of rocks would be dangerous on a day with fair weather, impossible in waters churned by the winds.

"I always think of California as a place for beginnings," she said, tugging on the fingers of her white glove. "But I suppose it's an ending for others."

He hadn't thought about endings here either, but he and Isaac had come too far for an ending. This was a new beginning for both of them.

He felt Mrs. Dawson turn toward him, but he kept his eyes focused ahead, at the promise of a harbor hidden deep under this fog. "Is Mrs. Payne coming to join you?"

He shook his head. "I'm not married."

"I see," she said. "Surely you have a woman waiting for you to return home, then."

"I'm not going back." Stella, he hoped, had already married Robert.

"You need a woman to help care for Isaac," Mrs. Dawson said. "And a wife to help keep you warm."

Was she propositioning him? The woman was about ten years his senior and attractive in her fashionable mauve dress, her dark hair brushed into a modern winged style, and a shiny salve polishing her lips.

When she smiled at him, he wrenched his gaze away, focusing back on the foggy gateway. She was comely, but she was also a married woman. "I heard California is already warm," he said.

"I heard it snows plenty in the mountains."

He inched away from her. "That's why I'm staying in San Francisco."

"You still shouldn't be alone."

He rubbed his hands over the rail. "Is Mr. Dawson waiting for you in the diggings?"

"Oh no," she said, waving her glove. "There's no Mr. Dawson. It's just safer traveling as a married woman."

"That's shrewd of you."

"You can't fool me, Mr. Payne." She scooted closer to him. "You may have been a deckhand on this boat, but you are clearly a gentleman. And I am a lady in need of companionship."

One day he wanted to marry, but he didn't want a marriage of convenience. Or to make promises simply to keep warm. One day, he wanted to marry a woman he loved. A woman who would dare love him in return.

"I'm afraid I have all the companionship I need."

"Of course—it's impossible to dig for gold when you're traveling with company." She looked back down at the white-capped waves. "Would you consider selling the boy to me? I've become quite attached to him."

He considered her words for a moment. He may not need a wife, but Isaac needed a mother.

"I'd pay you a good sum," she continued.

"What if you didn't pay me anything?" he asked. "What if you adopted him?"

She stepped away from the railing, her smile slipping. "Why would I adopt him?"

"You said Isaac needed someone to care for him."

"Without a husband, I need someone to care for me."

"Ah." The woman didn't want a son. Isaac would remain in slavery with this woman until she found a husband. Then he'd be dispensable. "I'm afraid he's not for sale."

"So I get nothing from you?"

"Well wishes as you search for gold."

"I'm not looking for gold." A smile returned to her lips again. "I'm looking for a husband so I can help him enjoy his gold."

"It seems I have liberated you, then." He tipped his hat to her. "I'm not here to look for gold either."

As Alden stepped away, he saw Mr. and Mrs. Webb along the rail, on the other side of the deck. Persila stood near them and so did Isaac. Persila held Isaac's hand as if she feared he might fall into the water, watching over him again like she'd done repeatedly as they worked together these past months.

Alden had tried to talk to her about freedom, about the possibilities in this new state, but she didn't seem to be able to entertain the hope of a future beyond serving the Webbs.

Isaac leaned against the railing, searching for a glimpse of the harbor. "Is it really California?"

"That's what Captain Crandall says."

"What will we do when we get on land?" Isaac asked. For the first time, Alden heard a tremor of fear in the boy's voice. They'd worked hard these past five months to secure their passage out west. And now the end—or beginning—was close at hand.

"I have a job waiting for me here."

"Will you hire me out?" Isaac asked.

Alden shook his head. "I'm hoping they might have work at the office for you too."

At least until he found Isaac a good home.

An albatross flew over their ship, diving into the bay, and the land began to clear in front of them, breaking free of the fog. He saw sand hills at first, covered by scrubs of evergreen, and then the harbor with a forest of ship masts huddled together below a hill, like weeds sprouting out f muddy soil. Above were the façades of buildings, stair-stepped up, and clusters of shanties and tents on each side.

San Francisco.

Everything looked grimy yellow from this vantage point. Dank. But it was home, and he was glad to be here. He would learn to work alongside Judah. And he and Isaac would be free from slave masters and ship captains alike.

The clipper dropped anchor near the pier, and Captain Crandall ordered his crew to extend the gangplank, but Alden and Isaac were officially done with their work. Alden had left his trunk back in Boston, so all he and Isaac carried were two carpetbags.

His legs wobbled as the wood below him on the gangplank seemed to sway.

"Why am I still rocking?" Isaac asked, his eyes wide.

"It will stop soon," Alden reassured him. "Our bodies don't know we've landed yet."

Isaac reached for the rope railing. "I hope my legs figure it out soon."

Persila trailed the Webb family down the gangplank. While almost everyone else had a look of jubilation on their face, she looked terrified to discover what this new land held.

"Are you going straight to the Mother Lode?" Alden asked Mr. Webb.

The man looked at him with the same disdain as many of the other passengers on the ship, but then he saw Isaac and seemed to realize that Alden was a kindred spirit of sorts: the only other man on the *Pharos* who'd brought a slave into

California with him. "We're going to Sacramento City for a week or two first, then we'll travel to the goldfields. Where are you headed?"

"I'm staying here in San Francisco."

Mr. Webb nodded at Isaac. "Are you selling him?"

"No," Alden replied. "Are you selling Persila?"

"Not yet."

Alden lowered his voice, pretending to confide in the man. "I was worried about bringing a slave to a free state."

"There's no need to worry," Mr. Webb proclaimed. "I heard there are plenty of slaves out here, digging gold for their masters."

Alden groaned inwardly.

"Once we strike it rich, we'll buy us a fine mansion and live as good as anyone else."

While the Webbs collected their freight, Alden slipped up beside Persila. "You can find me at 316 Stockton Street," he said. "I will do everything I can to fight for your freedom."

"You fight for Isaac's freedom," she said before kissing the boy on his head. "I'll be praying for you both."

Isaac looked as if he might cry. "I'll be praying for you too."

He and Isaac strolled off the pier, into a hodgepodge of adobe buildings, wooden warehouses, saloons, and hotels. The hulls of old ships were used as foundations for some of the buildings,

185

and canvas was draped as roofs over others. The streets were crowded with men it seemed from around the world, speaking different languages. He only saw one woman, and she was dressed like a man, with sporting pants and a black frock coat.

Mrs. Dawson would find a husband soon. Perhaps before the day's end.

"Fresh fish!" a vendor yelled on one side of the street. Another yelled that he was selling candy, oranges, and pears—a tray secured by suspenders over his shoulders displayed his wares. There were chickens in cages at an open market, quarters of animals hanging overhead. The smell of roasting meat clung to the salty sea air.

Isaac glanced up at him.

"We'll eat soon," Alden promised him.

They pushed through the crowds of people as they climbed the dirt road up to Judah's office on Stockton. It was located in a two-story white-washed building, the sign overhead displaying the names of Garrett and Baer.

Alden checked the address again before he and Isaac stepped into a bank, complete with two teller booths and an office on the side.

He slid the envelope across the counter. "I received a letter from a friend at this address."

The teller read the address and stepped back, saying he would return.

Isaac's nose was pressed against the glass

window in the lobby. It seemed everyone else in this city was in a rush to their destination, as if they had someplace important to go. But this address was supposed to be *terminus ad quem*—the journey's end for Isaac and him.

The teller returned to the counter. "Mr. Fallow used to rent an office upstairs, but he's no longer here."

"Do you know where he went?"

The man shook his head, slipping the envelope back to him. "My employer says he left a year ago. Probably went to the goldfields."

Alden stared down at the letter with dismay, then stuffed it back into his pocket, mumbling a thanks to the clerk before turning toward the door.

Judah had been so resolute with his offer; Alden hadn't considered that the man would have left San Francisco before he arrived.

Why hadn't he told Alden where he'd gone?

Despondent, he leaned back against a post. What would he do if he couldn't find work? Even if he found Isaac a home, there wasn't enough money left for his return passage to Boston now.

He prayed San Francisco wasn't an ending for them after all.

Chapter 22

Sacramento City
May 1854

Isabelle knelt on the grass by her aunt's grave, a bouquet of wild lupine in her arms. She laid the pale yellow and purple flowers beside the dried ones she'd brought here last week. Then she'd kissed her fingers and held them against the cool marble stone.

Aunt Emeline rested beside her husband in City Cemetery, her grave marked with a simple epitaph.

Emeline Labrie

Loving Wife, Faithful Servant, Daughter of God

April 1797–February 1854

The words pierced Isabelle's heart again. Three months had passed since Aunt Emeline had gone home, but it seemed like years. The anchor in Isabelle's life had been cut loose, and she felt like a ship lost at sea, drifting through a storm.

When she was younger, she used to watch other families with wonder until God brought a family to love her too. Her aunt and uncle had cared deeply for her well-being and for her dreams. For almost a decade, she had belonged.

The trinket box that Aunt Emeline had given her was hidden in the room under her desk at the hotel, and she wore two keys around her neck now—one for the lockbox with revenue from the hotel and the other for her aunt's box. That key was a consistent reminder of her aunt, but she still couldn't bear to open her gift. Nor could she visit the cottage on the knoll above the cemetery, even though Nicolas and Sing Ye had invited her to dine with them.

Soon, she'd told them. Soon, she could step into the cottage, knowing that the woman she'd loved was gone. And soon, she hoped, she'd be able to press forward confidently in this world on her own.

Her guardian was gone now, but she couldn't continue drifting. She would have to find strength to stand on her own feet and face whatever was next, knowing the God of Aunt Emeline and Uncle William—the God who sent His son—was with her too.

Standing, she wiped the tears from her eyes and began to walk back between the scrubs and iron fences and the mishmash of wooden and marble tombstones. The spring sun was welcome relief from the doldrums caused by the winter's rain. The storms had come swiftly into California and were already gone.

Still Ross hadn't returned home.

She'd received two more letters from him in the past months, a repetition of his previous words. He'd found gold. He couldn't wait to marry her in the spring.

But April had passed, and she'd begun to wonder if perhaps there was another woman in Marysville vying for his attention. Ironic, given he already had two women waiting for him in Sacramento.

She walked through the cemetery's gatehouse, and wind rustled the branches of a lone tree as she neared the street. Several blocks ahead, the Sacramento River bent toward the busy wharf. She could see the twin stacks of one of the steamboats that brought supplies and Argonauts alike from San Francisco. The paddle wheels on the sides of the boat churned the water, lapping it against the banks. A steady rhythm between man and nature.

She and Fanny had slipped into a comfortable rhythm as well, working together to accommodate their guests at the Golden. In lieu of a friendship, they'd developed a polite camaraderie, never stepping back into the mire of what had or had not happened between Isabelle and Ross. After Aunt Emeline died, Fanny stopped asking questions about the past, and Isabelle was grateful that she didn't have to answer the inquiries. She was quite content just sipping tea together each morning, reading the papers, knowing that Fanny would be gone soon.

She'd finally told Fanny that she received word that Ross was in Marysville, but instead of going to find him, the woman opted to stay in the city. Fanny had said she preferred to wait and enjoy the fruits of Ross's labor when he returned.

When Isabelle reached Fourth Street, she turned right. Lorinda Washburn, the only dressmaker in Sacramento, lived in a small house on this street, and as Isabelle passed her window, she saw Fanny inside, being fitted, it seemed, for a new wardrobe.

Fanny had no money to pay for clothing, but she'd still been visiting Lorinda about once a week, placing orders that she wouldn't be able to redeem until Ross returned. Reality didn't seem to daunt her. Fanny was convinced that Ross would take back the hotel, and she was preparing to take her place as hostess.

Sighing, Isabelle walked into the lobby. If Ross were able to buy back his half, she'd transfer the entire ownership of the hotel to him. No matter the arrangement, she couldn't work alongside him and Fanny.

Stephan was helping Janette in the kitchen, preparing for dinner. He had retrieved a box from the steamboat that arrived this morning—a buttery *queso chanco* from Chile, chocolate from Domingo Ghirardelli's company in San Francisco, and almonds from Spain. Janette was focused on her preparations of a *torta caprese* for dessert, a chocolate almond cake powdered with sugar.

"Have you seen Fanny?" Janette asked, her dress and hair powdered with sugar as well.

Isabelle nodded. "She'll be back soon."

"She's been gone all morning."

Janette complained more often these days about Fanny's long absences, and Isabelle couldn't blame her. The person who labored the least among them was living in the best rooms, seeming to do what she pleased. If Ross wasn't planning to return, Fanny needed to go find him.

The lobby bell chimed, and Isabelle hurried to the next room. As she moved through the dining room, she pressed her hands against the chignon she'd twisted at the nape of her neck, checking the loose curls that fell on each side of her head. Then she straightened her gray day skirt and white blouse.

When she rounded the corner, she saw the back of a man dressed in a blue flannel shirt, jean trousers, and high boots pulled up almost to his knees. The typical attire of a miner. But then she stopped in the archway. Frozen. She knew the shape of those shoulders, the dark-blond hair that had grown long over his collar.

Nine months after walking out of the Golden, Ross had returned.

She stepped back, poised to run away, but it was

too late. He spun on the heels of his boots, his lips breaking into a smile. Then he rushed across the lobby to her, arms outstretched.

Before she could speak, he wrapped her in his arms. Kissed her lips.

Stunned, she stepped away, her stomach ill. She'd rehearsed this moment for months, and yet she couldn't seem to remember what she'd intended to say to the man in front of her.

He was grinning, oblivious to her reluctance. "I'm sorry I didn't make it back before April," he said. "Did you get my letters?"

She nodded slowly.

"I felt like I was close to something big, and boy, was I." He dug into the pocket of his coat and removed a buckskin pouch. Inside was a small nugget of gold. "I wanted to surprise you."

He handed the gold to her, and she stared down at her hand, her palm open. "I can't accept this."

His grin faded. "But I found it for you."

She held the nugget out toward him. "I'm sure your wife will appreciate it."

He lowered the bag in his hands, studying her face instead of the gold. "Have you changed your mind?"

"No."

"I thought you would be faithful, no matter how long I was gone."

She curled her fingers over the nugget. "And I thought you were an honest man."

He shook his head. "You're not making sense."

"You asked me to marry you, Ross."

"And it's something I intend to do. This afternoon, if possible."

"You might want to speak to your wife about it first." Outside the window, she saw Fanny strolling slowly up the walkway, a white parasol propped up over her head to ward off the sun. "She's been waiting for months for you and your gold."

Moments later, Fanny opened the door. When she saw Ross, she shrieked and rushed toward him, flinging her arms around him. As she clung to his neck, Ross looked over at Isabelle. She saw the shock in his gaze. Dismay.

Fanny had been telling the truth. And it seemed he hadn't ever intended to make good on his promises to the woman he'd left behind.

"How I've missed you," Fanny said, stepping back, though her hands remained on his shoulders.

He dropped back against the counter. "I've—I've missed you too."

"I wanted to surprise you." She took a breath. "I didn't think you would ever come back."

She kissed him and then let go, giggling when she realized that Isabelle was in the room too. Her gaze fell to the nugget in Isabelle's hands.

"Look what Ross brought for you," Isabelle said, holding it out.

Fanny squealed as she reached for it. "You did find gold."

His smile was strained. "Of course I did."

She examined the piece. "How much more did you find?"

"Plenty, but it's all in dust," he said, speaking as if every word pained him.

Fanny smiled up at him again. "Now we can buy back your hotel."

Reaching for Ross's hand, Fanny led him around Isabelle, back toward the rooms where she'd been staying. Isabelle slipped over to her refuge behind the counter. She thought about hiding upstairs in her room, locking herself in until Mr. and Mrs. Kirtland left the hotel, but she wouldn't be able to hide for long. Instead, she tried to busy herself by writing a letter to a shop in San Francisco.

An hour later, after taking a bath and changing into the clothes of a businessman, Ross returned to the lobby. "Fanny is packing," he said. "Can we talk upstairs?"

They walked up to the third floor, to the sitting area in the center of the lodging rooms. He sat on one of the damask-covered chairs, and she leaned back against the wall beside the window.

Ross was one of the most handsome men she'd ever known, but any affection between them was gone. "You should have told me you were married."

He shifted on the seat. "Fanny and I never should have married. We had completely different dreams."

"I heard her father paid you an ample sum as a dowry," she said, crossing her arms. "Must have helped with your journey west."

"I'd wanted to come to California since the first time I heard about the gold."

"And you needed his money to do it."

He glanced toward the window before looking back at her. "I planned to send for Fanny, before I met you and Emeline."

"You used my aunt and me, like you used Fanny and her father," she said, refusing to accept the blame for his indiscretion.

"That's not true."

She glanced across the room at the elegant furnishings and Oriental rug that she and Ross had acquired in their first year as partners. "You never ran a hotel before this one, did you?"

"No," he admitted, "but I think we did a fine job managing this one together."

She couldn't disagree, but she didn't need his assistance in running the hotel any longer. "How much is your nugget worth?"

"Not enough to buy back my partnership in the hotel."

She brushed her hands over the curtain. "It's better that way."

"I suppose it is."

That nugget of his wouldn't last long at California prices, but she hoped he would use it wisely, much more wisely than he'd treated the women in his life. "Perhaps you and Fanny could invest in another establishment?"

His eyebrows climbed. "And compete against you?"

"There's plenty of business to go around."

Ross stood up. "I never meant for you to find out about Fanny."

"I would have found out at some point," she said. "Much better to do so now than after we married."

"I wish—" he started, but she stopped him.

"Fanny wants to make you happy."

He shook his head. "She wants to make herself happy."

Isabelle moved toward the top of the stairs. "I suppose, in one way or another, we all want happiness."

Ross stepped toward her, his gaze intense. Her stomach fluttered the way it did when he first told her that he loved her—and she hated herself for it. He had deceived her, wronged her, and yet she still felt her resolve flitting away.

"You're right, Isabelle," he said quietly. "We both deserve to be happy too."

She reached for the polished newel post, willing herself to be strong.

"I'll divorce her," Ross declared. "Then we can marry."

Stunned, she tried to process his words. "You would put her out?"

"No. I'd buy her passage to New York," he said. "She'll find a wealthy man to marry there."

Fanny had come to California like so many, with great expectations about the happiness they thought gold could buy. She'd envisioned an affluent husband and a lavish hotel to call her own. A life of riches and grandeur without the hard work.

But even if Fanny agreed to return east—and even if Ross truly loved Isabelle—she would never again consider marrying him, not even to fill the vacancy left in her heart.

She longed to be with someone who would cherish love and integrity more than money, who would choose to do right, even if it cost him a dream. Someone who would guard her secret with his life and would love her for who she was, not who she pretended to be.

"I need someone who will be faithful," she told him. Like Uncle William had been to Aunt Emeline.

"I'll be faithful to you," he said, trying to reassure her, but she shook her head.

He searched her face one more time, as if he might find a way to influence her otherwise, but she'd made up her mind.

"Can Fanny and I spend the night here?" Ross asked as he followed her down the steps.

It would be hard to find a decent place to stay in a city already bursting at the seams, but she didn't want to prolong this disaster any longer.

"Just until tomorrow."

He nodded. "We'll be out at daylight."

Ross left the hotel as customers streamed inside for dinner. She hoped he was searching for a temporary place to live, but with gold lining his pockets, the gambling tables would be a persuasive distraction. She hadn't suspected it before, but it seemed that Ross liked to gamble after all.

After helping Stephan serve dinner, she checked on Fanny. The woman was sitting on the made bed, her trunk open in front of her, a crumpled handkerchief in her hands.

Fanny didn't look over at her. "Ross said he doesn't have enough gold to buy back his share of the hotel."

"That's true," Isabelle said, sitting in the rocking chair by the window. "There's typically more money to be had in providing goods and services to gold seekers than in actually finding gold."

Fanny blew her nose into the handkerchief. "You could loan us the money, Isabelle. We'll pay you back."

"I can't go into partnership with Ross again."

Fanny dabbed at her swollen eyes and then dropped the handkerchief back into her lap. "Then partner with me. We could continue operating the hotel together."

She considered the woman's words. It was never her intent to work alone, but a business partnership was a precarious affair, even with someone you trusted. While Fanny firmly appreciated the finer things in life, she didn't want to work to provide hospitality to their guests. A partnership with her, Isabelle feared, would mean Fanny and Ross would continue living right in these rooms, enjoying the food and safety in this hotel, with Fanny too preoccupied to help in the kitchen or upstairs in the guest rooms.

And if a boy like Micah ever came into the hotel again, she felt certain Fanny would be the first one to alert Rodney that they had a runaway.

She took a deep breath. "I can't partner with either of you, Fanny."

Fanny sat up straighter, her tears drying. "I know you two were lovers."

Isabelle cringed. "I didn't know Ross was married."

"I wrote him every month," Fanny said. "Surely you must have suspected."

"He said the letters were from his sister."

She snorted, turning the handkerchief. "I'm willing to overlook what you've done in the past, if you will help us with our future."

"What I've done . . ." Isabelle's voice trailed off.

"I believe the people of Sacramento deserve to know the truth about the proprietor of the Golden Hotel."

Isabelle stared at the woman, appalled at her threat.

"What will they say when they discover you had an affair with a married man?" Fanny asked, the tears gone.

Aunt Emeline would say it didn't matter what people thought because the past didn't define her. She too was a daughter of God. Fanny's attempt to slander her wouldn't change who she was—or who she wanted to be.

She rocked back and forth in the chair. "I can choose to forgive Ross, but I can't overlook what he's done to both of us."

"Ross said we have to leave in the morning."

"You need to begin again as husband and wife."

Fanny's eyes narrowed. "It's selfish of you to put us out like this."

"I'm not putting you out. Ross has enough money to provide for you. I'm certain he will find work at another hotel soon."

Fanny stood up, brushing the wrinkles from her dress as she walked toward the door. "Is there any food left from dinner?"

"I believe so."

She leaned against the doorpost, seeming to prop herself up against it. "Ross and I are going to start a grand hotel together. One much finer than the Golden."

"Then I shall come have dinner at your place."

She would miss having the companionship of

another woman, but she was relieved that this ordeal was almost over. Perhaps with Ross and Fanny out of her hotel, starting their life together, she might be able to begin dreaming again on her own.

Chapter 23

Panama City
May 1854

Victor paced around the tent as he waited for Levi to purchase his passage out of Panama City—though the word *city* was much too civilized for such a vile place.

He wiped the sweat off his face with his long sleeve, wishing he could strangle the proprietor of his hotel back in Boston, the man who'd told him to take the shorter journey across the isthmus instead of traveling the full distance around South America.

The trip through the jungle had lasted a week. The wait on this side was almost two months now.

He'd deal with the Boston proprietor once he retrieved Isaac and returned home.

Rounding the tent again, he saw the growing line up to a makeshift ticket office under a tree.

Panama was a repository of both hungry gold seekers and natives siphoning money from those held prisoner here. The few claptrap hotels were full so he and Levi had been forced to sleep in a tent and listen to drunk men fighting outside, along with the discord of cracked bells clanging incessantly day and night.

The boredom was horrific, the only brothel filthy, and he'd had to pay natives to dig jiggers out of his toes. He'd taken to playing Old Sledge for entertainment, but not even that held his attention for long. Gambling, he decided, was for fools.

Stopping, he looked out again at the gray hull of the ship that arrived last night.

For weeks, he'd watched as dozens of ships passed in the distance on their way north. He'd watched and waited for one of them to come into port, but those that did stop rarely had room for more passengers.

Then, last night, a steamer finally anchored offshore. Word spread like fire through town that they were offering passage for twenty people, all of whom would be sleeping on the floor during the voyage up to San Francisco.

He and Levi concocted a plan. He'd spent the night in their tent, guarding their things from looters who'd like nothing more than to relieve them of their possessions. Levi stood in line to purchase tickets for both of them. Unlike Victor, Levi said he didn't mind waiting.

The line began to disperse, and he heard several

men talking as they passed. The tickets were gone.

But not for him. All his possessions inside the tent were packed, and now he waited in earnest for Levi to return. By this afternoon, the sea breeze would be cooling his arms again. And in days, he would be in California.

Levi crossed between piles of rubble until he reached the tent, a slip of paper securely in his hands.

Victor held out his palm, but instead of putting the paper in it, Levi returned Victor's money. Victor stared down at the banknotes. "What is this?"

"I'm sorry, my friend," Levi said as he tucked the paper into his satchel. "They only had one ticket left."

Victor stiffened. "You purchased it for yourself?"

"My employer is waiting for me."

"I have important business in San Francisco!"

Levi shrugged. "There will be another boat."

Victor's fingers curled slowly over the banknotes, his mind racing. "We must celebrate your good luck, then," he finally said.

Levi opened up the flap to their tent. "I only have an hour."

Victor smiled, eyeing the man's satchel. "That's long enough."

Chapter 24

San Francisco
May 1854

A dozen men—mostly miners and sailors—crammed into the dank room where Alden and Isaac had rented overnight space on the floor. Thankfully, Isaac fell right to sleep on a mat. The stories the men around them told weren't fit for the ears of a child. Or for a gentleman.

He didn't want to listen to their tales of depravity, but as a rain shower pounded against the roof, he was glad for the shelter. And for the meal they'd found in an eatery near the bank. He and Isaac had feasted on freshly baked bread—something they hadn't tasted since Boston—and an Italian stew called *cioppino* made with white wine and a mishmash of seafood from the Pacific.

He tried to sleep, but his mind raced instead with fear. In the past few hours, his plans for the future had disintegrated, and he wasn't sure how to put the pieces back together so he could either find Judah or obtain work for both him and Isaac.

Until he left Virginia, he hadn't realized that fear often accompanied the freedom he'd desired. Was this the reason so many slaves never even attempted to run away? The unknown was a frightening place.

"Did you hear what happened to that free Negro over on Market Street?" one of the boarders asked the other men.

Alden turned toward them on his bedroll.

"He was kidnapped and sold into slavery, like that Solomon Northup fellow back east. Two other men saw it happen, but they were both Negroes so the judge wouldn't let them testify."

"We should go get him," another man declared, clearly intoxicated.

"You got to find him first."

A third man spoke. "If we'd keep the Negroes out of California, then we wouldn't have these problems."

"Someone should have kept you out of California."

As the men argued about the institution of slavery, Alden realized he couldn't tell anyone else about his intentions to find Isaac a home in California. Until Isaac was adopted, feigning his enslavement was the best way to protect him.

The men around him finally succumbed to sleep, but his own rest was fitful, with the serenade of snoring and rustling, men entering and leaving at all hours, the saltwater breeze filtering through cracks in the walls until the first rays of sunlight trailed the wind.

Alden woke Isaac early. He needed to find work

so he could provide food and a decent place for both of them to board. They drank black coffee for breakfast at a local stand, then searched for plain, ready-made clothing that would define them as neither gentleman nor slave. Alden took what remained of his wardrobe to a local laundry. Isaac tossed his holey trousers and shirt into a rubbish pile.

People stared at them as they walked through the streets. At first Alden thought it was because of Isaac's darker skin color, but the sidewalks were full of miners, fishermen, and businessmen from all around the world—China, Mexico, the Sandwich Islands. The farther they walked, the more he realized that people were probably staring at Isaac because he was a child. The busy streets were as void of children as they were of women.

Alden practically tugged Isaac up one more hill to the bathhouse. He'd found another law office listed in the city directory, and he hoped Judah had either relocated or the attorney at the office— a Mr. Clement—might know where he went. After bathing, they would set out to find the address.

"I don't need a bath," Isaac insisted outside the establishment's front door.

"We both need a bath."

"Miss Persila made me bathe two weeks ago."

"And she'd make you take another one if she was here now, with soap and fresh water."

Isaac sighed. "I miss Persila."

"Perhaps we will see her again soon."

Isaac contemplated that thought. "I suppose I should take a bath, just in case we do."

"A splendid idea."

After Alden washed and shaved—and Isaac appeared to have at least rinsed off—they visited a barber to trim their hair. Then they set out on their quest to find the law office, locating it a block away from the wharf, as if the lawyer was waiting to settle the disputes that brewed at sea.

The office on the third floor was small but clean. Mr. Clement waved them into the room, toward two cane chairs, but he didn't look up from his paper for several more minutes.

When he did, he glanced curiously between Alden and Isaac before homing in on Alden. "Is the boy your slave or a runaway?"

"He's with me," Alden said simply.

"Has someone been harassing you about the slave laws?"

"I'm trying to determine the law."

"We're still establishing law in California," Mr. Clement said. "Unfortunately, most people here would rather string someone up than take their cases before a judge."

"I thought slavery was illegal."

"Officially, slave owners can only bring slaves into this state if they're just passing through, but I know Southerners who brought slaves here back in '49 and haven't left yet." Mr. Clement drummed his fingers on the paper. "How can I help you?"

"I'm actually looking for work as a lawyer."

"Have you practiced before?"

"Not yet, but I finished more than two years at Harvard Law School."

Mr. Clement shook his head. "The judges around here don't care one whit about law school. They won't hear you until after you've been admitted into the bar."

"I need to apprentice first."

"I don't have any time to train an apprentice," Mr. Clement said, looking back down at his paper. "You best find work doing something else."

"Do you know a man by the name of Judah Fallow?"

Mr. Clement glanced back up. "Last I heard, Judah went to Sacramento City."

Hope began rising inside him again. "How do I get to Sacramento City?"

"If you take a paddle wheeler up the river tonight, you'll arrive by morning." Mr. Clement nodded toward Isaac. "Best keep your eye on him. Passions around here are high on both sides."

"I'll do that," he said, before thanking the man.

He would collect his laundry later today and go back to the wharf with Isaac to find one of the paddle wheelers. Perhaps he had a job waiting for him in California after all.

Chapter 25

Sacramento City
May 1854

As Isabelle sipped her morning tea, Fanny's angry words stung her ears. And her heart. She wanted to be a faithful servant like Aunt Emeline, not selfish.

Sometimes it was hard to make sense of what was right and what was wrong, but it seemed to her that Fanny was being the selfish one. How could the woman expect more from Isabelle than she'd already given? And why would she want her husband working alongside a woman he'd claimed to love?

The Kirtlands had left an hour ago, neither of them saying good-bye to her. Relief flooded through her at their departure. Fanny's presence had been a heavy weight on her heart these past six months, a constant reminder of Ross's deception. And now they were both free.

She'd never wanted to operate this hotel on her own, but with Stephan and Janette's help—and the two Chinese women she'd hired to clean the rooms—she could do it.

As she finished her tea, it occurred to her that she needed to visit Judah Fallow. Right away. The lawyer had visited her twice at the hotel this spring, asking her to sign some papers in his office for Aunt Emeline's estate, but the very signing of papers seemed like she was saying good-bye once again.

Now that Ross had returned, she needed to finalize everything about the ownership of the hotel. She didn't know the particulars of how one would contest a will, but she guessed the Kirtlands could figure it out.

After assigning the daily chores to the maids, Isabelle unhooked her favorite straw hat from the lobby wall and tied the pale-blue ribbon under her chin. Then she boarded a horse-drawn omnibus east to J and Twelfth Streets, where Judah had hung his own hat in a building shared with a dry goods store. His door was locked; a sign on it said the office would open by eleven. She didn't want to spare an hour for idleness, but it seemed she had no choice.

Instead of returning to the hotel, she decided to walk further east until she came to Burns Slough. Sutter Floral Gardens was located near this bank, a respite at the edge of a dusty city devoid of much color or pleasant fragrance. Jacob Knauth had designed a pleasure garden here with serpentine walkways that wove between the plots of flowers he'd brought with him from Europe. Arbors covered several walkways, their vines dotted with clusters of green grapes, and two summerhouses stood among the gardens for people to retreat to during the summer heat.

Before she returned to Judah's office, she ordered a bundle of flowers to be delivered to the hotel that afternoon. It was a new season for her, and she intended to celebrate with an abundance of color. New life.

At ten minutes after eleven, Horace Potts—Judah's young clerk—walked across the interior corridor of the building, his boot heels clapping on the wood before he unlocked the office door. Then he invited Isabelle inside.

The room was sparse, with its plain desk, cabinet stuffed with books and papers, and one wooden chair for clients. A curtainless window gave light, but the only view was of the back alleyway.

She sat on the stiff chair. "Where's Judah?"

"He went off to Columbia for the season."

She groaned. Why couldn't people here stay in one place? "He was handling my aunt's estate."

"Oh yes," Horace said. "He said he stopped by your hotel to request you sign some papers."

"He didn't tell me he was leaving town!"

"I'm sorry, Miss Labrie." Horace tugged on the drawer of a cabinet. "Judah left the papers here for you."

Horace rifled through a stack of envelopes until he found one with her aunt's name. Inside were two papers—a handwritten copy of Aunt

Emeline's will, and the deed to the Golden Hotel.

The will was exactly as her aunt had said it would be—the hotel and its assets were hers. The house was for Sing Ye. Aunt Emeline didn't mention the trinket box or any other assets in her will.

"I just need you to sign the bottom of the will to show you've read the document and agree to take over ownership of the hotel."

As she wrote her name on the paper, the finality of it dropped like an anvil on her chest. Then it seemed to take wings and fly away. Aunt Emeline was gone. Ross was gone. And now the hotel was hers.

Taking a deep breath, Isabelle took the deed in her hand. Then she thanked the young man and turned to take her leave.

Outside the building, she stopped to rest on a bench along the sidewalk, leaning back to savor the warm rays of sunshine on her face, the crisp parchment paper secured by the tips of her gloves. More women were coming to Sacramento, but there was still less than one woman for every ten men, and only a few women were overseeing businesses on their own. But she'd managed the hotel successfully while Ross was gone. She would continue the legacy of the Labrie family here in California—a tradition of working hard, serving others, helping those in need.

She would improve the legacy too. She'd hire

more Negro and Chinese women, and with Fanny gone, perhaps she could harbor more runaways. Stephan could help them find passage up to Vancouver Island.

Her heart beat faster at the thought. At the renewed hope for her future.

Mr. Bridges had left Sacramento, resigned to return to Texas without his slave, and as long as she didn't draw attention to herself, no one would suspect her of using the finest hotel in Sacramento to help former slaves.

She opened her eyes again, ready to face her future firmly on her own. When she looked up the planked street, she saw a man walking toward her, a young Negro boy at his side. The boy was just a few years younger than Micah.

Sighing, she rose to her feet, straightening the ribbon on her hat. Unlike hers, the future of this boy was completely controlled by whoever chose to own him. Her heart saddened at the thought of him being enslaved in their free state.

Before she took a step, her gaze traveled to the gentleman beside the boy. He was a few inches taller than she was and quite distinguished-looking in his black waistcoat and white shirt. His hair was parted neatly in the middle, and his face was clean-shaven—an anomaly in a city where most men grew beards.

When the man met her gaze, her heart seemed to stop. It had been years since she'd seen him, but she knew exactly who was walking toward her. Alden Payne—Mrs. Duvall's younger brother.

Stunned, she couldn't seem to move her feet, couldn't even find her breath. She had expected Ross to return to Sacramento, but she'd never thought she would see anyone from the Payne family again. Never thought any of them would ever leave Virginia.

She fought to breathe so she wouldn't pass out on the sidewalk. Fought the urge to run.

Had anyone else traveled west with him?

She dropped her head as they passed, gazing down at the deed in her hand. Mr. Payne wasn't likely to recognize her, but she couldn't risk it.

Once he and the boy entered the building, Isabelle picked up her heavy skirt with one hand and rushed back to the hotel. Her heart racing, she locked the doors to the lobby and hid the deed under her desk, inside the metal lockbox with her gold and other valuable papers. Then she sat down on her chair, unable to move again.

Finally she was free, untethered in a sense, to begin dreaming again. Why was her past coming back to haunt her now?

Instead of dreaming, all she wanted to do was take the next steamboat out of Sacramento.

But this time, she had no one to help her run.

"How long is Judah going to be in Columbia?" Alden asked Horace. The clerk was at least five years his junior, but he seemed efficient. And trustworthy. Had Judah already given away the apprenticeship, thinking Alden wouldn't come?

"He'll be there at least another month. Two at the most."

"Are you his apprentice?"

"No," Horace said. "I'm just handling the paperwork while he's gone. Is he expecting your arrival?"

"Not for another six months."

"I'll send him a letter, but correspondence to the diggings is faulty," Horace said. "You should try your luck in Columbia as well while you wait. They're finding millions in gold out there."

After cashing in most of his banknotes in San Francisco for gold coins, he had enough in his wallet to pay for a month in this town. If he spent it on transportation to Columbia—and didn't strike gold—he wouldn't have the money to return.

"I think I'll wait here in Sacramento."

"Suit yourself."

"I need to find a room until Judah returns," Alden said. "A hotel fit for a child."

The man glanced down at Isaac. "There's only one decent place in town, but I don't know if they'll take—"

Alden stopped him. "I'll try our luck."

The man's directions took them to a hotel located near the river. The building was three stories tall, built of brick with a white granite façade on the front. There were two balconies above the sidewalk, and lacy curtains pulled over the windows.

Isaac whistled when he saw the place. "It looks like a plantation house."

"I suppose it does."

"If they won't let me inside, I can sleep out back," Isaac offered.

"If they won't let you sleep here, I'll join you outside."

He hoped the people would be welcoming. And he hoped the accommodations were much different from the place they'd stayed in San Francisco.

Isaac hopped up onto the walkway, lugging his heavy bag with him. His new trousers needed to be hemmed, but he was quite proud of his store-bought clothing and neat haircut. Alden had purchased him calfskin boots as well, but Isaac refused to wear them, carrying them instead in his luggage.

A bell chimed when Alden opened the door, and inside the lobby, he found a woman sitting behind the counter.

"I wanted to inquire—" he began, but stopped talking when she looked up at him, his words jumbling in his mind. It had been months since he had been near such a beautiful, well-bred woman. A lady.

Her dark-brown hair was pinned back at the

nape of her neck with curls draping over both of her ears, and she wore a pale-blue summer dress, the kind of dress the women back in Virginia would have worn to a garden party. The women back home would be aghast at her suntanned arms and face, but here it would be almost impossible to fight the rays of sun. And the sunlight did something magical with her eyes as well as it streamed through the window. Their caramel color was flecked with gold.

On second thought, the beauty of the women he knew back east didn't even compare to the lady before him. He guessed the men in Sacramento were as intrigued by the gold in this woman's eyes as they were by the dust they found along the rivers.

He managed a smile—the silence growing awkward between them as she moved out from behind her desk, then stood tall before him at the counter. Hostile.

Was she angry that he'd brought a Negro boy into her hotel?

Isaac stepped forward beside Alden, standing on his tiptoes so he could look over the counter. "This is a right pretty place you have."

Her demeanor shifted as she smiled down at Isaac. "Thank you."

Isaac grinned back at her. "It smells like lemons in here."

"Do you like lemons?"

When he nodded his head, she rang a bell.

Her smile vanished again when she looked back at Alden. She didn't seem to have a problem with a dark-skinned guest, but clearly she had a problem with him.

"Would you have a room available for us, Mrs.—"

She didn't offer her last name. "Unfortunately, we are completely full."

Isaac pointed up at a list of rules on the wall. "We won't drink liquor or spit on the floor," he said confidently. "And we'll take a bath at least twice every week."

She looked surprised at his ability to read. "I'm certain you would make a fine guest, but there's simply no room."

"I can sleep in the alley," Isaac offered.

Her lips opened to speak, but a Negro steward, dressed in formal attire, walked through the entrance at the side. "Did you need me, Miss Labrie?"

She nodded, pointing down at Isaac. "Could you bring my friend here a glass of lemonade?"

"Of course." The steward bent down, talking to Isaac. "Are you staying at the hotel?"

Isaac shook his head sadly. "You don't have any room for us."

The steward glanced up at Isabelle before looking back at Isaac. "Fortunately, we just had a room open on the third floor."

Miss Labrie's eyes narrowed again as she faced the steward. "I'm afraid that room is already taken."

"Our guest on the third floor is moving to a new place."

Miss Labrie looked back at Alden. "Please excuse me while I consult with my employee."

"Of course."

After Miss Labrie left with her steward, the only sound remaining was the slow tick of the clock on the wall. Outside the window, he heard the whistle blast of a steamboat, the clank of wagon wheels plodding over boards in the road.

And he realized that his world had finally stopped rocking.

Isaac turned toward him. "Did you say something mean to Miss Labrie?"

"Did you hear me say something unkind?"

"No, but—I'm pretty sure that Missus Eliza liked me better than that Miss Labrie likes you."

"It was nice of her to offer you lemonade."

"You can have a sip of mine." Isaac straightened his collar. "Maybe it will make you sweeter."

"I didn't do anything wrong."

"You have to compliment a woman, Master Payne. Or she'll think you don't like her."

"I'm afraid a compliment from me would have made her more angry."

"Or it might have gotten us a room," Isaac

replied. "I don't want to go back to that hotel in San Francisco."

"Me either."

"Then think of something nice to say when she returns."

Chapter 26

Sacramento City
May 1854

Isabelle paced in the kitchen between the wooden counter and oven. Stephan stood quietly by the bundle of flowers delivered from the gardens that afternoon, waiting for her to speak.

She was angry at her steward. Angry at herself.

She was supposed to keep her loathing of slavery secret, and yet the resentment inside her flared, jetting up like a waterspout. If she couldn't control her anger, Alden might remember her too.

She shuddered to think what might happen if he did remember.

Years ago, Isabelle used to watch him when he visited the Duvalls, wondering if he would choose to follow in the way of his brother-in-law and father or if one day he might emancipate the people he owned. But Alden had grown up now, becoming another Master Payne. Apparently, he'd selected California as his residence over the

Virginia plantation, and he'd brought the horrific institution of slavery west with him.

No one here suspected that she'd once been enslaved. Her skin—even slathered with the cucumber-and-lemon cream—might be a shade darker than some of the people from the East Coast, but other women's skin darkened here in the sun. In Virginia, Mrs. Duvall had called her a mulatto—a constant reminder that while her skin was a light olive color, Negro blood ran through her veins. In the Southern states, she would always be considered a slave.

But Aunt Emeline hadn't called her a slave. She'd called her beloved—helping lighten her skin, purchase a new wardrobe, educate her with a private tutor so she could escape her past. Reinvent herself as a treasured niece. With the power of a new name and wardrobe, Isabelle became a new person. And with the love and care of her adopted uncle and aunt, she thrived.

She wanted to be faithful to help children like Isaac, but she didn't want Mr. Payne staying in her hotel, didn't want to hear any stories about his life in Virginia or live with the constant threat of something sparking his recollection. Nor did she want to be reminded about the horror she'd left behind or the memory of the baby she'd held in her arms for a glimpse of a moment before he slipped away.

She unwrapped the string holding together the

parcel of flowers, trying to focus on the beauty of the coral chrysanthemums, lavender peonies, and creamy-white iris. She couldn't allow herself to journey back again in her mind, to the pain buried deeply in the recesses of her heart.

Even if Stephan didn't know about her past, he shouldn't have stepped in like that, undermining her authority in front of Alden and his boy.

Finally, she looked back up at him. "I don't want them staying here."

"Them?" he asked cautiously. "Or is it just the master you don't want in the hotel?"

"The master," she retorted. "I don't want him or any other slave owner as a guest."

"But we can do more good if the boy and his master stay right here, under our roof, than if they stay in another hotel."

She shook her head. "I won't be an accomplice to the evil."

"But what if we could overcome the evil?" Stephan lowered his voice. "We could help the boy escape."

"If he went missing like Micah, Rodney would put us both in jail."

"We'll find a way," he insisted.

She wanted to be faithful like Aunt Emeline, but if her past were exposed, it would ruin everything for her here in Sacramento—her reputation and her business. No one would want to stay in a hotel run by a Negro—a former slave—no matter how elegant the décor or delicious the food. And much worse, Alden might put her back into chains and return her to Victor Duvall.

She shivered. So much had changed in the past nine years, yet it didn't matter in the eyes of the law how strong or intelligent or capable she was. The color of her skin didn't even matter. Negro blood lapped inside her veins, flowing down from her mother's side of the family.

The blood siphoned from her father didn't count. Men could legally impregnate any of their slaves—married and maiden women alike—in order to add to their chattel. The more slaves to sell, the more money to be had. And somehow, they were able to deny these slaves were also their children. They sold their sons and daughters without grieving the loss.

She picked up two of the mums, slipping the stems into a vase.

But what if Stephan was right? What if she could help the boy in her lobby find freedom? She'd been angry when Fanny accused her of being selfish, but in this case, perhaps it was true. A great opportunity had been set before her— she could not only help a child but also free a Payne slave from the torment of his master.

But what if they sent her back to Virginia in his place?

The vase shook when she shuddered.

It would be worth everything, she told herself,

if this boy could be free. Redemption, in a sense, for what she had lost.

Thank God she hadn't told Ross about her past before he had left Sacramento. She couldn't allow herself to think he might have used it against her, but if Fanny found out, she might have used the information to her advantage.

She would have to find a way to obtain freedom for this boy while keeping her secret intact.

She pumped water into a pitcher at the sink and added it to the vase before speaking again. "Will you register them for me?"

Stephan nodded.

"They can stay—as long as they obey the rules."

"Of course." Stephan stepped toward the door. "We'll find a way to help the boy."

After she finished arranging the flowers, Isabelle fled into the rooms vacated by Fanny and Ross. There were no more guests to register for the hotel, and dinner guests wouldn't begin arriving until five.

Sitting on the rocking chair, she swayed back and forth, looking out at the herbs growing in the courtyard between the buildings. And the aching began to bleed out of the recesses inside her.

She'd tried so hard to escape the memories when she'd left the Duvall house. The memories returned to her some nights, in her nightmares, but it was daylight now, and they still returned with a vengeance, the realities of what happened years ago pressing against her chest, feeling as if they might suffocate her.

The hatred in her heart was still there, with a vengefulness that she'd never imagined. The guilt and shame—though Aunt Emeline told her over and over that she had done nothing wrong.

But her aunt didn't know everything. She didn't know about the baby Isabelle had brought into the world but couldn't keep alive. The baby her milk should have sustained.

She rocked back and forth again, and tears filled her eyes, unbidden.

Victor was a wicked man. She knew that now. With Uncle William and Aunt Emeline's help, she'd learned what was right and loving and good in a family. But the most painful memories from Virginia weren't the ones of Victor. The hardest ones were of the morning she'd lost her son.

The day of his death and the ones that followed bled together in a collective blur. She'd experienced true happiness for the first time in her life when she held her child in her arms. For the first time, she too had family, like the Paynes. Someone to belong to. Someone to love her in return.

But she'd been too young to care for him.

Incompetent.

That was the word Mrs. Duvall used as the carriage bumped along the road that warm spring day. It was a word that had stitched itself to her heart and her mind. Any tugging on the thread ripped at her very core.

On that terrible journey, her mistress had given her something for her pain, something that plunged her into a dark sleep. When she woke again, she was in a soft bed in Baltimore. Mrs. Duvall was gone, Aunt Emeline sitting at her side.

Blinking, she glanced around her room. Stephan had already moved her trunk down from the top floor to the foot of the double bed. Inside, buried under clothes and a coverlet, she found the baby blanket she'd crocheted before her son was born—an ivory-and-teal pattern from yarn left over from a blanket she'd made for Mrs. Duvall when the woman thought she was expecting.

Isabelle lifted the blanket and nuzzled her cheek against it. This memento was all she had left of her beautiful boy.

Someone knocked on her door, and she tucked the blanket back into her trunk before closing the lid. Then she wiped her eyes with a handkerchief.

She had to hide again behind the façade that had become so familiar in Uncle William and Aunt Emeline's care. Not that they required her to pretend; they just saw her as someone she was not. As the woman she—and they—wanted her to be. A woman she needed to become.

When she opened the door, she found Mr.

Payne's boy waiting for her. In his hands was the stem of a rose—a delicate peach-colored flower that was just daring to unfold.

But she never bought roses from the floral garden. They reminded her too much of Victor Duvall.

She eyed it skeptically. "Where did you get that?"

"From a man selling them outside." He held the stem out to her. "Thank you for letting us stay."

"I'm glad you're here," she said, taking the rose from him. The fragrance was as delicate as the color. The aroma of beauty and spring.

He held out his hand. "My name's Isaac."

"It's nice to meet you, Isaac." She reached out her hand to shake his. "My name is Isabelle Labrie."

"You have an awfully pretty name."

She smiled. "I'm glad you approve of it."

"And you serve the best lemonade I've ever tasted."

She tilted her head. "Do you need something?"

"Just to say thank you." He paused, and she waited for him to give the real reason for his visit. "And to let you know that Master Payne is a fine man. He treats his slaves right."

She nodded warily, not about to argue the evils of slavery with a child, especially if he thought his master was kind. When the time was right, she and Stephan would offer him the freedom to become his own master. To treat himself with even more respect than his owner did.

"He better keep treating you well."

"Yes, ma'am."

"And if you need anything"—she tapped on the door—"you know where to find me."

He smiled. "And if you ever need anything, you know where to find me too."

"That's right, I do."

Sadness flooded her heart again as she collapsed down on the bed, clutching the rose in her hand. If her son had lived, he would have been about Isaac's age.

Chapter 27

Sacramento City
June 1854

Lobster salad topped the dinner menu, followed by turnip soup, warm dinner rolls, cantaloupe slices garnished with sprigs of mint, and coconut cake for dessert. The Golden Hotel food was better than any Alden had tasted since leaving Scott's Grove, and breakfast and dinner were both included with the price of a room.

An accomplished pianist entertained them with Mozart's works as Miss Labrie fluttered around the dining room like an elegant butterfly, welcoming her guests, pouring wine, offering Chilean coffee to accompany dessert.

Gentlemen—including the mayor of Sacramento City—filled the twelve tables, accompanied by several ladies dressed as fashionably as their matron. Isaac was the only child in the restaurant, and the only Negro seated for the meal. The patrons politely ignored him.

Miss Labrie smiled at each guest who came through the door—smiled at Isaac, even—but she never once smiled at him.

Clearly, he'd offended her, but he couldn't recall what he might have done to deserve her contempt.

"*Bonsoir*, Monsieur Walsh," Miss Labrie sang as she welcomed a man standing at the arched entrance. The tables were filled, but she still waved him through the door. "We will find the perfect place for you."

Moments later, Stephan carried a small table and chair out from the kitchen and set them beside the piano. Miss Labrie covered the table with a white cloth and filled a goblet with wine.

"We've missed seeing you," she said to her new customer, her smile gracious again.

Mr. Walsh smoothed out his mustache with the tip of his finger before taking a sip of the wine. "I decided to return to the goldfields for a season."

"Did you have any luck?" she asked as Stephan brought the tableware and silver for his place setting.

"I always have luck." He took another sip. "But I have missed your restaurant very much. There is no decent food to be found in the foothills."

"I'm glad you've returned safely home."

He set the goblet back on the table. "Has your Mr. Kirtland returned as well?"

Alden saw the flicker of sadness in Miss Labrie's eyes. Or was it frustration?

Mr. Walsh didn't seem to notice.

"Why are you staring?" Isaac whispered.

When he looked back at his companion, he missed the answer to Mr. Walsh's question. "I was observing. Not staring."

And wondering. Why was a woman so beautiful and intelligent still unmarried in a land filled with wealthy, lonely men? Perhaps it was because she was intelligent. She could keep the profits made from her hotel, no husband threatening to take it from her.

Then again, perhaps she was planning to marry this Mr. Kirtland when he returned.

"Do you think Persila is all right?" Isaac asked.

"I hope so." Alden took another bite of the creamy coconut cake. He'd been inquiring around the city to see if any of the hotels had registered a Mr. and Mrs. Webb, but he'd yet to find them here.

"I wanted to tell her that I've bathed twice now."

Alden smiled, looking back at Isaac. "She'd be quite pleased to hear that."

Stephan stepped up to their table with a pot of

231

coffee. The thin man, clothed in a black swallow-tailed coat and white gloves, reminded him of Thomas. "How are you both faring?"

"Very well," Alden replied, his stomach mercifully full. After five months on the ship, he would be forever grateful for a good meal.

Stephan poured them both a cup of coffee. "Are you traveling to the interior soon?"

Alden shook his head. "Not unless I have to."

"What are your plans?"

"I need to find work here in the city. At least for a month or two."

"We had a recent vacancy here," Stephan said. "I could ask Miss Labrie if she'd consider hiring you."

Alden forced a smile. "She'd never agree to that."

Stephan returned his smile. "I wouldn't be so certain."

Miss Labrie's private sitting area was on the first floor of the hotel, beside the restaurant. Inside was a high-backed settee, polished table, and three upholstered chairs. Along the papered wall was a small library of books in a glass case.

Two doors led into the room—the one from the dining room and the other, he assumed, into Miss Labrie's bedchamber.

An hour after breakfast, the woman entered through the restaurant door. She carried a bone china teapot in one hand, and in her other hand, her fingers laced between the handles of two matching teacups.

She wasn't surprised to see him—Stephan had arranged the meeting—but she was clearly not happy about spending time with him.

She held up the pot of tea. "Would you like some?"

"Yes, please." Alden unhooked one of the cups from her finger and placed it on the table. She poured the tea into both cups, then stirred a spoonful of honey into hers. She didn't offer him anything to sweeten his tea, and he didn't dare ask.

He took a sip and almost choked on the bitter, earthy flavor. It tasted like dried tobacco leaves.

"It's a Chinese tea," she explained.

"It probably tastes better with sugar."

She ignored his slight. "I'm told you need a job."

"I'm looking for temporary work. I have an apprenticeship with Judah Fallow when he returns to town."

Her gaze remained on her teacup. "Does Judah know you own a slave?"

"He knows that I attended law school," he said, setting his half-full teacup back on the table. "He asked me to work for him."

"He may change his mind once he finds out about Isaac. He's known in Sacramento for being a staunch abolitionist."

"It seems the abolition laws are a bit muddled here."

Her arms stiffened, the teacup perched on her lips for a moment before she lowered it. "A muddled law doesn't make something right."

Sitting back in his chair, he realized his offense to her was a misunderstanding. She seemed to abhor slavery as much as he did, and she believed him to be the exact person they both despised. No wonder she was hostile to him. He wished he could tell her the truth, but as long as free blacks were in danger here, he had to guard Isaac.

He leaned toward her again, anxious to change the topic. "Your steward said you might have some work."

She took another sip of tea. "Sometimes I need to order supplies in San Francisco. Stephan was traveling there for me after—" She stopped herself. "There are rumors about free blacks being kidnapped in the city and sold into slavery. I can't risk having him travel anymore."

"I can travel to San Francisco for you," he offered. "And I can help make repairs around the hotel and retrieve shipments down at the wharf as well."

She studied the teacup in her hands. "Whoever I hire will also need to help Stephan and Janette in the kitchen."

He couldn't help but smile. What would his mother think, knowing he'd earned his way around

Cape Horn working in the galley? And now this woman was offering him the opportunity to earn his keep by working in a kitchen as well. Work, he'd realized, that could be even more grueling than his time in the fields.

She glanced briefly up at him. "You've probably never even been inside a kitchen, have you?"

"Actually, Isaac and I are both well acquainted with kitchen work."

Her eyebrows slid up. "You want me to hire him too?"

"We work as a team," he replied. "And it will keep him out of trouble."

She considered his proposition. "I suppose I have enough work for both of you, but I won't pay you for Isaac's work."

"That's hardly fair—"

"I will keep seventy-five percent of both your earnings for room and board, and I will pay Isaac the additional twenty-five percent directly for his work." She paused, looking up at him again. "If he wants to buy his freedom with the money, he shall."

The gold in her eyes gleamed in the light, and for a moment, he thought he might have seen those eyes before. In Massachusetts, perhaps? Or was it back in Virginia, when he was a boy?

Miss Labrie refocused on her teacup. Even though she talked confidently to him, she didn't like to meet his gaze.

He cleared his throat. "Isaac's well-being is my business."

"If I hire you, he becomes my business too."

Silence draped between them for several moments, and then he finally agreed to her terms. "We will work for you until Judah returns."

"You may need a position after he returns as well."

"I suppose I'll determine that later this summer."

She glanced up at the clock on the wall. It read nine o'clock. "I need you to go to San Francisco this afternoon."

"Will Isaac come with me?"

She shook her head. "I'll need his help here."

"I'll rely on you to treat him right."

She stood up. "I treat all my employees well."

Chapter 28

Sacramento City
July 1854

The sun in California was just as heinous as it had been in Panama. Victor sold his coat to a man traveling to New York, but he'd kept the hat. Anything to keep the blasted afternoon rays off his head.

He was close now to finding Isaac; he could feel it in his bones. Soon he would retrieve the boy, and then they would return to Virginia. Triumphant.

He couldn't wait to see Eliza's face. He'd have to sketch the image of his wife, her eyes bloated with shock.

Or perhaps he would try his luck at the diggings here first. He'd learned plenty from Levi and others on the ship. Isaac could squeeze into places that no grown man could. He could make them rich.

Then he would return to Virginia even wealthier than John Payne. He wouldn't even need Eliza anymore. Or men like Levi, who tried to cheat him.

He'd purchased a vial of opium along with a bottle of brandy for his acquaintance back in Panama City. Then he'd gained passage for himself through the Golden Gate.

After San Francisco, he'd taken a paddle wheeler up the winding Sacramento River until he arrived in this city that stunk of soot and saltpeter, but as he moved away from the wharf, the walk through the city began to energize him, the knowing his search was about to end. He carried the letter from Mr. Fallow that was addressed to Alden, stopping several workers in town to show the address. He finally found the law office a miserable twelve blocks away.

"I've just come from Virginia," he explained to a scrawny-looking clerk inside. "I need to find Mr. Fallow."

"Mr. Fallow is a popular man," the clerk muttered.

Victor licked the crease of his lips, stepping forward. "Has someone else been looking for him?"

The man's eyes narrowed under his spectacles, and he hesitated before answering Victor's question—a telltale sign that he was about to lie. "Plenty of people around here need an attorney."

Victor swallowed hard, grinding his fists together to contain his frustration. "I'm looking for one man in particular," he said pointedly. "His name is Alden Payne, and he's traveling here from Boston to work for Mr. Fallow, accompanied by a slave."

The man shrugged. "Mr. Fallow will return in a few weeks. Perhaps he will have seen your friend."

The clerk was clearly lying to him. Either Alden and Isaac had already joined this Mr. Fallow or they remained in Sacramento, waiting for his return.

"If Mr. Payne hasn't arrived yet, he will be here soon," Victor said. "It's urgent that I speak with him."

The man looked back down at the book on the desk, completely uncooperative. "If your Mr. Payne visits, I will pass along a message."

"There's no need to inform him, but once I find a tolerable hotel, I'll bring you the address so you can notify me."

The clerk looked up again. "If you're looking

for a place to stay, there's a new establishment in town, catering specifically to gentlemen like yourself."

Victor lifted his chest. "What's the name of this place?"

"The Kirtland House. It's over on the corner of G and Third Street."

He picked his bag up off the floor. "If Mr. Payne arrives, you can find me at the Kirtland House, then."

The man gave a sharp nod. "I will let you know if he appears."

Chapter 29

Sacramento City
July 1854

An urgent knock woke Isabelle from her sleep. She didn't remember her dream, but her cheeks were wet, her pillow damp. In the weeks since Alden and Isaac had arrived, she had awakened often to a bath of tears, to the return of her old nightmares and then the tremendous sadness of what she'd lost.

While they were still in Baltimore, Aunt Emeline would come into her room after the nightmares, softly humming the hymn about God's amazing grace. As a younger woman, she had embraced those lyrics, letting them settle into all the hidden places, in those dark corridors that she dared not open to anyone but a God who loved her.

Now, in these early morning hours, she hummed the lyrics again on her own, trying to remind herself of all the blessings she'd gained in the past nine years. A family, for a season. Her freedom. A profession she enjoyed and a place where people respected her. And most important perhaps, the means to help other slaves whenever God brought someone like Micah or Isaac her way.

The knock continued, growing louder, and she reached for her dressing gown, wrapping it securely around her waist. Then she lit a candle and hurried across the sitting room to find Stephan standing on the other side of the door, fully clothed.

"What is it?" she whispered.

"We need your help."

She scanned the empty dining room behind him. "Who needs my help?"

Stephan motioned to the side, and a Negro woman stepped into the candlelight. "This is Persila."

Isabelle suppressed a groan, but she couldn't stop the tears that flooded her eyes again. The woman's hair was matted, her clothing torn and dirty. Blood trickled down from her right ear, and her face was bruised. "Who did this to you?"

"My master," the woman said painfully, leaning against Stephan to stand. "He thought I stole money from him."

"Did you steal something?"

"No, ma'am. Master Webb lost most of his money gambling, but he can't tell his missus what he done."

Her hands trembled with anger. It was a familiar story, both of men losing their money in the gambling saloons and of slave owners venting their fury on their slaves.

Isabelle opened the door wide. "I'll help you clean up."

"There's no time." Stephan glanced back over his shoulder. "We need to hide her."

Isabelle directed the woman toward the room behind her. "You can rest on my bed for a moment."

When she left, Isabelle turned back toward her steward. "Where did you find her?"

"I saw her yesterday near the riverfront. When her master was distracted, I told her about a safe house for runaway slaves."

As much as she wanted to know the location of this house, she knew it would be better for all of them if it remained a secret. "Did she come tonight?"

He nodded. "Mr. Webb passed out, and she was able to escape."

She was glad Stephan had brought her here,

but the rugged hiding place between the walls downstairs was no place for an injured woman. "Can you take her back to the house?"

"It's no longer safe," he said, shaking his head. "Rodney is there, searching every crevice. Her owner is spitting mad."

"It looks like he already took out his rage on her."

"Unfortunately, there's more to be had."

Isabelle shuddered. They had no choice, then. "I'll hide her right now."

But there was no time to move the woman to the lobby. Someone began pounding on the front door of her hotel, the sound thundering across the dining room. A tremor shot down her spine, and when she looked back at Stephan, she saw fear reflected in his eyes.

"Take her through my window," she urged, pulling him into the sitting room. "Sing Ye will hide her until you and your friends find another safe place."

She didn't want to endanger Sing Ye, but she would want to help. And Isabelle prayed that Nicolas would want to help too.

"I'll take care of whoever's at the front door," she said, trying to assure him.

Stephan hesitated for a moment, clearly torn. "I fear they'll harm anyone who gets in their way."

She nudged him forward. "I won't get in their way."

The hammering rattled the glass windows, and she realized whoever was out there intended to enter her hotel whether or not she unlocked the door. Best that she let them in on her own terms. She called out that she was coming, though she doubted anyone could hear her voice over the incessant noise.

In the lobby, she set her candle on the counter and lifted the window curtain. Outside was the sheriff with one of his two deputies. Once Rodney saw her, he stopped pounding.

She resituated her dressing gown, as if he'd just awakened her, before opening the door. Both men stormed into her lobby.

She reached for her candle and held it to her chest. "What's happened?" she demanded, her voice brimming with concern.

"I'm sorry, Miss Labrie," Rodney said. "We have to search your hotel."

She followed him into the dining room. "What are you searching for?"

"We're looking for another runaway."

Her eyes narrowed. "Do you think I'm collecting people?"

"I surely hope not, at least not other people's property, but seeing as Mr. Bridges never did find his slave, I have to start here."

She glanced up at the staircase. "Can't it wait a few more hours?"

"I'm afraid not." He waved a piece of paper in

front of her. "This is a warrant from the judge."

"You'd think the judge would wait until the sun rose to begin issuing warrants."

Rodney shrugged before turning to his deputy. "You take the top two floors, and I'll search the dining room and cellar."

"But my guests are still asleep," she insisted.

"They'll have to rise early this morning."

She followed Rodney as he looked under each table and through the kitchen, praying the darkness would hide Stephan and Persila until they reached the cottage.

The sheriff didn't ask permission to enter her private quarters, but he did instruct her to light the oil lanterns in both rooms. He glanced around at the furniture in the sitting area, but when he stepped into her bedchamber, his eyes fixated on the window. It was open, about an inch, and a stripe of copper-red streaked across the white-painted windowsill.

"What is this?" Rodney asked, striking his finger through the fresh blood.

She froze, her lips pressed together.

He swung toward her. "Miss Labrie?"

She leaned forward, studying the smear. "It appears to be blood."

"Do you have any recollection as to how it got here?"

When she didn't answer, he sighed. "I suppose we'll have to find out in court."

The bell of her lobby chimed, and she hurried back toward the front door, the sheriff behind her. Several of her guests lined the staircase, looking down at them. She tried to reassure them with her smile, even as her heart was pounding, knowing that they all might vacate if they found out what she had done.

When she arrived in the lobby, all the pounding in her heart seemed to crash in on itself. There were two more white men before her—the second deputy and a man she assumed to be Persila's master. Secured in the deputy's hands was Stephan, his hands tied behind his back. And Mr. Webb gripped Persila's upper arm.

Tears streamed down the woman's cheeks, and Isabelle wanted to hug her, give her the same hope that Aunt Emeline had given her, but she could do nothing for Persila or her faithful steward right now. The men that held them were much stronger than she—and the law was on their side.

Loneliness gripped her. And fear.

How could she help them now?

Rodney studied the man secured in the deputy's grasp before looking back at her. "It appears that your steward was an accomplice to this crime."

"It depends on what you think is criminal."

"I'm sorry, Miss Labrie." Rodney opened the front door for his deputies. "Take Stephan and this woman to the jailhouse."

Mr. Webb didn't release the woman. "She's coming home with me."

Rodney shook his head. "Not until she goes before the judge."

Mr. Webb looked as if he might fight the sheriff, but he relented, releasing Persila to the sheriff's care. "I'm following you to the jailhouse," he said.

Rodney didn't speak to Isabelle again, but when the door closed behind him and his men, she knew his inquiry about her involvement had just begun.

Chapter 30

Sacramento City
July 1854

The accommodations at the Kirtland House were modest but sufficient. Last night, the proprietor's wife had flaunted her beauty over dinner, regaling him with stories about her hometown of New York, telling him to call her Fanny instead of Mrs. Kirtland. He had an appreciation for fine food and an even greater appreciation for the familiarity.

Mr. Kirtland hadn't extended the same courtesy in the use of his first name, but he seemed delightfully unengaged with the comings and goings of his friendly wife.

Victor removed his leather portfolio from the

plain bureau and took it down to breakfast with him. If Fanny wasn't available for hire, perhaps the women in the Sacramento brothels would be more accommodating than the ones in Panama. Or the woman he'd paid back on the ship.

After breakfast, he found Mr. Kirtland in the cramped lobby, drinking a cup of coffee at his desk. His hair was askew, his eyes streaked with red as if he'd been up and perhaps away from the hotel for most of the night.

Victor smiled to himself. Perhaps he wouldn't have to pay the wife after all.

When Mr. Kirtland saw him, he set down his cup. "Did you sleep well?"

Victor shrugged. "Well enough."

"This town never seems to sleep."

Victor sat in the chair beside the desk, the handle of his leather portfolio case secure in his hands. "How long have you and your wife lived in Sacramento?"

"I arrived here in 1850, but I spend half my year in the goldfields."

"Does Mrs. Kirtland run this establishment while you're gone?"

He took a sip of coffee before shaking his head. "We just purchased this house from a man on his way to look for gold. It's a constant ebb and flow here of people moving between the city and diggings, depending on the weather."

Victor leaned forward. "I'm actually looking for

someone who's either here in Sacramento or out in the mines."

Mr. Kirtland raised his eyebrows. "Is it your wife?"

Victor snickered. "I wouldn't be searching for my wife."

The proprietor didn't laugh. "Who are you looking for?"

"My slave." He slipped his drawings of Isaac out of the portfolio and spread them across the desk. "Someone kidnapped him and brought him to California."

The man picked up a sketch. His eyes flickered as he looked at Isaac's portrait, his lips pressed together. Then he dropped it.

Victor leaned forward. "Have you seen him?"

Mr. Kirtland pushed the sketch away. "No."

"Are you certain?"

"Of course I'm certain," the man snapped.

Victor slowly collected the pictures. First the law clerk and now this man—why did people keep lying to him?

Fanny swept into the room, smiling at him before looking at her husband. "There's a big trial down at the courthouse this afternoon."

"We have plenty of work to keep us occupied here today," Mr. Kirtland said.

"But I have a new gown to wear," Fanny insisted. "And this is an opportunity for us to find better clientele for our house, like Mr. Duvall here."

Mr. Kirtland sighed like a man who'd repeated a conversation one too many times. "Running this house well will attract the best clients."

"Nonsense," she said, clapping her gloved hands together. "We need to be socializing with the residents of this city."

"It's not like attending an opera," the man said, clearly frustrated with his wife. He opened a ledger on the desk and began to review it.

His disinterest didn't stop her. "The sheriff caught a runaway slave last night," she continued. "Lorinda said this will be the biggest trial they've had around here in ages."

Victor clutched his portfolio to his chest, processing her words. Was it possible the law had found Isaac before he did? If so, what would they do with him?

"And you'll never guess who they think is involved," she said, leaning closer to the men as if they were conspiring together.

Mr. Kirtland glanced up from his work. "President Pierce."

"Of course not," she said, clapping him on the shoulder.

"Then I can't imagine who it might be."

"Your Miss Labrie."

The man spilled his coffee on the ledger. "That's ludicrous!"

"Not according to Lorinda," she said, seeming quite pleased that she had secured her husband's attention. "Frankly, it doesn't surprise me one bit. Another slave disappeared at the hotel while I was staying there."

Mr. Kirtland looked as jarred as he had when he saw the sketches of Isaac. Yet his demeanor remained resolute. "I don't have time to go to a trial."

She stuck out her bottom lip. "But I need someone to escort me."

Victor glanced over at Fanny, her lips still puckered in a pout, before looking back at the proprietor. "Perhaps I could accompany your wife," he offered.

Mr. Kirtland studied him for a moment and then waved his hand. "By all means—be my guest."

Fanny promptly recovered her enthusiasm. "You are a saint, Victor Duvall."

After Fanny rushed out of the lobby, presumably to retrieve her new gown, Mr. Kirtland motioned him closer to the desk. Victor thought he was going to warn him in some way, tell him to treat his wife like a lady.

"She always gets what she wants," Mr. Kirtland warned.

He nodded, understanding. "I never let a woman control me."

Mr. Kirtland leaned back in this chair. "We're all controlled by something."

Victor disagreed. "Only if we give our power away."

He promised to escort Mrs. Kirtland to the trial, but didn't say he would escort her home. If the law had found Isaac, he wouldn't leave the courthouse without him.

Rain poured on Sacramento all morning, a methodic trickle that turned the planked streets into streams of mud. Rodney had locked Stephan and Persila in the jailhouse until the trial, and no amount of pleading on Isabelle's part would convince the judge to release them into her care.

Judge Snyder hadn't jailed her, but he made it quite clear that he would do so if she didn't appear at the courthouse again by two. The ultimatum wasn't necessary. She wouldn't run away from her steward or the woman he'd tried to rescue.

Mr. Webb had already secured one of the two attorneys left in Sacramento. The other lawyer would gladly take her money, but he wouldn't fight well for them—only Judah had the reputation for opposing slavery, and she didn't know where to find him.

Because they were Negroes, the law wouldn't allow Persila or Stephan to testify this afternoon, even to defend themselves against the charges. But the judge would let Isabelle testify, and she didn't need a lawyer to speak the truth.

After today, every resident in Sacramento would know that she opposed the institution of slavery, but no one must find out that she was also a runaway slave. If her secret were exposed, Persila and Stephan wouldn't have anyone to speak on their behalf.

She dressed in a simple black gown, and the keys to both her boxes hung around her neck. In her hands, she carried the small Oxford Bible that Aunt Emeline had given her long ago. She would pretend that her aunt was in the courtroom with her, praying as she spoke.

When she opened her door, the dining room was empty except for Isaac. He was sitting at the piano, fingering the keys.

She brushed her hand across the piano's rosewood case. "Have you ever played?"

He flashed a smile. "A few times."

"You're welcome to practice on this."

"Thank you," he said, his smile growing. "Are you walking to the flower gardens?"

She shook her head. "I have an appointment to keep."

"I can watch over the hotel while you're gone."

Turning, she glanced up at the staircase. "Where is Mr. Payne?"

He tilted his head, a quizzical look straining his eyes. "He went to San Francisco yesterday."

In all the confusion, she'd forgotten that she had sent him on a steamboat with instructions for commissioning a seamstress to make new tablecloths for the dining room. And now he wouldn't return until this evening—much too late to manage the place in her absence.

It had been a strange position for her, delegating work to a member of the Payne family. She'd thought it might give her some sense of satisfaction, justice, even, for what had happened to her as a girl, but Mr. Payne willingly agreed to do even menial chores these past weeks without complaint.

She sat on the piano bench beside Isaac and listened to him play a simplified version of "The Watchman." While she appreciated Mr. Payne's willingness to work hard, the fact remained that he owned a slave. And her affection grew every day for the boy sitting beside her.

"Is Mr. Payne still treating you kindly?"

"He always treats me kindly."

"I'm glad to hear it," she said and waited as he played a few more notes. He played well for a child but especially for a slave, typically banned from an owner's piano.

"Have you ever thought about what it would be like to be free?" she asked.

"Think about it all the time, but Master Payne treats me as if I'm free."

"As your owner, he could sell you at any time."

"Master Payne wouldn't do that," he said, returning his hands to his lap.

"Unfortunately, it's happened many times to slaves with decent owners."

He nodded. "My old owner gave me away, and I was plenty glad of it."

"When you're ready, I can help you find a place where you'll be completely free."

"Thank you, Miss Labrie."

"And now . . ." She listened as the clock in her room struck one. Sing Ye may not have heard about the trial yet, but perhaps she would assist Isaac at the hotel. "Can you ask my friend to help you look after the hotel until Mr. Payne or I return? Her name is Sing Ye—Mrs. Barr."

"Where are Stephan and Janette?"

"Janette's not working today, and Stephan . . ." She hesitated. "He has been detained for a few hours."

He seemed to contemplate her words before responding. "Missus Barr and I will take good care of this place."

"I know you will."

After she gave him the address, Isaac skipped off between the tables toward the front door. Then she stood slowly and began her short walk to the courthouse.

How was she supposed to stay hidden in the shadows now?

Chapter 31

Sacramento City
July 1854

"I call to the stand Miss Isabelle Labrie."

Victor strained his neck, trying to see the woman walking toward a chair beside Judge Snyder, but the courtroom was so crowded that he couldn't see much beyond the sea of gawking heads. The trial, it seemed, was more entertainment than a circus in this town.

The runaway slave wasn't a child. It was a woman named Persila, the slave of a man who'd thundered multiple times during the past two hours against the injustice in California's justice system. Persila was his slave—he had the ownership papers to prove it. And if he were back in Georgia, Mr. Webb said, there would have been no trial. He'd have taken his property home early that morning and punished her privately for her offense.

Until yesterday, Mr. Webb said, he'd treated his slave with remarkable care, spoiling her with a light workload and the best of food. But then his slave had gotten jealous and lied to his wife. No court, he declared, should interfere in a domestic dispute.

Before calling Miss Labrie, Mr. Webb's lawyer had drawled on about the fact that his client was a visitor from the Southern states. He pontificated about the Fugitive Slave Act, which penalized anyone caught helping a runaway. Mr. Webb interjected often with his own opinions until Judge Snyder said he'd heard enough. Then he took a long recess before anyone else gave testimony.

During the recess, Fanny had chattered on like the lawyer about the threat of trying to integrate a group of people who clearly didn't understand the difference between right and wrong. As she talked, he'd contemplated his own situation. Isaac may need direction, but he was plenty smart. And he knew right from wrong. When he found the boy, would the courts in California expect him to go before a judge and convince them that his own slave—his son—belonged to him? Were there others here who might assist runaways, like the abolitionists on the East Coast?

Perhaps he needed to be more secretive about his venture for now, keeping the sketches to himself while he searched. Mr. Kirtland had seen Isaac someplace, and he intended to find out where. No one would deter him from finding the boy.

"Do you have representation?" the judge asked Miss Labrie.

The room quieted as the woman spoke, her

voice refined by a European accent. "I have decided to represent myself."

"That's an interesting choice," Judge Snyder said.

"One I feel entirely capable in making."

"Then tell us your perspective on what happened early this morning."

"Certainly," Miss Labrie said, seemingly oblivious to the murmuring around her. "I had a guest arrive at my hotel before daylight. A woman badly beaten by a man claiming to be her owner."

"I am her owner," Mr. Webb howled from his table.

The judge slammed his gavel. "You've already given testimony, Mr. Webb, and a whole lot of nonsense on top of it."

The crowd laughed.

"She pretends to be French, but she's really from Baltimore," Fanny whispered.

He almost snorted at Fanny's critique. She may like to talk about her childhood adventures in the city of New York, but she was clearly raised someplace in the South.

"Continue your story, Miss Labrie," the judge said.

"My guest needed care for her wounds, but she also had a man chasing her. I was afraid for her life, so I instructed my steward to secure her in a safe place until I could determine who had injured her and why."

The attorney spoke next. "Were you not suspect when you saw her dark skin?"

Victor strained his ears to listen above the rustling.

"My steward is a freed black. I thought this woman might be free as well."

"You asked your steward to hide her from the sheriff?"

"I didn't know at the time that Rodney was knocking on my door."

The attorney snickered at her response before he continued to badger her. "There are rumors around town that you intended to marry an already married man."

"I don't know what that has to do with—"

"It tells us what type of woman you are," he stated, playing to the audience. "What type of decisions you make."

"My past decisions are not relevant to this case," the woman replied.

"But I think they are, Miss Labrie. I think your choices speak to your character as a person who isn't as trustworthy as your fine gowns and demeanor might display. In fact, I suspect that you're hiding more than just a slave."

As he waited for the woman's response, Victor glanced across the heads of the men in front of him. Were they as fascinated by this Miss Labrie as he was? By her confident speech? He wished he could see her face. He imagined her appearance was as exotic as her voice. And a challenge to all the men in town.

"What exactly do you think I'm hiding, Mr. Martin?"

"Probably many things, but let's start with the truth about this morning."

"I've already explained to you what happened."

Mr. Martin paced beside the table. "You lied to the sheriff."

"I didn't lie."

"You didn't tell him about the runaway."

"He never asked me if I had seen a runaway— or a woman, for that matter."

"Another deputy found Mr. Webb's slave being carried by your steward, a block away from the hotel."

Victor stood on his toes again, trying to see the woman on the stand as well as the slave.

"I believe I've already explained that I thought Persila was going to be harmed. And I remain resolute in my assumption. If this court returns her to the man in front of me, he will hurt and possibly kill her."

"Conjecture, Miss Labrie. It's not for you or me to surmise about the future."

"But if he injures Persila further, it will be on my conscience, as it should be on yours."

"I abide by the law of man," the attorney said. "No matter what my conscience says."

"Perhaps you should abide by God's law instead."

259

The judge struck the gavel again. "In this case, we will all abide by the law of California."

Straining his neck, Victor saw the profile of Miss Labrie, turning toward the judge. "It seems that the laws in our state keep shifting."

"They are growing and changing, with the rest of the state," Judge Snyder said.

"Then you have the power to change this too, for the sake of an innocent woman who only wants to be free like you and me."

The judge shook his head. "That's something I cannot do."

The debate continued for another hour, the back and forth. And somewhere in the midst of the arguments, Victor grew bored of it all.

He needed to be searching for Isaac while most of the city was packed inside here—or perhaps he should be back at the hotel with Fanny, if her husband was as oblivious to her activities as he supposed.

Alden panicked when he stepped into the Golden. Miss Labrie was typically at the front desk at this hour while Janette, Isaac, and Stephan were preparing the evening meal. Instead, it seemed that Miss Labrie and Isaac and everyone else at the hotel had disappeared.

He walked outside, around the corner of the alleyway to see if Isaac or one of the others might be working on Miss Labrie's herb garden in the courtyard, but there was no one outside either.

As he looked over at Miss Labrie's window, his heart seemed to stop. What if the trip back to San Francisco was just a ruse? It was possible that Miss Labrie sent him away in order to snatch Isaac. She wouldn't kidnap Isaac to sell him, but he could imagine her stealing Isaac to set him free.

He should be thrilled if Miss Labrie were able to find a good home for Isaac, but if he was honest with himself, he didn't really want Isaac to leave —the boy had become like a younger brother to him. Isaac needed a family, though, and a sense of stability that Alden couldn't provide.

He sat down in the front lobby, shaken. He would find Miss Labrie and tell her the truth. Then he'd find Isaac so he could say good-bye.

Outside the window, he saw a petite Chinese woman pause next to the lobby door. She was dressed in a silky pink dress, her head covered with a white parasol. When she opened the door to the hotel, Isaac rushed inside.

Alden hopped up from his seat.

"You're home," Isaac exclaimed, giving him a hug.

"I thought—" Alden started, vastly relieved. "I thought you might have gotten lost."

Isaac was grinning when he stepped back. "Miss Labrie asked me and Missus Barr to take care of the hotel in her absence."

He looked over at Mrs. Barr. Unlike Isaac, the

woman wasn't smiling. "Do you know where Miss Labrie is?"

She twisted the handle of the parasol. "I'm afraid I do."

"And Stephan?"

She nodded her head, but didn't tell him where either Miss Labrie or Stephan had gone. Alden's sentiments shifted again, alarm filling his chest once more. The sail of his emotions had risen and fallen rapidly today, like a ship trying to ride out a storm.

"Isaac—could you start setting the tables for Stephan?"

"Yes, sir."

Once Isaac was gone, Mrs. Barr told him all that had transpired. Miss Labrie was on trial for helping a runaway slave. Stephan was on trial for assisting her.

He had no doubt that the accusations against them both were true.

Mrs. Barr gave him directions for the courthouse. He may not have passed the California bar yet, but he needed to do something to help Miss Labrie and Stephan and hopefully this runaway slave.

"Isaac can take care of himself, but—"

"I'll watch over him," Mrs. Barr assured him.

"Thank you."

The wood-framed courthouse was five blocks from the hotel, over on I Street. By the time he arrived, streams of people were flooding out of the building, the spectators chattering, some even laughing. There was no solemnity after a fateful verdict. No whispering about what was going to happen next.

Perhaps the judge had thrown out the case. Or perhaps Miss Labrie and the others had even won.

When he found Miss Labrie and Stephan by themselves at the front of the courtroom, their faces sober, he knew instantly that there'd be no victory celebration.

Where were the men and women who frequented the Golden's dining room? Where was Mr. Walsh and the Mr. Kirtland he'd inquired about? Surely, someone in this city should be here alongside Miss Labrie and Stephan, letting them know they weren't alone.

Alden reached for a chair to join them at the table. "Mrs. Barr told me about the trial."

Miss Labrie met his eyes, the gold flecks dull in the fading light. "Was she at the hotel?"

"She and Isaac will take care of the guests." He glanced at her and Stephan, at the exhaustion etched into their faces. "Did the judge find you guilty?"

She nodded slowly. "He fined Stephan and me each a thousand dollars for assisting a runaway."

It was an enormous sum of money, even by California standards. "Do you have the money?"

She nodded again.

"What happened to the slave?"

Tears filled her eyes. "The judge returned her to the man who'd beaten her."

Alden leaned forward, his hands pressed together. "Why are you helping this woman?"

"Because it's the right thing to do," she said. "No person should be owned by another."

He studied her eyes again, the rawness in them heartrending. And he felt her pain keenly, like on Christmas morning, when it seemed as if his own heart had been ripped open.

"I have no doubt that her master will make his ownership known tonight," she said.

He glanced over at Stephan. "It will be even more dangerous for you to help a slave now."

Stephan's eyes flashed with a renewed fervor. "I won't desert Persila, no matter what the court says."

Alden stared at him, his emotions swept back in the gale. "Persila?"

Miss Labrie wiped the tears from her cheeks. "Do you know her?"

"Is she owned by a man named Mr. Webb?"

Stephan nodded.

Alden stood up, his hands trembling. "They were on my ship to San Francisco." Back in Virginia, he'd waited too long to help Benjamin, but he wouldn't make that same mistake with Persila's life. "Where is Mr. Webb staying?"

"At a boardinghouse on Seventh Street."

"If you'll excuse me"—he stepped back—"I'm going to pay the Webbs a visit."

Stephan stood up beside him. "I'm going with you."

Alden eyed the man for a moment and then nodded. "First, I need to speak to the judge."

He and Stephan found Judge Snyder walking between the oilcloth walls of a corridor, heading toward a back door.

"Excuse me, Your Honor," Alden said. "I would like to request a retrial."

"On what grounds?"

"Neither Persila nor Miss Labrie had proper representation during the first trial."

The judge straightened his top hat. "Miss Labrie chose to represent herself."

"Because she didn't have time to secure an attorney."

When he reached the door, the judge turned toward him. "Are you an attorney?"

He shifted his hat in his hands. "I attended Harvard Law School."

"Have you passed the California bar?"

"No, Your Honor."

"Once you pass the bar, you can bring any case you want to my court."

Alden stepped back. "I will do that," he assured the man.

He and Stephan left the building to find the Webbs. If the courts wouldn't protect Persila, they would have to find a way to do it themselves.

Chapter 32

Sacramento City
July 1854

All Isabelle wanted to do was escape into her bedchamber and pull the covers over her head, like she'd wanted to do after her son died. Persila was out there tonight with a man who hated her yet refused to let her go. It wasn't about the money. It was about power—a power that refused to be satiated, no matter what Persila did to subdue it.

Instead of returning to the hotel, Mr. Payne and Stephan had gone to visit Mr. Webb. What they planned to do next, she didn't know. She only prayed that Stephan would be safe. And Mr. Payne —she wasn't sure what to think about that man.

He'd unnerved her this evening with his determination to help Persila. A slaveholder attempting to rescue a slave. It didn't make sense.

Maybe her resolution not to trust him was about power for her too. Even if he feigned kindness, she wouldn't give him or anyone else who owned slaves an ounce of power over her heart. She'd learned early never to trust a slave owner. No matter what Mr. Payne did, she couldn't trust him either.

She'd expected to find Sing Ye and Isaac at the hotel when she returned, but she hadn't anticipated Ross waiting for her in the kitchen. She hadn't seen him or Fanny since they left her hotel, though she'd heard he used his gold to buy a boardinghouse about six blocks away.

Had he come to revel in her misery?

She didn't invite him into her sitting room, choosing to speak with him in the front lobby while she sat behind her desk—above the vault that held the deed for the hotel and the money she needed to pay the judge.

He leaned against the counter. "I heard you've had a hard day."

"One of the worst of my life."

"The fugitive slave law should be abolished."

She shrugged, knowing he'd say anything to get what he wanted from her. "It's too late to change it for this woman."

"Fanny has been talking about returning to the East Coast," he said.

"Are you going back?"

"It doesn't matter what I decide. She's leaving with or without me."

She swept a loose curl back behind her ear. "I thought she wanted to run an establishment of her own."

"She likes the idea of being the proprietor of a fashionable hotel, but she's not too keen on keeping up a boardinghouse."

"I'm sorry to hear that," she said, though she wasn't surprised. She doubted Fanny would want the responsibility of being a proprietor for long either.

"She thought she'd be living in luxury here, but I don't even have enough money to buy her passage home."

Ross's gaze dropped to the floor. He knew where she kept her savings, knew that she had enough gold to pay for multiple tickets back to the East Coast. She wouldn't have much money after she paid the judge, though. Perhaps that's why he came now, before she paid the fine.

"Hopefully you'll have time, then, to reconcile your marriage."

He sighed. "I'm afraid there's nothing left to reconcile."

In his eyes, she saw the hope that she might not only give him money but also change her mind and marry him after Fanny was gone.

"You should save your money and return with her. Perhaps New York really is the place you belong."

He stepped closer, his gaze intense. "My place is here in California."

When she didn't reply, an awkward silence crept between them.

"You'll have to excuse me, Ross. I'm afraid I don't have any more conversation left in me."

"I understand," he said, but still didn't leave.

"There's one more thing . . ."

"What is it?"

"There's a man staying at my house who showed me the oddest thing today."

She didn't want to take the bait. "Is this important?"

"He said he was searching for his slave."

She sighed, the weight heavy on her heart. "It seems as if everyone is looking for a slave."

"This wasn't just any slave," he said slowly. "It was the picture of a child, but the eyes—they looked just like yours."

She clutched the edge of her desk as she considered his words. It felt as if she were back on the ship to California, the room rocking back and forth. She tried to refocus her gaze. Calm her voice. Still, everything seemed blurry.

"What is this man's name?" she asked, her voice trembling.

"Victor Duvall."

In that moment, it felt as if the entire ship slammed into a rock.

Ross took his leave, but she didn't even realize he'd gone until the bell chimed across the room.

Nine years had passed since she had left the Duvall house. Nine years of a new life for her, learning and working as a freed woman.

Had Victor been searching for her all this time? And had Mr. Payne come to Sacramento as well to find out if she belonged to the Duvalls?

But that didn't make sense. Mr. Payne knew exactly where she was.

If her old master found her, he wouldn't hesitate to do exactly what Mr. Webb had done to Persila. He would beat and humiliate her, then take her back before Judge Snyder if he must.

And there was nothing she could do to fight him.

She slid her chair back and hurried to lock the lobby door. Like Persila, she had to run before her master found her.

Fanny giggled like an elf as she slid off her high-topped shoes and tossed them next to the bureau. He wished she'd given the slightest contest, but she'd followed him willingly up to his room, to the edge of the horsehair mattress on his bed.

Victor hushed her when she giggled again. "Mr. Kirtland will hear."

She dangled her stockinged foot in front of him, the shadow of it dancing on the wall in the lantern light. "Ross won't be back for hours."

"And you're not concerned about your guests?"

"We don't have silly rules here, like at Isabelle's place."

He locked the door and sat down beside her on the ticking that covered the mattress. The entire room stank of camphene from the lamp. "Who is Isabelle?"

She wrinkled her nose, her pretty lips crunched together in a pout. "That awful Miss Labrie at the Golden Hotel."

His mind wandered back to that confident, pure lilt in the voice of the woman who'd publicly disputed the act of slavery. Miss Labrie, he was certain, would prove to be more of a challenge than the woman beside him.

And less inclined to brain-numbing drivel.

She reached for his arm. "I don't want to think about Isabelle."

"Neither do I," he lied.

She laughed again, twirling her foot until it knocked the leather portfolio off the bureau.

He dove for it, placing it back on top of the dresser. "Don't touch that."

She ignored his words, bending toward it. "What is it?"

He shoved her hand away. "I said don't touch it."

"You shouldn't keep secrets from me." She crossed her arms, seemingly offended.

"I'm not here to banter, Fanny."

Scooting away from her, he fumbled with the three buttons on his pleated dress shirt. Then he took it off. He'd finish what he started, and then he'd go visit this Isabelle.

When he looked back over, Fanny had his portfolio in her lap. The flap was open, and she was staring down at the sketch of Mallie.

271

Irate, he yanked the portfolio out of her hands, the papers scattering on the floor.

"Fool," he mumbled as he dropped to his hands and knees, shoving the papers back into the case. He had tired of the woman's silliness long ago. Unlike Mr. Kirtland, he did not intend to let her or any other woman control him.

He placed the portfolio inside a drawer this time. If she tried to open it, he'd make certain she remembered that no matter what he asked, she must obey.

When he returned to the bed, Fanny wasn't smiling anymore. Instead, her gaze was focused on the drawer. "Why do you have a sketch of Isabelle?"

His eyes narrowed. "What?"

"I said—" Looking up, she studied his eyes for a moment before shrugging. "Never mind."

He reached for her arm. "Tell me what you just said."

"Let me go," she said, shaking her arm to break free.

But he wouldn't let go until she told him the truth. "What about Miss Labrie?"

"I—I just wondered why you had a portrait of her."

He squeezed her arm as he mulled over her words. Then he let go.

After all these years—was it possible that Mallie was right here in Sacramento, hiding behind the title of Miss Labrie? Her skin was almost as light as any white person's, and her beauty would enchant all the men in this city. Add to it a cultured accent and perhaps an education, and she would be free to move in circles that would have rejected her back in Virginia.

He clasped his hands together, the reality of it pouring over him.

Not only was he close to retrieving Isaac, but he would be able to regain Mallie as well—a refined, beautiful woman who must do as he pleased.

His family was all right here, waiting for him.

Was that the reason Alden brought Isaac to Sacramento? Had Mallie somehow orchestrated this to reunite with her son? Oh, it was perfect. There would be a reunion all right, just not what Alden or Mallie were expecting.

He pulled the white shirt back over his head and quickly rebuttoned it.

She sat up straighter, rubbing her arm. "Where are you going?"

"I'm finished playing games, Fanny."

"I wasn't playing a game."

"You've been distracted." He stood, taking the portfolio from the drawer and then reaching for his frock coat and wallet. "But I've heard that Miss Labrie is more than accommodating."

When she swore at him, the pieces seemed to fall into place: Mr. Kirtland's recognition when he

273

saw Isaac's face, and then his denial. Victor knew the proprietor had been lying, but he hadn't seen Isaac after all. He'd seen Mallie.

It was impossible for any man to forget her eyes.

He stopped by the door. "Perhaps I will find your husband with Miss Labrie as well."

He heard the glass shatter, felt the heat of the lantern's flames, but they didn't burn him.

A steady coolness flooded over him as he asked someone outside for directions to the Golden Hotel. Finally, after all these years, he would recover what was rightfully his.

Chapter 33

Sacramento City
July 1854

They found the Webbs residing on the second floor of a boardinghouse built of rotting wood and covered with rusted tin. In the corridor outside their door, Alden and Stephan listened as Mr. and Mrs. Webb yelled at each other about their money, their future, their only slave.

Alden's mind flashed back to his former nursemaid, cowering in his father's room, and he wondered where Persila was in the midst of the fighting.

If he heard Persila cry out, he'd break down the door.

In the past weeks, he'd inquired after the Webbs at all of Sacramento's hotels and most of the boardinghouses. There was no sign hanging at the front of this house, but even if there had been, he never would have suspected the Webbs would rent a room in such a run-down place. But perhaps they flaunted their power over Persila for this very reason. Perhaps because they owned little else.

When they heard feet stomping toward the door, Alden and Stephan backed farther down the corridor.

"You best be done with that mending when I return," a man shouted before slamming the door. Then he hurried down the front steps.

Stephan stepped forward and knocked on the door.

Mrs. Webb's face was a pasty white blotched with red. Strands of graying hair fell from her bun, and there were several holes in her dressing gown. Her gaze slipped over Stephan, landing on Alden. "What are you doing here?"

"We've come for Persila."

She cackled. "You think you can just take her?"

"If you're unwilling to negotiate a deal."

Her eyes narrowed. "What sort of deal?"

"That depends on you, Mrs. Webb. My friend and I are hoping for a reasonable one."

He held her gaze even as he positioned his foot against the door to prop it open.

"What if I don't want to negotiate?"

Alden shrugged. "Then we'll just take her."

"You can't do that."

He glanced over at Stephan, and the two of them elbowed their way past her, into the cramped room.

"Get out," Mrs. Webb cried behind them.

Persila was sitting on the floor, mending items from a basket. The Webbs, it seemed, had found another way to generate income from her work.

"Hello, Persila," he said.

Her eyes lit when she saw the men, but her gaze plunged quickly back to her mending. Stephan sat on the frayed rug beside her while Alden faced Mrs. Webb.

"Would you like to discuss the terms?"

Mrs. Webb eyed her and then looked back up at him. "I won't take less than five hundred."

"Dollars?"

"Of course, dollars."

"Do you have her papers?" Alden asked.

Mrs. Webb removed a canvas portfolio from the bureau and took out two sheets of paper. Alden perused them slowly. They must hurry before Mr. Webb returned, but he wanted to make the woman before him nervous. He suspected that she'd already spent the five hundred dollars in her head.

"Alden?" Stephan urged.

He glanced down at Mrs. Webb, the papers

secured in his hands. "We will purchase her for three hundred dollars."

Mrs. Webb laughed again. "Five hundred."

He sighed as he inched back. "Then it seems we can't compromise. You'll have no slave and no money."

She stopped laughing when he bolted the door behind him. "If you steal her, Mr. Webb will send the police after you."

"The police won't find us," he assured her before looking around the room. "What shall I use to tie you up?"

Her face paled.

"I'm sure Mr. Webb will be back soon to rescue you."

She shook her head. "He won't return for hours."

Stephan looked as relieved as Alden about that news.

"Are you certain you don't want to negotiate?" he asked.

Mrs. Webb crossed her arms. "I'll take four hundred."

Alden stalled again, even though he knew his answer. He and Stephan had discussed their plan as they'd walked here. If they pooled resources, they had four hundred between them, with a small reserve left.

"I think we can compromise with four hundred as long as there are no more delays." He nodded at Stephan, and the man rushed from the room.

"While my colleague collects the money, please fetch Persila and me a cup of tea."

Mrs. Webb grumbled all the way to the door.

Persila dropped her mending back into the basket after Mrs. Webb left, and he took Stephan's seat on the floor. His stomach clenched when he examined the blood matted on her face and the cut above her eye. Even if they didn't respect Persila, the Webbs—or the judge for that matter—should have given her the opportunity to clean her wounds.

"I'm sorry I didn't find you earlier."

Her gaze widened. "You were looking for me?"

"Of course," he said. "Isaac insisted that I tell you he's had multiple baths since we stepped off that ship."

She managed a small smile. "How is that boy?"

"As precocious as ever."

"Tell him that I miss him."

"I will."

"Alden—"

"What is it?"

She fidgeted with the thread beside her. "I'm not worth four hundred dollars."

"You're worth much more than that, but it's all we had to offer."

She looked back up at him. "You could buy a lot for that money."

"But your freedom is priceless, Persila."

"The Webbs don't deserve any more money."

"No, but I don't want you to live as a runaway." He leaned back against the window shade, glancing at the strips of faded paper dangling from the wall and the three pallets set up on the floor. "How did the Webbs acquire enough money to buy you in the first place?"

"Master Webb won me gambling." She pulled her knees up to her chest. "And he's going to come after me when he returns, even with new papers. He needs my income to keep gambling."

Alden checked the timepiece in his pocket. It was 5:15. "There's a paddle wheeler leaving for San Francisco at six. You and Stephan can both travel up to Vancouver Island, where everyone is free."

As her smile grew wider, he took her hand. "One day soon, I'd like to send Isaac up to live with you so he can be free too." In some small way, he hoped Isaac might also help replace the child Persila had lost long ago.

"Oh, Alden," she said, squeezing his hand. "I adore that boy, but he would be devastated to leave you."

"He needs a good mother."

"And a good father." She laughed softly. "All you need to find is a wife."

The door opened, and Mrs. Webb shuffled inside with two cups of tea. She reluctantly handed both of them to Alden, and he gave the second cup to Persila, though neither he nor Persila dared to try it.

"When will your man be back?" Mrs. Webb asked.

"Stephan will return soon." It wouldn't take him long to locate Alden's dwindling supply of money and say good-bye to Miss Labrie.

As the three of them waited in silence, he prayed Stephan would indeed return soon. If he and Persila didn't leave on that boat, Mr. Webb and a crowd of sympathizers might find them. At the very least, the man would drag them back before the judge, refuting the sale of his slave. The worst scenario involved some rope and a tree.

Minutes later, there was a frantic knock on the door, and Mrs. Webb opened it.

"We must hurry," Stephan insisted.

Mrs. Webb didn't move. "I'll go at my own pace."

"The city is on fire."

Mrs. Webb leaped toward the window, and when she yanked up the shade, Alden saw smoke billowing several blocks away. They had no time left for games.

"Do you have the money?" she asked.

Stephan nodded, but he didn't hand it to her. Instead, he dug into his carpetbag and gave Alden the little money left from his stash, along with several pieces of paper, a pen, and inkwell. Alden dropped the gold coins in his pocket and drafted the manumission paper on the bureau, trying not to think about the loss of time or the looming fire.

"Good riddance," Mrs. Webb said as she signed it.

The remaining transaction happened at lightning speed. After they paid Mrs. Webb, Persila eagerly ripped her old ownership papers into pieces.

Mrs. Webb glanced back out the window. "Here comes my husband."

The two men and Persila fled down the back steps and raced through the smoky street, toward the wharf. The waiting paddle wheeler gave a long blast on its horn.

With the fire, it might leave early tonight.

"I bolted the iron shutters and door at the hotel," Stephan told him as they ran. "No one was inside."

"Where did Miss Labrie and Isaac go?"

"Probably to her aunt's cottage near City Cemetery. It's up on the knoll."

They stepped onto the wharf, and Alden sighed with relief when he saw the paddle wheeler still moored at the other end.

As they raced across the long pier, the deckhand untied the mooring line from a piling. Alden shouted, but if the man heard, he ignored them, signaling for the captain to leave.

Persila cried out as the steamer slid away, but Stephan sprang forward, leaping onto the deck. Then he stretched out his arms for Persila. Alden swept her up and passed her across the watery divide.

Both Stephan and Persila waved as the boat began paddling briskly toward the coast. Then Alden turned, hurrying toward the cottage on the knoll.

Chapter 34

Sacramento City
July 1854

Isabelle didn't light a candle in the sitting room. If Victor could track her to Sacramento, he could easily locate her aunt's home. Better to stay in the dark tonight, pretending that no one was in the cottage. Perhaps Stephan could help her gain passage with Persila up to Vancouver Island tomorrow. Then she would give him the keys to her hotel.

After Ross left the hotel, she had found Isaac in the kitchen. While he retrieved his and Alden's things, she'd thrown some clothing and personal effects into a carpetbag. She should have left Alden a note on her desk as well and salvaged her money and Aunt Emeline's box from their hiding space, but her mind had been all muddled.

Sing Ye had come with her and Isaac to the cottage but hadn't stayed with them. Nicolas took her to visit a friend who lived on a rancho outside of town. He feared backlash from today's trial, and he wanted to keep his wife safe. Aunt Emeline would be pleased, knowing how much Nicolas cared for Sing Ye.

And her aunt would be praying all night if she knew Victor was in town.

Nicolas had asked her and Isaac to join them on the rancho, but she'd said she thought it best to wait here for Stephan and Alden, to see if they needed further assistance with hiding Persila. She would never forgive herself if something happened to Sing Ye because of her past or her current work.

Isaac was sprawled out on the woven rug below her, one of Aunt Emeline's books clasped in his hands. It was too dark to continue reading, but he was still trying to make out the words in the faint promise of starlight.

Aunt Emeline would be so pleased, knowing this Negro boy was in her home, reading her books.

Isaac glanced up at her. "Do you smell smoke?"

She sniffed. There was a faint scent of smoke in the air, but Sacramentans often disregarded the ban on fires during the dry summer months. Strange that Rodney wasn't as compelled to stop those who ignored this law as he was to enforce the one about runaway slaves.

"Someone must be burning trash," she said.

He reluctantly closed the book, resigned it seemed to the loss of light. "How many books are in this house?"

283

"At least twenty."

He sighed. "I wish I could read every one."

"I'm sure Sing Ye would let you borrow any of them," she said. "You can read my books back at the hotel too."

He could have all of them after she left for Vancouver Island.

"I will take good care of them."

"Does Mr. Payne know you can read?" she asked.

"Of course."

"I don't mean Alden—" She hesitated. It seemed odd to use the man's first name. "I mean Alden's father. Master Payne."

"That Master Payne doesn't know me at all."

"Did your mama teach you to read?"

"No," Isaac said. "She left right after I was born."

Isabelle's heart twisted. She couldn't imagine leaving her son.

"My mistress said she took off with another slave."

She considered his words in the darkness. How sad it must be for a child to learn his mother ran away. Devastating. "I'm sorry that your mama left you."

"She didn't leave me, Miss Labrie. She left slavery."

"Of course," Isabelle said. And how could she blame the woman? Her heart probably ripped in two, leaving her child in search of freedom.

284

Perhaps she had escaped with her husband. Perhaps Isaac's parents were planning to come back one day to rescue their son.

"Master said my mama was a princess."

"I'm sure she loved you very much."

"I would have loved her too." He paused. "My nursemaid said she would be proud of me, learning how to read and play piano."

"Any mother would be proud to have you as her son."

"One day, I'm going to find her. And I'm going to take care of her too."

"Isaac,"—she straightened her skirt—"you said your mistress told you that your mother ran away."

"Yes, ma'am."

Mr. Payne hadn't mentioned a wife, but after her experience with Ross, she knew it was quite possible that he too had left a family behind in Virginia.

"Is Alden married?" she asked.

"No, ma'am, but a woman on our ship sure wanted to marry him."

When Isabelle breathed the air again, the smoke seemed heavier. Acrid. Then the clang of the town's fire bells resonated through the room.

She jumped up from her seat, her heart clanging with the bells. The last time Sacramento City caught fire, it took almost every building with it.

She raced over to the window and saw the center of town glowing an eerie orange. She had to return to the hotel before the flames reached K Street and destroyed everything inside, including Aunt Emeline's box.

Her body trembled at the thought of discovering Victor below, but she couldn't let her fear stop her from saving Aunt Emeline's gift and the money she needed to start over. In the chaos, the smoke, she could slip back into the city and rescue her things without Victor seeing her. Then she would return to this cottage.

She knelt down beside Isaac. It would be too risky to take him down near the fire. She needed to move swiftly, through the alleyways to avoid the blaze and the man who wanted to destroy her as well.

"I need you to stay here and watch the house," she told him.

"Like I did with the hotel?"

"Exactly. The fire shouldn't come this way, but if it does"—she pointed east—"follow this street outside town, to the floral gardens. I will find you there."

He reached for her hand. "Miss Labrie?"

"Yes, Isaac?"

He leaned over, kissing her cheek. "Don't get too close to the fire."

Smoke poured down K Street, curling between the empty buildings and abandoned wagons. Flames followed close behind the smoke, but

286

unlike its predecessor, the flames showed no mercy. They devoured the wooden structures faster than Moby-Dick destroyed Ahab's boat.

A crowd of people watched the flames from the street, listening to buildings explode in the distance when barrels of gunpowder ignited. Victor pushed through the mob, rushing up one more block, his leather portfolio tucked safely under his arm.

He'd walked the streets for far too long tonight, trying to find either the Golden Hotel or someone sober enough to give him accurate directions. It wasn't until he'd found a man headed to fight the fire that he discovered the hotel was near the wharf. A brick-and-granite edifice in a long queue of wood.

He gritted his teeth as he stared at the structure. The front door was shuttered with iron. He'd come so close to finding Mallie, and now it seemed like she'd escaped him once again.

The smoke burned his throat. Stung his eyes. Lifting his loose shirt up over his mouth, he watched the fire in the distance, the flames casting a hazy glow through the curtain of smoke, the roar of destruction shaking the ground.

He wouldn't stop searching, for her or for Isaac. He would find them both after the fire subsided, and they would return to Virginia together, as a family, even if he had to shackle them together for the entire journey home.

Oh, the rage in Eliza's face when the three of them walked through the door. He'd triumph without saying a word.

Heat radiated between the buildings, and the smoke almost drove him back toward the crowds. But then he saw her—an apparition in a cloud sustained by the fire. And he couldn't move.

He'd worried that Mallie might outgrow her beauty, but she was even more beautiful now than she'd been as a girl. And Mallie was his. He'd inherited her. Subdued and trained her. He would treat her as a lady. Eventually. First, she must be taught a swift lesson as a reminder: he owned her, for the rest of her life.

As she held up her lantern, checking the iron shutters, he stepped toward her. But then she seemed to disappear into the smoke, along the back of the hotel.

He smiled in spite of the heat. The alley was the perfect place to waylay her. No one in the crowd would see him take her. Or hear her scream.

He moved swiftly into the alleyway, searching for her light. She may have outwitted him before, but he wouldn't lose her now.

Chapter 35

Sacramento City
July 1854

Flames engulfed the planks on G Street, the roar of thunder echoing across town as buildings collapsed in on themselves, spraying a storm of embers across the stunned crowd. Alden pushed through hundreds of bystanders watching the destruction, trying to make his way up toward Isaac and Miss Labrie.

He didn't get far. As the volunteer firemen lined up on the streets, one of them asked him to help pull the heavy fire engine with its canvas buckets, leather hooks, and one-hose reel toward the flames. Alden grabbed one of the drag ropes and joined the men.

Another crew fought the fire inside buildings with their axes, blowing their brass trumpets when they needed help. The rest of the volunteers pumped water through the engine's hose or hauled up buckets of water from the river to douse flames. Shards of glass blew out from the rubble of saloons around them, liquor exploding in a turquoise blaze. The courthouse was consumed in minutes.

As Alden worked alongside the firemen, he

prayed that Miss Labrie and Isaac were safe in the cottage, that Stephan and Persila would find their way to freedom without complication, that the volunteers could contain the fire before it consumed this tinderbox of a town.

As the first rays of dawn crept through the haze, Sacramento City was subdued into a fenland of smolder. The Golden Hotel was still standing, thanks to the swollen slats of iron on the windows and front door, but he couldn't attest to its structure. The wooden buildings on both sides of the hotel were destroyed.

Once the fire was contained, he hurried away from the wharf, following Stephan's directions to the cottage far from the center of town. No one answered his first knock, but when he called out, Miss Labrie opened it. Her dress was covered with soot, her hair tangled in curls. In her arms, she clutched some sort of box.

He glanced over her shoulder and saw a mound of canvas bags, but he didn't see anyone in the room. "Is Isaac here?"

"He's asleep."

He sighed with relief, grateful they were both safe. "Is he okay?"

She nodded.

"Thank you for taking care of him."

He'd thought Miss Labrie was lovely the first time he'd seen her at the hotel, but she looked even more beautiful in the faint morning light, covered with the ashes from the fire, than she had looked in her tailored gowns, serving the elite of Sacramento. The fire, it seemed, refined both her strength and beauty.

"Come inside," she urged. "Quickly."

When he stepped into the sitting room, she slid the metal bolt behind him, locking the door. And the niggling thought haunted him again. He was almost certain that he'd seen her before, somewhere in years past, but it was as if his memory was veiled by smoke as well, like a dream that had faded away.

She glanced toward the curtain drawn over the window. "Where is Stephan?"

"He's with Persila."

"Were you able to rescue her?"

"We were."

"Thank God." She collapsed onto the sofa, the wooden box secured in her lap. "I need to see Stephan this morning."

"I'm afraid he's already gone."

"What do you mean, gone?"

"He and Persila were able to board a paddle wheeler when the fire started."

She took a deep breath. "Are they traveling to Vancouver Island?"

When he nodded, her shoulders fell. "I'm happy for them, but"—she looked down at the rug— "I wish I could have said good-bye."

"Stephan asked me to thank you for all that

you've done. He said he intends to find a boy named Micah up north, and I have a suspicion that he intends to marry Persila too, if she'll have him."

"I hope she will. He will treat her with honor and respect." She smoothed her hands over the box. "I'm confused about one thing, Mr. Payne."

He sat in the chair across from her. "What is it?"

"Are you or are you not Isaac's owner?"

He contemplated his words before he spoke. "I'm his guardian."

"Is he a freed slave?"

He crossed his legs, leaning back against the stiff upholstery. "It's a bit complicated."

"I don't think freedom is complicated at all."

Miss Labrie was an advocate for slaves, and she was fond of Isaac. Perhaps it was time to tell her the truth.

"Isaac isn't free according to the law, but I figure that the law here doesn't need that information."

"You don't have his papers?"

He shook his head.

"Nor can he buy his freedom," she said, seeming to speak more to herself than him.

"He doesn't owe me anything."

"A slave hunter could steal him away."

"No one here knows he's run away," Alden said. "As long as people think he's my slave, he'll be safe."

"You and I both need to stay in the shadows, then."

"Forgive me, Miss Labrie, but it doesn't seem like you've been living in a shadow."

She gave him a shaky smile—the first time she'd ever smiled at him. "All is not as it seems, Mr. Payne."

He pointed toward the stack of bags. "Are those from the hotel?"

She nodded. "I need to leave this morning."

"The Golden is still standing," he told her. "If the structure is safe, Isaac and I can help you restore it."

"I'm not going back to the hotel."

He leaned toward her. "What's wrong, Isabelle?"

She didn't correct him when he used her first name, didn't even seem to notice that he'd said it. "There's someone in Sacramento trying to harm me."

He pressed his hands together. "After today's trial, you probably have many people angry at you."

"It's more than that," she said. "It's someone from my past."

He could hear the fear in her voice, and he understood.

She stood back up, clutching the box to her chest. "I'm going to purchase a stagecoach ticket."

"To where?"

"It doesn't matter."

"You need someone to go with you."

She shook her head. "There's no one—"

"Isaac and I were thinking about going to Columbia," he said.

"To see Judah?"

He nodded. "If he hasn't moved on."

"I suppose I could go to Columbia too. For a season."

"How much, exactly, does a stagecoach ticket cost?" he asked.

When she told him, he wanted to kick himself. Almost all his money was now in Mrs. Webb's pockets. "I'm afraid Isaac and I will have to stay here after all."

She eyed him curiously before speaking. "I owe you and Isaac for your work at the hotel."

"We haven't made nearly enough to purchase tickets."

"You can pay me the rest later."

He didn't want to take a loan, yet he needed to find Judah. And if someone was trying to harm Isabelle, he could protect her as well.

"I'll find work in Columbia, whether or not it's with Judah," he said. "When does the stage-coach leave?"

"At ten."

"If the hotel is still standing, I'll have to retrieve my things."

There was strength in her smile this time. "Isaac carried your things here."

He returned her smile. "Perhaps he's my guardian as well."

PART THREE

Whoever dwells in the shelter
of the Most High will rest
in the shadow of the Almighty.
Psalm 91:1

Chapter 36

Sierra Foothills
August 1854

A flock of silvery birds crested beside their stagecoach and then glided back down toward a lake in the valley, the water glistening like gold in the afternoon sunlight. Yesterday, the stagecoach had rumbled across a plain composed of scrub oaks and channels of river. Then it began to climb up into the foothills west of the Sierra Nevada.

The smoke from Sacramento's fire was far behind them now, though they'd seen the black smoke from several camps in the hills. The trail of fire, their driver called this rock-studded road.

In the distance, Isabelle could see the jagged Sierras, each peak still dusted with snow. The town of Columbia lay somewhere below these mountains, at the edge of a wall that no stagecoach could climb.

The indigo ripples beyond them reminded her of the sea billowing and crashing in a storm. It seemed impossible to travel through these foothills by coach, but as their party jostled up and down this narrow road, the two miners who'd joined them said they'd taken this route many times. They'd arrived safely to their destination each time—only once had they been robbed. They said this with pride, as if they'd somehow cheated fate.

There was no Rodney out here in the wilderness to deter bandits from relieving stagecoaches of their gold, though the revolvers the two miners carried along with the driver's double-barreled shotgun might send them running. While her luggage was belted onto the top of the coach, she'd packed the iron lockbox with her gold coins and Aunt Emeline's gift in a valise made of tapestry and tucked it securely under her skirt.

While Alden attempted to read a book on the bench beside her, Isaac's nose was pressed against the dusty glass. This morning he'd watched the fog pooling on the valley floor, and once it lifted, he'd counted the clouds flitting past them in the wind. Now he was searching for bear or wildcats in the fir trees, neither of which she hoped he'd find.

Outside her window were clusters of wild peas and blooms of mustard, weaving threads of lavender and yellow between the trees. For three years, she'd heard the stories about the mining towns from her guests, earning her living from people seeking the gold hidden in quartz veins at the base of the Sierras, but she'd never once visited the interior.

What would it be like to live in this wilderness, so far from the elegance in her hotel?

She never expected to leave Sacramento City, but now that Victor had found her trail, she could never go back to the place that had become home. An image of a bloodhound flashed into her mind, its tail curled up, droopy ears sweeping the ground.

Victor could spend his days in the remains of the city if he wanted, his hunting nose to the ground, but he wouldn't find her. She hadn't left a trace of her whereabouts or even told Sing Ye where she had gone.

Her one regret when they'd left was not saying good-bye to Sing Ye, but it wouldn't take Victor long to knock on the cottage door. Better for Nicolas and Sing Ye to tell him that she'd simply disappeared.

There was freedom ahead for her now. An opportunity to start over again on her own. She had the resources to buy a new hotel if she wanted or tuck herself away in hiding until she journeyed up to Vancouver Island on her own.

"You'll like Columbia," the miner named Samuel told them. "They're digging out thousands of dollars' worth of gold each week, and it doesn't seem to be slowing down."

"How exactly does one make a claim there?" Alden asked.

"You find a plot of open land, ten feet by ten, and stake it off," Samuel explained. "All you need is a shovel, pail, and a decent rocker to start your mining."

"Doesn't seem like there would be much land left to claim," she said.

"There's plenty of land away from the town. My little claim has already yielded about four thousand in gold."

Alden shook his head. "Sounds too good to have any truth to it."

" 'Tis true enough, but four thousand doesn't last as long in the mining towns as in other places."

The other man elbowed him. "That's because plenty of establishments in Columbia are more than willing to strip you of your find."

"How long have you two been married?" Samuel asked, clearly wanting to change the subject.

"Oh, no—" Alden started, but Isabelle interrupted him.

"For ten years."

Isaac turned swiftly toward her, his eyes wide, but neither he nor Alden disputed her.

She should have discussed this with Alden before she claimed to be his wife, but she feared what might happen if word spread that an unmarried woman was arriving in this town. And if Victor did decide to look for her out here, she didn't want anyone to remember the name of Isabelle Labrie.

"Not many ladies venture out to the western slope," Samuel said.

"More will come," she assured him.

"I certainly hope you're right."

Alden glanced back down at his book, and in her window, she saw his reflection. She'd thought him handsome when they were younger, with his firm jaw and kind gray eyes. Even in his youth, Alden had been almost as tall as Victor. Now he would tower over the man.

A long time ago, Victor had claimed that he loved her, said that she was his rose blossoming in a field of weeds. Then he would lock her door, and she knew what was next. She'd fought him as a girl, everything within her crying out against what she was certain must be wrong. Even when her master said it was right.

In the end, no matter how hard she resisted, Victor had won. He didn't care that he hurt her. And no one else cared when she pleaded for help in the darkness. She was a slave, subject to punishment for her refusal to breed.

When she shivered, Alden glanced over at her, but he didn't say anything. She'd been scared when she was younger that Alden might hurt her too, but—gratefully—he never seemed to really see her.

If Alden couldn't find Judah in Columbia, perhaps he'd try his hand at mining gold. She would select a new name for herself, both first and last. The two miners in the stagecoach knew her as Isabelle—or Mrs. Payne—but once they all dispersed, she doubted she would see them or even Alden again.

Strangely enough, she would be sad to say good-bye to Alden. Back in Sacramento, she'd equated him with the rest of the Payne family, but now it seemed his opposition toward slavery matched her own. He had worked with Stephan to free Persila, and he wanted Isaac to be free as well.

Her heart ached at the thought of saying good-bye to Isaac, one more farewell in a string of losses these past months. But once Alden found a home for him—or the laws changed—Isaac would be free to seek out an education as he grew into a man.

She glanced down at Alden's book.

La Loi. The Law.

It was a French book, translated by a British man, that he'd obtained in Aunt Emeline's cottage. The English had abolished slavery twenty years ago, thanks to reformers like William Wilberforce, who spent his life fighting the institution.

If only the United States would follow suit, granting every man, woman, and child the same opportunity to embrace freedom. But it would take someone strong like Wilberforce to change these laws, someone courageous enough to stand up to the injustice around them.

Someone willing to sacrifice his or her own freedom in order to set slaves free.

Chapter 37

Sierra Foothills
August 1854

Alden stared down at the book in his lap, but he didn't turn the page. Isabelle had surprised him in many ways, but he'd been shocked when she announced their marriage to the men traveling with them.

Her declaration was a veneer, of course. Another layer to hide behind. He understood why she needed to slip into this role. Like Mrs. Dawson said, the title of marriage was a reasonable way to fight off unwelcome advances from men desperate for female companionship. In contrast to his thoughts about Mrs. Dawson, he quite liked the idea of being married to Isabelle.

The woman sitting next to him was beautiful and confident. Brave and compassionate. Elegant and aloof. If only he could gently peel back each layer under her lofty air, get to know what was hidden deep inside. If only he still had the income and status to engage her.

Back east, he would have pursued Isabelle Labrie with his whole heart, but she wouldn't have to ward off advances from him here. Now that she realized he was a proponent of freedom, she was civil to him, but she'd made it clear that there was nothing personal between them.

He turned the page of his book, trying to refocus on the words: "Each of us has a natural right—from God—to defend his person, his liberty, and his property."

He agreed with Frederic Bastiat. God had given each of them a natural right to defend their lives and their liberty.

The murky area in their country's law was the definition of property. Mr. Webb and his own father would say that they had the right to defend their property, including their slaves, discounting the fact that they were stealing away another person's liberty.

Greed—legal plunder, as Bastiat called it—was the root of many of their problems. When lawmakers made laws for personal gain, it perverted the whole system. Legal plunder meant injustice for people who'd been stripped of their natural rights.

People like Isabelle were working to give these natural rights back. Stephan said she'd heroically defended Persila, a stranger to her until Stephan brought her into the hotel. Alden admired her greatly for her public and personal stance.

The stagecoach was descending into the valley now, toward a river that streamed down from a lake flanked on both sides by willow trees and clumps of driftwood. On one of the banks was a makeshift mining camp of canvas tents and wooden rockers scattered across the landscape. The driver said they were spending the night at this camp before fording the river and finishing their journey to Columbia.

If he couldn't find Judah in Columbia, he'd either find work in town or mark off a claim outside it. There would be no fancy hotel for him and Isaac. He'd be happy if they could afford a tent with the little of his money that remained.

The coach stopped a few yards from the camp, and the passengers all stepped swiftly out into the fresh air. It was warm here, but nothing like the heat in the city. Instead of smoke, it smelled like wild honeysuckle and pine.

The driver already had a tent pitched for his passengers, and several men from town sold them a quarter of antelope to roast. The river cascaded down a waterfall from the lake, but here the water loped peacefully around boulders beside the tent, pooling in the middle before it continued downstream.

Samuel rushed toward the river, splashing water on his head and hair. "Let's take a swim."

The other men agreed before turning warily toward Isabelle.

She pointed back toward the tent. "I'll wait in there until you're done."

Isaac eyed the river. "I can wait in the tent too."

Alden shook his head. "You need a bath."

"So does Miss La—"

Alden interrupted him. "I'm sure Mrs. Payne doesn't want to go swimming with us."

Isabelle laughed. "Perhaps you can bring me a basin of water so I can wash off inside."

Isaac checked the river again, and Alden realized that he'd probably never been swimming before. His mind wandered back to the hours he and Benjamin spent swimming in their pond and the creek nearby, at the fun they'd had racing and diving and pretending to ward off snakes. Every boy, in his opinion, should know how to swim.

Alden lowered his voice. "If you can learn to read, you can easily learn to swim."

Samuel filled a basin for Isabelle, and she took it into the tent. Then the men stripped down and plunged into the cold pool. Mossy boulders surrounded their swimming hole, water rushing over each rock. The men swam toward the middle of the river, but Isaac stood on a shallow ledge, splashing himself to cool off.

Alden called for Isaac to join them. When the boy shook his head, Alden swam back to persuade him. So much had changed since Isaac had sat perched on the back of Eliza's carriage, determined not to move. He'd grown in the past seven months, in stature and in experience. Now he needed to conquer this river.

"I'll stay beside you," Alden said.

Isaac glanced back at the shore behind them,

and for the first time, Alden noticed something on the boy's right shoulder blade. It was a red scar shaped like the bud of a rose with the letter V inside.

Anger flared inside him. How could Victor take a branding iron to a child—his son—searing the skin as a reminder that Isaac would always belong to him.

Isaac turned back around, and Alden blinked, trying to refocus his gaze and the thoughts coursing through his mind. "You can't learn to swim unless you jump in all the way."

Isaac scanned the surface. "It's too deep."

Alden lifted one of his arms and dipped it into the water. "If you paddle like this, you won't need the ground."

Isaac waded a few inches deeper, testing the water. Then he stepped into its depths. He struggled at first, grappling for air. Alden saw the panic in his eyes, but still he waited, a few feet away, for the boy to catch his stride.

In seconds, Isaac's head was firmly above the water, the fear in his eyes fading away as he swam in circles. Then he paddled toward one of the large rocks until his feet found stability again. "I did it!" he exclaimed.

Alden returned his smile. "Yes, you did."

"Persila would be proud of me."

"Definitely. Another bath, and you learned how to swim." Alden stood in the water near him, carefully choosing his next words. "Guess who I saw in Sacramento City before we left?"

Isaac's eyes grew wide. "Persila?"

He nodded.

Isaac splashed the water. "I want to see her!"

"I know you do, and she wanted to see you too, but she was on her way out of town."

"With the Webbs?"

"No. She was going north."

"By herself?"

"With Stephan." Alden smiled. "She had her freedom paper in her hands."

"She'll be safe forever, then."

"Yes, she will. I told her that you were safe too and that you'd found work in the city."

Isaac dragged one hand through the water, the wave slapping against a rock. "We can't work at Miss Lab—your wife's hotel any longer."

Alden smiled. "No, but we'll find other work in Columbia."

"Do you really want to mine?"

"Perhaps for a season."

"Maybe we'll find a field of gold after all."

"Or at least enough gold dust to buy our food."

Isaac stepped toward the shore. "I want to eat right now."

"Then let's build a campfire."

The men tossed a towel between themselves to dry off, then slipped on their trousers, securing them over their chests with suspenders. Before

310

Isaac put on his shirt, he called out toward the tent. "We're finished, Missus Payne!"

Isabelle opened the tent flap. Her cheeks were pink, and her dark-brown hair hung loosely over her shoulders as if she'd just brushed it. "I wish I could have gone swimming with you."

Alden reached for a knot of driftwood, trying to rid his mind of the image of Isabelle swimming with him in the water.

As she stepped toward them, Isaac grabbed his shirt from the low limb of a tree. Isabelle's eyes locked onto Isaac's shoulder, to the raised scar that marked him a slave. Her lips rounded as she froze in place, and Alden thought for a moment that she might faint.

"Isaac," she finally said, her voice quivering. "I was curious—"

He shook his wet head, spattering her and Alden. Then he buttoned his shirt. "Curious about what?"

"Were you born on the Payne plantation?"

"No. I was born at the Duvalls'."

She knitted her fingers together in front of her waist. "You said your mother ran away when you were a baby."

Isaac picked up a piece of driftwood and tossed it on the pile. "Yes, ma'am."

"Do you know the name of your mother?"

Alden saw the boy smile, but he didn't hear Isaac's answer.

311

Isabelle backed away from him. "I'm so sorry."

"You didn't do anything wrong."

"I have to take a walk," she said, but it looked to Alden like she might collapse instead.

He hurried to her side and saw tears streaming from her eyes like the river water over the rocks. "Are you all right?"

She waved him off. "I just need a few minutes."

Then she hurried away from him and the mining camp, forging her own trail down the riverbank.

Chapter 38

Sierra Foothills
August 1854

The river rushed below Isabelle as she ran, but she didn't see the water. All she could see was the baby boy swaddled in her arms, his eyes gazing up at her with complete abandon. Like she would never leave him. He'd trusted her to care for him, and she'd left him to fend for himself with a man who was mad. And a woman who hated him.

She stumbled on a rock, hidden under the grass, and picked herself back up, the image in her mind shifting from the calmness in her baby's eyes to chaos. Crying. Mrs. Duvall arched over her bed, yanking her arm.

Blood streamed from a gash in her hand—a

wound from the rock—but Isabelle didn't stop to tend to it. Her heart—it beat so fast that she felt as if it might explode into a thousand pieces.

She hadn't suspected Mrs. Duvall or the midwife of lying to her. In her heart, she'd thought she had failed her baby. It was her milk or her youth or something she'd done wrong during the delivery that took him.

All along, she'd believed what Mrs. Duvall had told her, that her son was dead.

But Isaac had survived.

And he'd been forced to grow up in a snare of lies too. He thought his mother had abandoned him.

Isaac's mother wasn't a princess. She was a simple, broken woman, masquerading as the niece of the French couple who had rescued her.

At the time, she'd thought her mistress had done a rare kindness in helping her escape Victor's grasp, but really she'd stolen away Isabelle's son.

Oh, why had the woman lied to her?

But even as she ran along the bank, dodging the mesh of driftwood, Isabelle knew exactly why Mrs. Duvall had lied. Her hatred was venomous. Victor had abused Isabelle with his warped view of love, torturing her in the night hours that she feared. Instead of helping Isabelle, Mrs. Duvall had blamed her for her husband's obsession.

And that's what Victor had been. Completely obsessed. As if he would somehow find happiness if he humiliated her and then conquered her body, mind, and the depths of her soul.

Her hand traveled up to the pale pink lawn of her dress, and she cupped it over her right shoulder. The senior Master Duvall once promised that he'd set her free, but after his father's death, Victor made it quite clear that there would be no freedom for her. Ever. Then he'd branded her so she would never leave him.

The pain of losing her baby had seared her heart, but the branding iron scarred her in a different way. It was the constant reminder— long after her shoulder healed—that no matter where she went, she could never fully get away from the man who owned her. Even though she'd tried for years, the cucumber-and-lemon cream had done nothing to fade the brand of his rose.

Her toe caught another rock, and she stumbled again, collapsing onto a bed of grass along the bank. The rush of river had quieted to a gentle hum here, giving life to the crimson columbine that blossomed on each side.

Had Mrs. Duvall thought that by getting rid of the slave girl, her husband's affection would turn toward her? Or had Mrs. Duvall hoped to raise Isaac as her own?

The guilt that plagued Isabelle, haunting her dreams, was all based on a lie. She'd done nothing wrong. It was the Duvalls who'd conspired against her.

For so many years, she'd wondered what her son would have been like if he'd lived. What kind of man he would have become. Now it felt as if her baby had come back from the dead. Her stolen dream, the only person who'd ever really belonged to her, returned.

What a gift to see Isaac as a strong, smart, kind boy thriving under the care of a man who wanted the best for him. It was God's gift to discover that Isaac had circumvented the cruelty of his father and gained freedom as well.

She tugged on the ends of her loose hair, as if it would help her brain make sense of all that had transpired.

Alden had said their situation was complicated. Had he helped Isaac run away? Perhaps that was the reason Victor had traveled to Sacramento—to make a grand display of his power, taking both her and Isaac back to Virginia with him.

She shuddered at the thought of what he would do if he found them.

As the sun began to settle beyond the willow trees, she wrapped her arms around her knees.

No matter what happened, she would never let Victor take Isaac away from her again. She'd protect him from the Duvalls with her life, if she must.

Soon, after Victor was gone, she and Isaac would return to the city, and she'd take him up to safety on Vancouver Island. Until then, she couldn't risk telling him or anyone that she was a runaway slave. As long as Victor didn't find them, her façade would protect both herself and her son from harm. And keep them together for the rest of their lives.

A rustle in the grasses startled her, and she jumped, thinking it might be a wildcat, but when she looked up, she saw Alden walking toward her.

She sat up, wiping her eyes on her sleeves before climbing up onto the flat edge of a rock.

He studied her for a moment. "Are you ill?"

She contemplated his words. Her body was well, but everything inside her felt sick.

He found a seat on a rock near her, his head resting in his hands. "It's horrific what some slave owners do."

She nodded, wanting him to think her tears were for the horror of the branding alone. He could never know about the rose and letter that marked her shoulder as well.

"Isaac thought you were mad at him."

Her heart clenched. "Oh, no—"

"I told him that you just needed to exercise your legs since you weren't able to swim. He seemed satisfied with that answer."

She looked up into the swell of compassion in Alden's eyes. "Why are you different?" she asked.

"I've never tried to be different."

"I mean—" She had to tread cautiously, taking

care not to reveal too much. "You said your family owns slaves."

He picked up a stick and threw it into the river. "Unfortunately."

"Yet you helped Persila escape from her owner. And you said you want Isaac to be free."

"I've never been a proponent of slavery."

"What would your family say?"

His gaze settled on the water. "My father would say that I'm a coward. That I'm weak-willed and pitiful for entangling my emotions with people he considers to be property."

"I don't think you're a coward."

His eyes found her again, and he flashed a wry smile. "That's because you don't know me very well."

She wiped her eyes again, wishing she could tell him that she did indeed know him, back when she wore a linsey-woolsey dress and a cotton cap and spoke with the timid voice of a slave girl. "I think it's quite brave of you to bring Isaac west."

"I ran away from home," he said. "It wasn't the least bit brave."

She shook her head. "Running takes a lot of courage, especially when you choose to do it for the right reason."

His gaze fell to the blood still trickling on her hand. "You've hurt yourself."

"I'll be fine," she said. It stung a little, nothing else.

"We have to clean it."

"No."

Standing up, he reached for her good hand. If she were thinking clearly, she would have refused, but she followed him to the edge of the bank. He scooped cool water from the river and gently washed her palm. After the blood was gone, he wrapped his dry handkerchief around the wound and stepped back.

She stared at the gray cloth around her hand before looking back up at him. "Thank you."

"Isabelle," he started, locking her gaze. "If I were a gambling man, I'd bet a pile of gold that I've seen you before, long before Isaac and I came to California."

Her gaze returned to the handkerchief. "Have you been to Baltimore?"

"No—did you ever visit Boston before you came west?"

She shook her head. "I'm sure there are plenty of women who look like me."

"I don't think there's anyone else in this whole country quite as lovely as you," he said tenderly.

Her heart seemed to flip with his words, her fingers trembling. She didn't dare glance back up at him.

He cleared his throat. "I think it's very courageous of you to not only run a hotel on your own but help Persila escape as well."

She put her hands back down at her sides, hiding

them in the folds of her dress so he couldn't see them shaking. Plenty of men back in Sacramento City had called her beautiful—men desperate for female attention—but no one had ever called her courageous.

"I wish you would have met my aunt before she died. She was a truly brave woman."

When she looked back up at him, his gaze was still intense. "I wish I could have met her too."

"She would have liked you."

When Alden smiled back at her, it seemed as if everything would be fine now. As if he could take care of her and Isaac alike. She nodded back toward the camp. "I've never eaten antelope before."

"Me either, and I'm starving." He laughed. "There will be plenty of new things for us to try out here."

She trekked back through the rocks and grass, Alden at her side. It seemed like they both had run away from their pasts. Just as she'd worked to break free from the Duvalls, she needed to offer him the same grace if he sought redemption from the sins of his family.

It was a new season for both her and Alden now. And a new season, she hoped, for the boy back at the camp too.

No matter what happened, she would do anything she could to rescue her son.

Chapter 39

Sacramento City
August 1854

Sacramento City was still smoldering a week after the flames had been extinguished. The fire left behind charred skeletons of buildings on at least twelve of the city's blocks, the crumpled walls reeking of smoke and slag. Ashes shrouded the once-planked streets, and every structure that remained was blackened with soot.

Mallie's hotel had resisted the inferno, but the metal shutters and doors were welded together from the heat. Victor had walked down K Street every day since the fire, searching, but after he'd followed Mallie into the alleyway, it seemed as if she'd blown away with the smoke. Like she'd known he was looking for her.

But no one knew he was searching for Mallie except Fanny, and she'd disappeared as well, taking with her the cache of coins she must have stolen when she rifled through his portfolio. He'd hoped the fire had taken her life, but the only bodies found in the aftermath were those of three workers who'd perished behind the shutters of a mercantile.

According to the chief engineer of the fire

department, the fire had been an accident. He said it began when a guest knocked over a lantern at the Kirtland House. No one knew the name of the guest. And no one, it seemed, had guessed that the proprietor's wife had started the blaze.

Sacramento's residents had already begun to rebuild, but there was nothing to occupy Victor's time except to continue his search. The fire had burned everything he owned except his portfolio, his wallet, and the clothes on his back. A steamboat from San Francisco had delivered food and clothing yesterday, but he hadn't found out about the arrival until after their wares had sold at ridiculously high prices. He'd heard that a pair of boots went for fifty dollars. A readymade shirt for thirty.

The proprietor at his new place of residence—a man by the name of Louis Gibbs—was a cheat too, taking advantage of those made homeless by the fire. Louis's boardinghouse had burned down, but he'd hired a hungry crew for a pittance to clear his property while he retrieved enough canvas from San Francisco for a large tent. Then the man charged five dollars for a spot underneath it.

For seven days, Victor had slogged through dust that blew west from the valley, through the scorched streets and those that had dodged the fire. He visited the wharf every day to watch the passengers embark on the steamers, and he'd stopped by the Wells Fargo stagecoach office three times, asking if the woman known as Isabelle Labrie had been a passenger out of town.

As he searched for Mallie, he'd been looking for Alden and Isaac too. The firemen stopped the blaze before it reached Mr. Fallow's office, so Victor visited there almost every day as well. Horace had grown tired of his inquiries, as if the man had a hundred things to do in the absence of his employer, but he didn't particularly care if the man disliked him.

This morning, Victor paused outside the closed door of the lawyer's office. Someone had posted a notification on the wall beside it.

After he knocked, Horace called out for him to come inside. Then the man rolled his eyes. "Can't you read?"

Victor flinched. "Read what?"

"The sign." Horace stood up and marched toward the door, rapping on the paper nailed beside it. "Mr. Fallow. Has. Not. Returned."

"I didn't notice it."

"I will take down the sign when he returns. Until then, it's useless for you to continue knocking."

After Horace locked the door, Victor tore down the man's sign and crumpled it into a ball before stomping away, swearing under his breath. He was more than ready to leave this town in its dust and ashes and return east where people treated him like a gentleman.

Before he went to his home in West End, he'd travel to the office of the *New York Herald* and tell the editor exactly how unwelcoming the people in California were. He'd name names, show the people here in Sacramento that they should have treated Victor Duvall with dignity. Then he'd settle back into his comfortable farmhouse and wait patiently for his time to rule over Scott's Grove.

With the sign clenched in his hands, he marched up I Street until he reached the stagecoach office. "I'm looking for a woman I lost in the fire," he explained to the agent on the other side of the counter. "Her name is Miss Isabelle Labrie."

"A hundred people leave here every day," the man said coolly. "Going all different directions."

"I understand, but this woman would be hard to forget. She's French, you see, and has these beautiful brown eyes that will haunt a man."

"When did you see her last?"

"During the fire, over on K Street." Victor shook his head solemnly. "Isabelle and I were planning to marry, and then we were separated in all the chaos. I fear she might have traveled out to the goldfields, looking for me."

Another man stepped up to the counter. He was almost a foot taller than Victor and much more stout. "I drove a woman named Isabelle out to Columbia last week, but she was already married to a fellow named Payne."

His fingers curled around the paper. "Was she traveling with anyone?"

"A colored boy. And her husband."

Anger flickered at first and then roared inside him, hotter than the inferno that had blazed through this town.

"Seems like you were jilted," the agent said after the driver walked away.

Victor stepped back from the counter.

Had Alden traveled to California to marry Mallie? Were the two of them laughing together now as husband and wife?

He looked down at his hands, at the crumpled paper, and tore it into shreds.

Had Eliza arranged this secret meeting? She'd probably known all along about Alden and Mallie. Mallie hadn't run away from Victor. Alden had stolen her away and then he'd taken Isaac. And his beastly wife was probably at home, laughing about it all, as if it were all a grand scheme.

He'd left Eliza eight thousand miles ago and still her laughter stung his ears.

The law may acknowledge her as his wife—until death parted them—but he only needed her alive until John and Alden were gone. If he was patient enough, resolved, he could secure Scott's Grove and the two people he loved most in the world.

Good riddance.

That's what Eliza had said about Isaac, and it's

exactly what he would say about her after he inherited the plantation.

"How much is a ticket to Columbia?" he asked the agent, his voice calm again.

"A hundred dollars."

"That's outrageous!"

The man shrugged. "Gold prices."

Victor reluctantly lifted the wallet from his coat pocket and opened the brass clasp. Then he counted through the coins inside. Blast Fanny Kirtland. He didn't even have enough for one return passage to Boston, clear around Cape Horn, but right now, he'd spend every dollar left in his wallet if he must to find this semblance of a family.

He removed five gold coins and put them on the table. The agent slid them off the counter, into his till, then held out a ticket.

"The next ride to Columbia is in two weeks."

Victor choked. "What do you mean, two weeks?"

"I mean that is the next time we have a seat available on a coach going to the town of Columbia," the agent said, annoyed with him. "They've been finding gold out there by the fistful, and after the fire, it seems like half of Sacramento wants to go."

"How about taking a boat?" Victor asked. "Or a train?"

When the man snorted, Victor snatched the ticket out of his hand.

He'd find Mallie, and then he'd figure out a way home. This trip had cost him dearly—all the money left from his inheritance—but he was almost finished.

He felt like Captain Ahab, sniffing the scent of the white whale in the ocean. Except no rope was going to take him down to the depths of the sea.

Unlike Ahab, he was going to conquer this whale.

Chapter 40

Columbia
August 1854

The cypress writing desk in Isabelle's hotel room was similar to the one found in her aunt's cottage, the narrow drawer at the bottom folding out for miners to hide their gold. She removed Aunt Emeline's box from the hidden drawer and stared down again at the rose inlaid on the lid. Then she smoothed her hand over the skirt of her plum-colored working dress.

Unlike the silk and taffeta of a fashionable French woman, this calico was supposed to help her blend in on the crowded streets here in Columbia, but even dressed plainly, the miners and businessmen watched her and Isaac closely whenever they left the hotel to eat. Perhaps it was because she was a woman. Or perhaps it was because she was accompanied by a black boy. She'd only seen two other Negros since they'd arrived in Columbia, both of them freedmen working as miners.

She rested back in a chair, the trinket box on her lap. It would make Aunt Emeline so happy to know that she'd been reunited with her son—pleased that God was creating beauty from the ashes of her life.

Her window open, she could hear the crack of a wooden ball knocking down bowling pins across the street. Chickens squawked from a pen, men sang off-key in what she assumed was a nearby saloon, and in the distance, she heard what sounded like a trombone.

The town of Columbia was about the same size as Sacramento, but there were no tidy blocks or planked streets here. The town's center hosted hotels, saloons, dry goods stores, a bank, an assay office, and several eateries. A lovely frame home with its picket fence and flower garden was the crown jewel, the residence of the bank president and his family, but a mishmash of ramshackle tents and wooden buildings fanned out from Main Street, bleeding down into the gulch and up into the forested hills.

Miners seemed to be everywhere, carrying their shovels and picks back and forth between the diggings and saloons in town. The air here was cleaner than in Sacramento, the mountains blowing down a light coolness that stifled the summer heat, and the streets seemed to buzz with optimism. These were the men who still believed in the power of gold, unlike so many back in Sacramento, who'd lost everything in their quest.

It felt strange to be the patron of a hotel instead of the matron, but the Broadway Hotel was the finest establishment in this town. With Alden off trying to stake a mining claim, it seemed like the safest option for her and Isaac as well. She'd secured two rooms for them, connected by an inside door in case Isaac needed her.

Isaac was reading *Uncle Tom's Cabin* in the next room, a book he purchased with the money she'd paid him for his work at the Golden. Over the past week, she'd been continually amazed that God had seen fit to bring them back together again. And she wished that Aunt Emeline were here so she could ask her how to be a mother.

She brought the crocheted baby blanket with her, but instead of it bringing her sadness, it filled her heart with a deep joy. What she thought she'd lost had been found.

Now she needed to do one last thing before she stepped boldly into this new season of life. She needed to find out what her aunt had given her.

Her hands were resting on the lid when Isaac

poked his head into the room. "Are you hungry?"

She smiled, the joy flooding her heart again. "I am if you are."

"I'd like more oysters."

"Then we'll find you some." It wouldn't be hard. It seemed that every establishment in this town sold oysters along with champagne. She and Isaac ate their oysters with buttered bread and a bottle of root beer.

He pointed toward the box. "What's that?"

"It's a gift that my aunt left for me."

He rested on the edge of the bed. "What's in it?"

She looked at the boy sitting beside her in wonder, marveling at the genuineness in his brown eyes, the curiosity in his voice. She'd been worried this past week that she might see Victor in him, but Isaac was confident and kind and thoughtful. Nothing like the man who'd fathered him.

"I don't know what's inside."

He stared down at it. "Why haven't you opened it?"

"I suppose it's because I'm scared."

"Is there something scary inside?"

"No." She smiled at him even as tears formed again in her eyes. It seemed she'd been an open spigot of water the past week. "It's my aunt's last gift to me, and I suppose I'm afraid to say a final good-bye."

"But what if it's not good-bye?" he asked.

"What if there's something inside that will last forever?"

She blinked back the tears. "You sure ask a lot of questions."

"Master Duvall says I'm insatiable."

"Inquisitive might be a better word."

"But I don't get angry when someone can't answer my questions."

"Did Master Duvall"—she pressed a finger to the edge of each eye, trying to keep her tears at bay—"did he ever hurt you?"

The boy shrugged his shoulders.

Had Victor seared him with the brand when Isaac was too young for memories or had he waited until Isaac was older? If only she'd been able to protect him.

"I understand," Isabelle said tenderly. "Someone hurt me once too."

Isaac nodded his head, gazing down at the box again. "Why don't you open it now?"

She placed her hand on the cover, remembering that last day with Emeline when she'd told her aunt that she would treasure her gift. And she had treasured the box, just not what was inside.

Could she really open it now? Part of her wanted to unlock it, but part of her still wasn't ready.

Then again, if a fire ripped through this town like it had in Sacramento, she might never know what Aunt Emeline wanted her to have.

Taking a deep breath, she carefully pulled her

necklace with the two keys over her head. Then she used the smaller key to unlock the clasp.

She thought she might find jewelry or another valuable from her aunt, but there were only three pieces of a gray parchment paper stored inside, each folded in half.

Isaac tried to look over her sleeve. "What is it?"

"Papers," she said. "I haven't been able to read them yet."

He dutifully scooted away, waiting as he watched her.

The first piece was a letter from Aunt Emeline, written in her elegant script.

Dearest Isabelle,

I'd hoped to be with you until the day you married, but it seems God is calling me home soon. Enclosed is my last gift to you—the story of where He intertwined your life with mine.

William and I had a daughter once, born before we left Marseille. She was a beautiful girl who died when she was two. We mourned our loss deeply, our hearts broken. A year later, we sailed for Baltimore in a desperate attempt to escape our grief.

I learned quickly that grief trails a person, no matter where they go, but when we opened our home in Baltimore to men and women searching for freedom, God began stitching together the ragged pieces of our hearts, healing us from the inside.

Then He brought you.

Eliza Duvall showed up at our door late at night, her coachman carrying a beautiful young woman who was grieving just as deeply as I had done. You reminded William and me so much of our Rose, and we rejoiced at the opportunity to love you as our own. Never once did we want you to think we tried to replace our daughter with you. We loved you for the woman you were—and the woman we prayed you would become.

Eliza Duvall returned to our house in 1849, asking for money. We gave her a small sum, but William and I feared that she would return again and again for more. Or much worse, that she would tell whomever had harmed you where you were.

William left for California that summer, and you and I followed soon after. The loss of William tore my heart too, but it was a different kind of grief than losing Rose. William died a hero, trying to provide a safe place for our family.

The book of 2 Corinthians says where the Spirit of the Lord is, there is liberty. He never meant for you or anyone else to be enslaved by another. He meant for you to be redeemed and restored in Him. The perfect Father.

Forgive me for not giving you the enclosed documents before, Isabelle. I never thought of you as anything other than a daughter of God, loved for exactly who He made you to be. Compassionate. Clever. Charming.

Cling to His wings—the wings of an eagle—so you can fly. Forever free.

Lovingly,
Aunt Emeline

Isabelle unfolded the other pieces of paper. The first one was a bill of sale for a slave girl named Mallie, purchased for eight hundred dollars. The last paper stated that the slave girl had been set free.

Isabelle wiped her tears with her sleeve. The Labries hadn't just harbored her; they'd purchased her. But never once had they treated her as a slave. They'd signed the paper for her emancipation long before they'd left Baltimore.

They'd bought her, and then they'd set her free.

"Do you still have to be scared?" Isaac asked.

"No." She tucked the letter back into the box and locked it. "I don't have to be afraid anymore."

Chapter 41

Columbia
August 1854

Victor's heart raced as he stepped onto the dusty street in Columbia. He felt like one of those bulls in Spain who'd been trapped in a pen much too long. The stagecoach ride here had been worse than sailing up to San Francisco, worse even than taking the dreadful bungo across the isthmus.

His legs were bruised, and he desperately needed a bath and a fresh change of clothes.

All he wanted now was to return to his clean chamber in West End, to his feather bed, with Mallie at his side. He'd spend all night reminding her of what she'd left behind. Then in the morning, Isaac would come in with the paper and coffee and read to them both. Mallie would draw him a hot bath, and he'd dress in a clean suit for a Sunday dinner of roast pork with cold pickles, tea buns, and a strawberry ice cream, made by that woman he'd bought back in Alexandria.

He hadn't tasted ice cream since he left Virginia.

The farmhouse would fill with his and Mallie's children, at least a dozen of them. He could picture them all together, crowded around the dining table, Isaac or another one of the boys reading a story to them as they ate.

Then he pictured Eliza, dressed in the home-spun uniform and cap of a maid, pouring cups of fine English tea for him and Mallie and their entire brood. The thought made him laugh—and made the gentleman standing next to him step away.

He had to stay focused. Before he could return to Virginia, he had to find Mallie and Isaac. Then he had to rid himself of Alden Payne.

Or perhaps he should remove Alden first.

A gun, he'd decided, would attract unnecessary attention. So he'd stolen a bowie knife from the man bedding next to him in Sacramento. And he'd practiced using it on the bear carcass they'd cooked last night at camp.

He stomped toward the assayer's office, across from an ice cream parlor and bookseller, ready to resume his inquiries. The two miners in front of him took an eternity to weigh their gold before he was able to step up beside the brass scales displayed on the counter.

"I'm looking for a man," he told the assayer.

"There are more than ten thousand men in town," the assayer said with a shrug.

"This fellow's named Alden Payne. He came to town just a few weeks ago with his wife and a slave boy."

The man wiped off the scale with a white cloth. "I saw a man with a Negro boy."

Victor leaned closer, trying to keep his fervor penned inside. "Where can I find him?"

"Last I spoke to him, he was mining in one of the gulches."

The last thing he wanted to do was stomp around the wilderness, searching among thousands of miners. "Any idea which gulch?"

"Nope, but if you wait long enough, he'll come back into town," the assayer said. "I'll tell Mr. Payne that you're looking for him."

"No need," Victor replied. "I'll find him myself."

He stepped back outside and scanned the street, looking at the felled trees on one side of town and the hills on the other.

In the past seven months, when he wasn't on the ship, he'd combed through towns and cities, hotels and boardinghouses. He'd quizzed countless clerks and assistants and visited all manner of offices.

It was finally time to end this search and go home.

Chapter 42

Near Columbia
August 1854

Alden loosened the dirt around rocks on his mining claim. When he first arrived in Columbia, he'd gone straight to the assay office to ask about Judah, but the assayer didn't know him. So he bought a wooden rocker and two bedrolls from a Vermont man who said he was done with mining.

Two weeks ago he staked a claim along a gulch that channeled snow and rain runoff in the spring. This area seemed to be the heart of gold country, with quartz veins threading from every direction, entwined in the creases around the boulders.

After Alden claimed his patch of land, Isaac had begged to help him dig for gold. Since there was no school for him to attend in Columbia, Alden thought it healthy for Isaac to work. Isabelle agreed, as long as half the findings went to his care.

In the past weeks of mining, they'd barely made enough to care for either of them, but he and Isaac worked hard, like they had back on the ship, except this time they worked for themselves. Together, they could operate the rocker—Alden dumped in shoveled dirt, and Isaac poured pails of water into what was called a riddle box to trap the large rocks. Then they'd rock the long cradle for as long as it took for gold to free itself from the gravel and fall into cleats called riffles below.

It was Isaac's job to open the slat and retrieve the gold.

Because the gulch was dry, they paid five dollars a day to the Tuolumne County Water Company for a ditch of water used to flush the gold away from the dirt. He and Isaac were bringing in about eight dollars in gold dust and flakes each day. There wasn't anything left after they bought beans, a tin of crackers, and salt pork, but at least, as Isaac once said, they were both fortunate enough to eat. And they didn't have to pay for lodging. After a hard day of digging, they washed off—thanks to the water company—and slept soundly in bedrolls under a tent housed between their four stakes.

If he didn't find Judah before the rains, he'd look for other work until they'd saved enough for passage up north. He hoped that Isabelle would remain in Columbia. He was getting quite used to the idea of seeing her in the evenings when he and Isaac walked into town.

The sun was beginning to set, but they could work another hour in the flicker of twilight. They'd found enough today to reward their labor with a decent meal at one of the eateries. Hope-ully Isabelle would join them.

As he shoveled another round of dirt into the rocker, he thought back again to those sacred moments along the riverbank where Isabelle had wept for Isaac's childhood. And he wondered again about her years in Baltimore. Surely she'd seen slaves there, when she was a girl. Perhaps, until she'd met Persila and then Isaac, she hadn't realized the cruelty of what a slave owner could do.

California was a new beginning for many people, yet they all carried the burden of their past with them, molded by the experiences of their youth. Isabelle had been cold to him back in Sacramento, but he'd glimpsed something from the depths of her heart on their trip here. And he couldn't stop thinking about her.

She'd said she was leaving Sacramento because someone from her past wanted to harm her. Was this the Mr. Kirtland that Mr. Walsh referred to back at the Golden? Or was it someone upset that she had sympathized with the plight of runaways?

As he and Isaac rocked the cradle, both mud and gravel poured down into the gulch. Then Isaac checked the riffles. "Look at this!" he shouted.

Alden kneeled down beside him as Isaac reached in through the cleats and pulled out a water-smoothed nugget of gold the size of a walnut.

A few of the nearby miners glanced their way,

and Alden swiftly picked up the pewter flask where they stored their gold dust and flakes. The mouth was too narrow for the nugget, so he pulled open the burlap bag where he kept coffee beans.

"Put it in here," he instructed.

Isaac dropped their gold into the bag.

Alden felt the nugget among the beans, but he didn't dare check on it. A nugget that big—if it really was gold—could launch a riot, and he didn't want to tempt any unsavory characters to try to steal it during the mayhem.

He tossed their shovel and pan inside the tent. "We need to get to the assay office before it closes," he whispered to Isaac.

They passed by dozens of claims along the gulch, greeting other miners as they hiked toward a treed hill. It was almost a mile back into Columbia, but if he and Isaac hurried, they could be there before the assayer locked his door.

"What should we do with it, if it's worth something?" Isaac asked.

"I'm going to pay back Isabelle for our stage-coach ride here, and then I'm going to find a way up to Vancouver Island."

Isaac hopped over a tree stump. "I like it here just fine."

"Yes, but it's still not as safe as it should be."

"Not safe for slaves?"

"For any black person."

As they neared the edge of town, they passed a

herd of mule deer grazing among the rugged oaks. Then they stepped onto a clay street between a row of shanties and a fandango house pumping out Spanish music.

Alden patted the bag tucked inside his coat one more time. He'd trade it in for gold ingots, then he'd pay back Isabelle and ask her to secure the rest in her locked room. Hopefully, the assayer would keep mum about their find. Around here, word about a nugget this big would travel faster than the flames in Sacramento.

Main Street was crowded at the end of day, the oil lanterns from boardinghouses and shops pooling the streets with light. A man stepped out of an alley, startling Alden. His clothes were tattered and smelled as if they'd been recovered from a burning heap of trash. Sympathy washed over Alden at first, but the sentiment turned quickly to shock. Then fear.

It wasn't just any vagabond standing in front of him. It was Victor Duvall, clutching a knife in both hands.

"Come here, boy," Victor told Isaac, but his blade was pointed at Alden.

Instead of stepping forward, Isaac inched toward Alden's side. Then Alden pulled him close. "What do you want, Victor?"

"What is rightfully mine."

"Put down your knife," Alden commanded.

A group of miners started to circle them, but

none of them stepped up to help until a black miner moved in beside Alden, telling Victor as well to drop the knife.

Victor held his hand steady. "Not until he pays for what he's done."

"What has he done?" the miner asked.

"He stole everything from me."

Alden clenched his fists, his arm secure around Isaac. "I didn't steal anything."

"You took the woman I loved, and then you kidnapped my son."

The miner took a step back from Alden.

"He's lying," Alden spat.

The miner shook his head. "Stealing people is a crime."

Victor moved toward him, the blade steady in his hands. "Where's Mallie?"

"Who's Mal—" Alden started. Then he stopped.

The crowd around him faded for an instant, and all he saw were hickory-brown eyes, laden with light. Those eyes, he remembered them now. They belonged to the beautiful slave girl back in Virginia, the one who used to bring coffee with jam and bread to his room early in the morning. The girl Eliza hated.

His stomach churned. Isabelle wasn't a French woman from Baltimore. Not long ago, she had been Victor's slave.

Had this man forced himself on Isabelle, like his father had done to Naomi?

He lurched forward to pummel the smirk off Victor's face, but the miner near him reached for his arm. In seconds, a horde of miners surrounded both of them, a wall blocking Alden from his brother-in-law.

"Let's take it before the justice of the peace," one of the men said. "Judge Roth will want to resolve this tonight."

Even as one man restrained his arm, Alden leaned down toward Isaac and whispered, "You and Isabelle must hide."

When Isaac didn't move, Alden nudged him away with his knee, praying the boy would run.

Chapter 43

Columbia
August 1854

Locked in the hotel room, Isabelle clung to Isaac on the edge of the bed, holding him like she'd done when he was a baby. And they cried together. Both of them were afraid of what Victor would do to Alden, afraid of what the man could do to all of them.

Even with the freedom papers hidden in the desk, she still feared Victor, but she wouldn't let Isaac return to Virginia as his slave. Now that God had brought her and Isaac back together, she couldn't bear being ripped apart again.

Isaac dried his tears on the back of his hand. "Why won't Master Duvall let me be free?"

"Some people—" she started to explain, but there was no good explanation for what Victor had done. And continued to do. "It seems this man doesn't like change."

"I think he's deranged."

"Perhaps you're right."

"All I did back in Virginia was read to him when he wanted and fetch his coffee."

She smoothed his curly hair back over his collar. "It's not about the work."

He turned toward the window and stared out at the darkness. Should she tell him that Victor was her former master too? And that Victor was also his father? Perhaps Victor had already told Isaac who'd fathered him.

He stood up, his shoulders slack as he slogged toward the door.

"Where are you going?"

He reached for the door latch. "To help Master Payne."

"You can't go to the court. Victor will take you away."

"I have to do something," Isaac said, the conviction in his voice as hard as the rocks bedded around Columbia. "He's only in trouble for helping me."

She patted the bed. "Stay here, Isaac."

"I can't. The miners might hang him."

"They only hang murderers and thieves."

"But Master Duvall said that Alden stole me."

She groaned before motioning him back to her side. "Let me show you something."

Kneeling down beside the desk, she folded back the panel in the drawer, revealing the hidden space. Then she took both keys from around her neck and unlocked Aunt Emeline's box, removing her bill of sale and emancipation paper.

Her secret could no longer be kept safe, but she was a free woman. Even the courts would respect that.

She prayed they would also let a mother keep her son.

She handed the remaining key to Isaac before showing him the lockbox. "This contains the rest of my money and the deed to the Golden. If I don't come back, you and Alden need to leave for Vancouver Island as fast as you can."

Tears filled his eyes again. "I'm not going north without you."

She kissed his forehead. Then she slipped a dress out of the bureau—an ivory silk with French lace on the sleeves—and while Isaac waited outside the room, she changed her clothing before walking alone to justice court.

Two lanterns poured light across the judge's small bench and thirty or so miners huddled together in the cramped space. Alden sat in a chair beside the judge, his jaw firm. Isabelle didn't see Victor nor did she allow herself to search for him in the crowd. Instead, she elbowed her way through the miners until she reached the bench.

The judge was middle-aged, with a thick beard, and wore a formal black gown that made him look as distinguished as the judge back in Sacramento. She stood confident before him, glad she had worn her silk gown. "I'd like to speak on behalf of the defendant."

The judge scanned her attire. "Are you his wife?"

Her gaze wandered over to Alden, and in his eyes, she saw compassion. And concern. He'd been caught in the middle, trying to do what was right in a system gone awry.

She faced the judge again. "No, we're not married."

"Then what do you have to say?"

"I don't believe Mr. Duvall wants Mr. Payne or even Isaac. I believe he wants—"

Behind her, Victor shouted out, interrupting her. "She has no right to speak in court, Your Honor."

The judge glared at him. "I will say who speaks in this court, Mr. Duvall."

For a moment, she felt like that twelve-year-old girl again, forced against her will to become what Victor had called his bride. The pain welled up inside her, battling the confidence that she wanted her clothing to portray.

346

Slowly she turned to face the man who had wounded her deeply with his twisted version of love. Victor looked smaller than she remembered, and instead of the fine suits he wore back in West End, his clothing was filthy. Threadbare.

But the smirk on his face, that shell of pride, had not changed. "The law clearly states that a slave cannot speak in a courtroom," Victor told the judge.

She lifted her shoulders. "I am not a slave."

"Or any Negro," Victor continued. Then he turned to look at her, a frightening smile on his lips. "Hello, Mallie."

The same greeting he'd given her every time he'd awakened her during the night.

She opened her mouth, ready to deny the claim of her ancestry, but how could she defend herself? Negro blood did run through her veins, pouring down from her mother's side of the family. But for the first time in her life, she felt the worth and dignity of her heritage. Even though her ancestors were victims of slavery, they had been courageous. The men and women before her didn't just survive; they had persevered in the face of injustice.

And she would persevere as well.

She didn't dare look over at Alden, but she turned back toward the judge and placed her freedom paper on the desk. "This is my emancipation."

The man didn't even look at the document. Instead, he studied her olive-colored arms. "I'm sorry, Miss—" he started, clearly confused about what to call her.

"Miss Labrie," she said boldly. In the power of that name, she was exactly who she'd chosen to be and who she wanted to become—a courageous, educated, free woman who feared no one but God.

"Are you a Negro?" he asked.

"My mother was of African descent," she said proudly. "Her skin was as light as mine, but the color of skin shouldn't matter in regard to one's testimony."

The judge pushed her paper back toward her, as if her freedom was meaningless to him. "Unfortunately, your ancestry matters very much under the confines of federal law."

She took her paper back, the value of it worth more to her than a thousand nuggets of gold.

"Do you still own her?" the judge asked Victor, promptly resigning her back to the equality of a cow or pig.

Victor nodded slowly. "She's been mine since she was twelve."

"How can you prove it?"

Victor walked forward, whispered something to the judge, and fear snaked through her again.

How was she supposed to defend Alden if the judge wouldn't let her talk? And how could she explain that the boy Victor wanted was her son? A boy who should stay with his mother.

"Your Honor—" she tried again, holding up her freedom paper.

"You can't speak on your own behalf."

"But I must."

"If you say another word, Miss Labrie, I will have you escorted to the jail." The judge paused, glancing around the courtroom. "Is there anyone here who can speak for her?"

Instead of someone answering the judge's question, an eerie silence replaced the rustling in the courtroom. Alden wanted to jump out of his seat and speak boldly on Isabelle's behalf as a witness, but he'd seen her as a slave back at the Duvall house. He knew that Victor had owned her. His testimony, he feared, would harm instead of help.

The lechery in his brother-in-law's eyes sickened him, but in Isabelle's eyes, he saw courage. The woman had walked through the fire, and she still continued to fight.

Passion is most powerful when bridled by restraint.

As the dean's words echoed through his mind again, he knew he must bridle his own fury and fight for Isabelle with words seared by truth.

In the lull of silence, he raised his hand. The judge in Sacramento wouldn't let him defend

349

Isabelle until he passed the bar, but Judge Roth might be different. Instead of speaking about Isabelle's past, perhaps the judge would allow him to defend her future.

"Yes, Mr. Payne?"

"I would like to act as Miss Labrie's counsel."

The man pressed his hands together in front of his face. "Are you a lawyer?"

"I attended the law school at Harvard College in Massachusetts."

"Have you passed the California bar?"

"Not yet."

Judge Roth studied Isabelle for another moment before looking back at him. "I think we could remedy that." He leaned back in his chair. "I can admit a candidate to practice law in this court, but if you want to practice anyplace else, you'll have to go before the Supreme Court in San Francisco."

"I understand."

For the next fifteen minutes, the judge grilled Alden on federal and state law, particularly when it came to the laws of slavery. Yes, he knew that California was officially a free state, though the laws about fugitive slaves applied here. Yes, he realized anyone caught helping a fugitive was subject to imprisonment and a fine.

Judge Roth made it known that he hadn't forgotten Victor's initial case against Alden regarding the stolen property, but he could help

Isabelle first and then defend himself and Isaac.

Alden pointed back at his brother-in-law. "Mr. Duvall has no evidence that this woman was once his slave."

"That's not true," Victor blurted out. "I have the deed with her name on it."

"You could claim any woman as your slave."

"Perhaps." Victor stepped up beside Isabelle and fingered the lace on her sleeve. "But all my slaves have been branded."

Bridled words escaped Alden. He wanted to strangle this maniac for scarring Isaac and Isabelle. Make him pay dearly for what he had done.

Victor touched Isabelle's neck, and she flinched. "Show them your shoulder."

Alden towered over him. "Take your hands off my client."

The judge agreed with a sharp nod. "Don't touch her, Mr. Duvall."

Victor lowered his hand. "Show them your mark, Mallie."

Isabelle shook her head, but this time, Judge Roth concurred with him. "We need to see it."

Alden slammed his fist on the desk. "This is a court of law, Your Honor."

"It is necessary."

When Isabelle looked at him, he saw the young slave woman again, a victim of her circumstances. He'd thought she was pretty back at West End as well, and in his youthful mind, he'd been a wretched soul, just as bad as Victor in his core. But he'd chosen to fight against the evil back then, and he'd fight now for the purity of the woman standing before them all.

Alden swept his arm across the courtroom. "We must all protect Miss Labrie's dignity."

Judge Roth seemed to mull over his words, and Alden wondered if the man had ever considered that a slave might want—or have—any dignity. But he finally commanded all the spectators to leave. The miners filed out grudgingly, the last one closing the doors. They didn't go far, though —a crowd of them remained outside, peering around the edges of the etched glass on the window.

Alden stepped behind Isabelle to block their view, and with her eyes focused on the floor, she slowly unbuttoned her bodice and rolled back the lace collar to expose her skin. Alden knew he would see the red V inside the rosebud, but still he cringed.

"I branded her myself," Victor said proudly. "When she was twelve years old."

Even the judge seemed stunned into silence.

"I want her and my other slave," Victor demanded.

"One slave at a time please, Mr. Duvall."

Isabelle looked over at Alden, and he could see the humiliation in her eyes. And a plea.

"May I consult with my client?" Alden asked the judge.

The man glanced at the clock on the wall. "You have two minutes."

Alden nodded before guiding Isabelle toward the window. At least a dozen men stared back at them, but Judge Roth didn't invite them back inside.

"I'm so sorry, Isabelle."

"I wanted to help you and Isaac," she said, buttoning up her dress. "Instead, I made a mess of it."

"We'll put all the pieces back together again."

"I have something to show you," Isabelle said, handing over the papers. "It's my bill of sale, from Eliza to the Labries. And this is my emancipation. The Labries wanted to make sure I would always be free."

Alden skimmed the papers, and then he smiled. They were fair copies—originals. "The judge may not let you speak, but he won't be able to argue with these."

"I have something else to tell you—" she started.

Judge Roth hit the gavel on his desk. "Time's up."

"This should be enough for now." Alden turned to the judge and placed the papers before him. "According to her former owner, and the state of Maryland, Miss Labrie is free."

Victor sprung forward, shaking his head. "I never emancipated her."

The judge read through the documents and then showed the bill of sale to Victor.

"Is this your signature?"

He barely glanced at it. "No, Your Honor."

"Then who sold her?"

The three men were silent as they turned toward Isabelle. And with great strength, she smiled back at them. She was the only one who knew the answer.

"Would you like me to consult with Miss Labrie again?" Alden asked.

"No," the judge said, growing frustrated. "Miss Labrie, who sold you?"

"Eliza Duvall," she answered clearly. "Victor's wife."

Victor's cheeks flooded with red. "It's illegal in the state of Virginia for a woman to sell her husband's property."

"That may be so," Alden said. "But we are no longer in the state of Virginia."

"I have something else." Victor reached for the portfolio he'd left on his chair. "It's the deed of ownership for Mallie. She and all my slaves were passed on to me after my father's death."

Isabelle held her breath as the judge reviewed the paper. When he looked up again, he seemed confused. "This isn't a deed of ownership."

Alden stepped forward. "What is it?"

"It's a deed of manumission, saying that the

slave girl named Mallie is eligible to obtain her freedom when she turns twenty-one."

Victor swore.

The judge looked over at Isabelle. "Have you turned twenty-one?"

"Yes, Your Honor."

Judge Roth turned back toward Victor, studying his ragged clothing. "Do you know how to read, sir?"

"I don't know what that has to do with—"

"You might ask someone to inspect any other deeds you have."

Victor placed a pile of papers on the desk. "One of these is the certificate of birth for Isaac."

The judge rummaged through the papers until he found it. Then he turned toward Alden. "As long as you and Miss Labrie produce Mr. Duvall's slave boy in the morning, I'll release you both with a fine."

Chapter 44

Columbia
August 1854

There she blows.

The words of Captain Ahab played in Victor's mind as he looked down on Mallie, sleeping in her hotel room bed, just like he'd found her many times back at her room in West End. He'd bribed one of the men downstairs to unlock her door, saying he'd had a fight with his wife and she refused to let him back in.

He didn't care what a measly justice of the peace said. Nor did he care about the ruling of any court of law or what his cursed father did to humiliate him.

Mallie was his white whale, his rose among weeds. He would not leave California without her.

Back in Virginia, no one would care about a manumission paper. They all knew Mallie was his, including Eliza. And Eliza would pay for stealing Mallie away and then lying to him.

He took a draw on the cigar he'd taken from one of the miners and let the smoke settle over her bed. Then he slid the bowie knife out of the sheath and held it up in the glimmer of moon. The light danced off it, a silver glint on the wall.

"Hello, Mallie," he whispered.

She awoke with a start, and her eyes grew wide with alarm when she saw him and his knife. She sat up, pulling her bedcovers over her chest.

"What are you doing here, Victor?"

"Master Duvall."

Her eyes narrowed. "I will never call you master again."

He set the cigar on her bed stand and sat beside her. "So you thought you could run away with Alden Payne."

"I didn't think any such thing."

He traced the line of her neck with the blade until it rested on her collarbone. "Were you seducing him too, under my roof?"

"You are mad."

The tip of the knife pressed against her skin. "I'm going to win, Isabelle. Alden can't have you any longer."

"I don't care if you kill me," she said, but her voice shook.

"Maybe I won't kill you," he said. "Maybe I'll just leave a few more scars."

"I'm not your property anymore."

"You will always be mine." He inched the knife slowly away from her neck and put it beside the cigar. Then he took his father's crumpled manumission paper out of his coat pocket.

"Do you know what this is?" he asked, holding it up in the moonlight.

She blinked. "I do."

He held it over the molten edge of his cigar. The heat licked at the paper until he blew on it. Then it turned into flames, consuming the deed. When the fire got close to his fingers, he blew it out, the embers scattering across the bed.

"You'll always be my slave, Mallie. And I will always be your master."

She clung to the bedcoverings against her chest, looking at him with a growing confidence that disturbed him. She'd often fought his advances, but she'd never looked him in the eye.

"What if we make a deal?" she asked.

He scooted closer. "What kind of deal?"

"I will buy Isaac from you."

"At what price?"

"At whatever price you'd like as long as you set us both free."

A laugh escaped his lips, and then he silenced himself lest he awaken someone in the neighboring rooms. "I want both of you, but if I had to choose one, I'd choose you."

"I see." She took a deep breath, her gaze still fixed on his face. "I'll go back with you, Victor, but only if you leave Isaac here. And you drop your case against Mr. Payne."

He contemplated her proposal. It would make things much easier if she would go willingly. He wouldn't really leave Isaac behind, but if he could appease her now, he would find Isaac—and her money—once he had her in chains.

Louis Gibbs had offered him six hundred| dollars back in Sacramento for a slave boy. It was enough to buy passage for him and Mallie on a ship out of San Francisco. Then they could begin filling the farmhouse with more children, all of them owned by him.

"Isaac can stay here with Alden," he said before leaning forward, slowly kissing her forehead. "You and I will leave in the morning."

She nodded her head.

"We'll celebrate Christmas at home this year."

• • •

Isabelle crunched her knees up to her chest and sobbed. It felt as if Victor's lips had burned her forehead, his knife piercing her heart.

She may no longer belong to Victor in the eyes of the law, but he wouldn't relent until she went back to Virginia with him. She had to protect Isaac. And Alden. She couldn't allow Victor Duvall to hurt either of them.

Her stomach rolled, her mind racing at the thought of being locked back in that chamber in Virginia—her personal slave pen, where she was subject at any hour to Victor's sick whims.

Mrs. Duvall would hate her even more now, and there was nothing she could do about it.

She rocked back against the pillows.

Some judges esteemed moral law over a federal mandate, but it seemed Judge Roth would never give Isaac to her, even in her freedom. Federal law recognized the bloodline of the female parent, not the father. Isaac had been born a slave, and if she'd didn't make a deal with Victor, her son would remain one for the rest of his life.

Victor desperately wanted what he couldn't have; she'd known it from the time she was a girl. The more she fought Victor, the more he refused to give up. If she willingly gave him what he desired, he lost interest for a season, basking in his power.

On their walk back to the hotel last night, Alden

had told her they would find a way to rescue Isaac, but only a miracle would help them now. Alden wouldn't understand why she had agreed to return with Victor, perhaps even if she told him the truth about Isaac, but no matter what she must endure, she could never let Isaac go back with him.

Thank God her son was alive and free. She would cling to the hope of his future.

Standing up, she walked to the window and looked at the brick building across the street. Alden had tried to secure the room next to hers last night, but the hotel was booked, so he and Isaac had stayed in a room above the bowling alley. For just a moment yesterday, as they stood before the judge, she'd seen something new in Alden's eyes. Wonder, perhaps. And dare she think it, something like love.

But she no longer trusted her instincts about love. Back in Sacramento, she'd thought that Ross cared for her and that Alden was a loathsome slave owner. Victor, it seemed, had messed up her ability to distinguish who she could trust and who was out to deceive her.

It was a foolish thought to think that Alden might care for her anyway. She was more than a tainted woman. She was ruined, as wrecked as the streets of Sacramento after the fire. Aunt Emeline might have called her Isabelle. Beloved. A daughter of God. But Victor would call her something else. Terrible names that no woman should ever hear, names she feared she would begin to believe again.

In the darkness, she prayed that Victor would make good on his word and leave Isaac here. And then she asked, if possible, that she could be free as well to raise her son.

By the time the sun rose, she had washed, dressed, and pinned up her hair. Alden knocked on the door at seven, and she opened it. He looked exhausted too.

"Could you sleep?" he asked.

She shook her head. "Not well."

"I saw your lantern early this morning."

"I was—" She paused. "I was praying."

"Me too."

She glanced behind him. "Where's Isaac?"

"I asked him to stay and read in our room."

"But the judge said—"

"We're going to fight this. I'll pass the bar and take it all the way up to the Supreme Court if I must."

She contemplated again telling him the truth about Isaac, but fighting for her son in court wouldn't work. The law wasn't on her side. She'd longed to hug Isaac one last time, but perhaps it was for the best. If she held him in her arms again, she might not release him.

Isaac was free now, and she wanted him to be free for the rest of his life, not worried about the mother he'd left behind. As much as she wanted to tell him the truth—that she loved him with all her heart—perhaps genuine love meant that she needed to let him go. That was the one thing that Victor had never been able to do.

She stepped out into the parlor and locked the door behind her.

"I'm sorry I didn't remember who you were until last night," Alden said as they moved toward the stairs.

She shook her head. "I was a different person back in Virginia."

"You were just as beautiful."

"I didn't feel very beautiful."

"I didn't understand—" He stumbled over his words. "I should have helped you back then."

When he stopped on the top step, she looked into his eyes. "You can't rescue everyone, Alden."

"Perhaps not, but I could have helped you. Please forgive me for not fighting for you then."

He hadn't done anything wrong, and yet she understood his shame. He was a victim of this institution as well. "You are forgiven, Alden."

His face warmed with his smile. "Thank you."

She followed him down the steps, and he offered his arm as they walked onto the street. For those brief minutes, she pretended that she really was Mrs. Payne. That she was honored and cherished by Alden. That she had a home to call her own with no fear of someone snatching her away. She pretended she could speak her mind in a court of law and rely on justice to protect her and her innocence.

But she was only a project to Alden, a defendant in need of a lawyer. Still, she feared he would be furious when he found out today what she'd offered.

Then again, he would only be angry if he cared.

Victor and the judge were waiting for them in justice court, but it seemed that all except two miners had returned to their claims this morning.

After they stepped inside, Judge Roth looked at the door behind them. "Where is the boy?"

Isabelle spoke first. "Mr. Duvall and I settled this dispute last night."

Alden swiveled toward her. "What?"

The judge looked up at her, sighing. "Do I need to remind you that you're prohibited from testifying?"

"I didn't realize discussing a bargain was considered testimony."

Alden stopped her. "I would like to buy Isaac, Your Honor. I will offer Mr. Duvall a fair price."

The judge looked at Victor. "Would you accept those terms?"

He shook his head. "I will only accept Mallie's terms."

"And what are those?"

"That she goes back to Virginia with me, in

363

exchange for the boy." He looked over at Alden. "Isaac is yours."

Alden stepped forward, his eyes panicked. "I will give you a thousand dollars for Isaac if Isabelle remains with him."

"I don't want Isaac anymore."

"Two thousand."

"That's enough, Mr. Payne," the judge said. "A deal has been struck."

Isabelle couldn't look back over at Alden. "He also agreed to drop the kidnapping charges against Mr. Payne."

Victor's face contorted, but he ultimately agreed that it was true.

Isabelle slipped a piece of paper onto the |judge's desk without a word. It was the freedom paper she'd written up early that morning, for Victor to sign.

"What does it say?" Victor asked the judge.

"It says that Isaac has been emancipated from slavery. From now on, he will be free and under the care and guardianship of Alden Payne."

Victor drew an X across the bottom line. Then he reached for Isabelle's arm, and she cringed as he led her toward the door.

Alden was close on her heels, reaching for her as well. "You can't do this."

"I must," she said, shaking him off. "Tell Isaac to use the key I gave him."

Alden stepped in front of Victor. "I'm not letting you leave."

Victor smirked. "I'll deal with you later."

Alden glanced back at the judge. "This isn't right."

"Step away from him, Mr. Payne," the judge commanded.

"Not until he releases Miss Labrie."

Instead of responding, Judge Roth nodded toward the other two men in the room. They flanked Alden, each of them taking an arm and pinning it behind him. He wrestled against the men as Victor moved around him, shoving Isabelle toward the door.

The judge sighed, pointing toward the wall. "Take him to the jail."

Isabelle braced herself against the doorpost. "But he's supposed to take care of Isaac."

"He'll only be in jail until you and Mr. Duvall leave town."

As Alden struggled to break free, she glimpsed the sorrow in his eyes, a rawness that spoke of fear. And a tender love.

She closed her eyes as Victor pushed her into the street, the image of Alden embedded into her mind. Her heart.

Alden did care for her, in spite of her past. More than she could ever have dreamed.

She'd cling to that picture of his love for the rest of her life.

Chapter 45

Columbia
August 1854

Brandy burned the lining of Victor's throat, inflaming his stomach, but it didn't stop the pounding in his head. The last two silver dimes in his wallet were spent and still there was no relief for his pain.

After all these years, Mallie was finally his, yet she wasn't as he remembered. The beauty remained, flourished even, but her respect for him was gone.

She'd fought him back in her hotel room, giving him a lump behind his ear. He'd wrestled her down and tied her to the post of her bed, threatening all manner of things if she screamed again, not the least of which was kidnapping Isaac if she didn't cooperate. He was still stronger than she—and a good inch taller—but she defied him with eyes that used to fear him, eyes now filled with disgust instead of awe.

And those eyes reminded him of Eliza.

He'd go back to the hotel room when the darkness came, after the brandy cured his head. Then he wouldn't care one whit about Mallie's eyes. He'd teach her to revere him again, and she wouldn't be able to fight back this time. Nor could she drain his power away. No matter what she did, he would remain in control.

When he was finished, Mallie would call him master again.

He took another swig.

Captain Ahab had triumphed in darting his whale before Moby-Dick took him down, but there was no victory for Victor yet. Nor was there any money left to take Mallie and Isaac on a coach back to Sacramento. He'd searched her hotel room for an hour, but all he found were two measly dimes.

If Eliza were here, she'd be laughing at him again. Was Mallie laughing too?

A new hatred began to burn inside him with the brandy.

He'd loved Mallie with his entire heart, doing everything to provide for her, love her, and she was laughing at him. Mocking him because of his ragged clothing, his incompetence. Because he couldn't read.

No one laughed at Victor Duvall.

Mallie was his, and she would pay for her scorn.

As he stood up from the bar stool, the tables and mirrors around him began to spin. Even the chandelier overhead rocked back and forth.

A man wearing a long overcoat slid onto the stool beside him. "It looks like you need another one," he said.

Victor dumped his wallet onto the counter. "I've used up all my resources."

When the man clapped him on the shoulder, Victor teetered back onto the stool. "I'll buy you another."

His new friend told him stories about his adventures and laughed at jokes that Victor didn't find funny. But he drank a third brandy on the man's bill. Then a fourth.

And suddenly nothing seemed to matter anymore.

Alden raked his hands through his hair, pacing alongside the wooden bench in the jail cell. The light had faded outside the barred windows, and a dank air settled over the bricks around him.

Back in the courtroom, he'd ripped off the bridle of restraint, trying to protect Isabelle, and now there was nothing he could do to help. He'd lose her too, just like he'd lost Benjamin.

He slapped his hand on the bricks.

Isabelle never should have agreed to return to slavery without consulting him first. They could have fought this together. With the money from his gold nugget, he could have convinced Victor to sell Isaac, like he and Stephan had done for Persila.

But once Isabelle offered herself, no amount of money would motivate Victor. A nugget of gold may pay for room and board and buy nice clothing and decent passage on a ship, but it wouldn't resolve this.

He clenched the iron bars on the door and shook them. He'd tried to pick the lock from the inside, like he'd done with his father's desk, but he needed a hairpin or needle to do it. The jailer had made sure he had neither.

He sank down to the bench, his head in his hands as despair filtered through the darkness, its talons piercing him. He had to stop Victor before he took Isabelle away, but he was useless as long as he was trapped in this cell.

Minutes passed and then another hour before lantern light trickled down the dirt path outside the cell. Then he saw a familiar face on the other side of the bars, a man smiling between his mustache and spade beard.

Judah Fallow had come at last, but after all this, Alden wanted to thrash him. "I've been looking all over for you!"

"I've been all over," Judah replied. "I heard you might need some help with the law."

"I wish you'd heard that news yesterday." Alden folded his arms over his chest. "The law here didn't do me or my client any favors."

"Clearly." Judah held up his lantern to look into the cell. "At least you've got the place to yourself."

After Alden told him what had happened in the courtroom, Judah groaned. "We sing about this sweet land of liberty, and yet the liberty is only sweet for a portion of our citizens."

"I'm terrified that Victor will kill Isabelle."

"If Judge Roth won't serve justice, then we'll have to serve it ourselves."

"She won't leave Victor," he said. "She's protecting Isaac from him."

"Then Victor will have to leave her."

Alden shook his head. "He'd never do that."

"I happen to know that your Mr. Duvall is at a saloon across town this evening, drinking away what seem to be his sorrows with an associate of mine."

Alden wrapped his fingers around the bars again. "But Victor got exactly what he wanted today."

"Getting what we want doesn't always make us happy."

"Can you help me secure his passage back to Boston?" Alden pleaded. "I have enough gold to pay for it."

"Keep your gold. As long as you make good on working for me back in Sacramento, that is."

"I'll gladly work for you."

Judah glanced back at the door. "The jailer will be here in a moment. I told the judge that Mr. Duvall is on his way out of town and that I'd keep my eye on you for the rest of the night."

Hope flooded him again. Perhaps it wasn't too late after all.

"Do you know where Isabelle is?" Judah asked. "I'll find her."

"Before we send him off, let's have a chat with your Mr. Duvall to make sure he won't bother her again."

Chapter 46

Columbia
August 1854

Darkness crushed Victor's head, and he struggled to breathe. Under his cheek was dirt. Grass.

He wrestled against the cuff of blackness, trying to open his eyes. But there was no light. Not enough air to fill his lungs.

Where was his friend from the saloon? The one who'd helped his headache go away.

He needed another brandy. Just one more sip to stop the pain.

He tried to push away from the dirt, but someone pressed a hand against his shoulder, pinning him to the ground.

"Don't move, Victor."

"Alden?" he slurred. Eyes forced open, he turned and saw fury raining down on him.

"Where is she?" Alden demanded.

He shut his eyes again. "You're in jail."

"Not anymore. Where's Isabelle?"

His entire body spun when he tried to lift his head. "Waiting for me."

There were others now on both sides of Alden, staring down at him. They rolled him over on the dirt and wrapped something tight around his wrists. He smelled hemp, like the rope that trapped Captain Ahab. Were they planning to toss him into the sea? If only he had his knife—

Alden shook his arm. "Where is she?"

His laugh sounded more like a gurgle. Alden still wanted Mallie, but he couldn't have her. None of these men could.

They lifted him off the dirt, and his head banged against something hard when they tossed him onto a wood platform. Then something else jabbed his neck. Straw. He started to itch.

Alden was in his face again. "Did you take her to a new hotel?"

"No—untie these ropes."

"You're not in a position to negotiate," Alden said.

Someone poured another drink into his mouth, and he welcomed the heat. Hopefully it would dull the pain.

"She's not in her room," Victor said.

"I know that."

Words then slipped out of his mouth in the muddle of darkness, against Victor's will. "She's next door."

• • •

No one answered Alden's persistent knock, but the lock on the hotel room door didn't stop him. He borrowed a nail from behind an oil painting in the parlor and picked it.

Isabelle's hands were tied over her head against the bedpost, her bare feet secured at the bottom. One of her eyes was swollen shut, and her cheek was mottled with purple and blue. A bandana was stuffed into her mouth, and the sleeve on her dress was shredded, as if she'd tried over and over to release herself from her bonds.

And she was so still. Like Benjamin.

His chest clenched as he stood over her with his lantern, blood boiling inside him.

Please save her, he prayed. He couldn't bear to lose someone else he loved.

And he knew it then, as he cut the rope off her wrists. He loved Isabelle Labrie with his entire heart. Loved her strength and her courage. Loved her willingness to risk her life to save someone else. Loved her resilience to overcome her past as she pressed boldly into the future.

He gently massaged the rope burns on her arms, begging God to breathe life back into her. Then he propped her head up on a pillow before cutting the leather strips that bound her legs. With water from the basin, he carefully cleaned her wounds. She moaned at his touch but didn't open her eyes.

"Isabelle," he whispered, easing back her hair.

She moaned again when he dabbed the water on the cut above her eye. Slowly, she opened her good eye, and when she saw him, she flinched. "You're not supposed to be here, Alden."

"I had to find you."

"Victor will kill you when he returns."

He leaned away from her, grateful to hear her voice. "Victor isn't going to find me."

"He'll come back," she whispered.

He shook his head. "Not this time."

She closed her eye and then opened it again. "Where's Isaac?"

He nodded toward the window. "In my room."

At least, he hoped that Isaac was still there, reading the book he'd started when Alden left for court this morning.

"You should stay with him until Victor and I are gone."

He lifted her from the bed, holding her close to him. "You're not going anywhere with Victor."

"It's too late."

He shook his head. "I'm not going to let him touch you again."

He extinguished the lantern, and she rested her head on his chest as he walked down the steps of the hotel, out into the street. A crowd of miners, loitering outside a saloon, glanced over.

When one of the men stepped forward, Alden

hung his head, seemingly disappointed. "Too much to drink."

The men left them alone.

Instead of taking Isabelle up into his room, Alden carried her toward the edge of town. There, he found Judah and his friends still waiting in the darkness.

"Isabelle," Alden prompted, nudging her hair with his forehead. "Please wake up."

She groaned again before lifting her head. Judah raised the lantern, and she opened her good eye wide enough to see Victor lying in the farm wagon, his arms and legs bound together.

"They're going to escort him all the way to San Francisco," Alden said. "A colleague there is looking for a deckhand willing to go east."

"He won't work," Isabelle whispered.

"The captain of the ship will make sure he earns his keep."

Judah stepped forward to close the end gate on the wagon, but Isabelle stopped him, reaching out her hand. "Please let me."

Alden stepped closer, and with Judah's help, Isabelle raised and locked the wooden gate.

"What are you doing?" Someone asked behind them, and he turned to see Isaac, staring up at him in the light of a kerosene lamp.

"You're supposed to stay in the room," Alden scolded.

"I've been wandering around all evening,

looking for both of you." He eyed Isabelle resting in Alden's arms. "Why won't you tell me what's happening?"

Alden nodded toward the wagon, and Isaac leaned forward to peek over the edge. Then his eyes grew wide. "Is that Master Duvall?"

Alden nodded.

"Is he dead?"

"No, just drunk. He won't ever bother you or Isabelle again."

Judah climbed onto wagon bench. "I'll see you back in Sacramento."

Alden nodded. "We'll return as soon as we can travel."

With the money from his gold find, he had more than enough to leave tomorrow, but he'd stay here until Isabelle's body healed. And then if she would have him, he hoped she might accept his proposal to legally become Mrs. Payne.

The three of them listened to the rattle of wheels across the rocks, bustling away from Columbia. Judah, he was certain, would make sure that Victor never bothered them again.

Isaac lifted his lantern. "Good-bye, Master Duvall," he whispered.

Alden turned, and when he looked down at the boy, he saw gold flecks amidst the brown of his eyes, reflecting in the light.

His mouth dropped open. He'd looked at the boy a thousand times in the past months, but he hadn't really noticed the color of his eyes. Isaac wasn't just a fellow slave owned by the Duvall family. Isaac was Isabelle's son.

No wonder she would do anything to rescue him, like Naomi trying to rescue Benjamin. Did Isabelle think he would condemn her for this?

Her eyes had closed again as she rested against him.

"You're free," Alden told Isaac. "Victor signed the papers."

"Completely free?"

"Forever," he replied. "Both of you are free."

Isabelle lifted her head a few inches. "I have something I'd like to say."

"You can say anything you want now."

Isaac took her hand. "Can you say it to me too?"

"Absolutely," she said quietly. "I want to tell you first."

Chapter 47

Columbia
August 1854

Every bone in Isabelle's body ached, but her heart was full. Alden had somehow acquired a dozen pillows, and he'd propped her up on all of them so she could rest while they talked. Then he brought over her lockbox and papers and the clothing left in the hotel room across the street.

Victor had assaulted her body, but it was the oddest thing. All the fear she'd had pent up inside her had dissipated earlier that day. As an adult, in the light of truth, she finally saw Victor Duvall for what he really was—a bitter, troubled, controlling man who would never be happy, no matter how many slaves he acquired for his kingdom.

A man who no longer held any power over her.

After Alden left to retrieve the last of her things, Isaac hopped onto the end of the bed. "Can we talk now?"

"Certainly." She smiled. "If you'll do me a favor."

"What is it?"

"Somewhere in the stack of things Alden brought over is a special blanket."

He searched through the pile until he found it, and she held her memories on her lap, stitched together with teal and ivory.

"Isaac,"—she took a deep breath—"I'm afraid your mother wasn't a princess. Nor did she run away with another slave."

He eyed her curiously. "How do you know?"

Tears began filling her eyes again. She prayed he wouldn't reject her when he discovered the truth. "Because I'm your mother. I birthed you when I was fourteen."

He inched closer to her, studying her face in confusion. "You're my mother?"

Isabelle braced herself for his disappointment. "I'm so sorry."

He swung his arms around her neck, hugging her. "I'm not sorry." Then he stepped away, concern draining away his grin. "Did I hurt you?"

"You haven't hurt me at all." Instead, joy washed over her pain, flooding the channels of grief carved inside her. "I never meant to leave you. Mrs. Duvall told me you were dead."

Isaac shook his head. "She's a wicked woman."

"I believe you're right." She held out the blanket. "I made this for you, before you were born."

He reached out his hand slowly. Reverently. "You made it for me?"

When she nodded, he clutched it to his chest. "No one's ever made anything just for me before."

"I'd like to make you lots of things in the future."

"You don't have to make me anything else." He looked down at the blanket as if it were crocheted with strands of gold. "I always wanted to have a mother just like you."

She leaned forward to kiss his cheek. "And I could not be prouder to have you as my son."

When she pulled him close to her again, all the years lost between them seemed to disappear into tears and laughter.

Minutes later, Alden stepped back into the room, carrying her valise filled with sundries. He glanced at the two of them. "You're both smiling."

"We've been talking," Isaac said, scooting away.

She wanted to reach for him, as if he might vanish again, but he knew the truth now and wanted to stay with her.

Alden searched her face. "I see."

Isaac hopped off the bed. "Miss Labrie is my mother."

Alden smiled with them. "I know."

"How did you know?" Isabelle asked.

"Your eyes."

Isabelle clasped her hands together. "I have a proposition to make."

Alden set the bag on the dressing table and collapsed into a chair. "I don't know if I can handle any more propositions."

"It's an important one," she said. "Instead of going back to Sacramento, I've decided to go to Vancouver Island with the other freed slaves. And I—I would like to take Isaac with me."

Alden leaned toward her. "You don't have to worry about Victor. Judah will make sure he's on that ship going east."

"But he might return one day, and if he did— I can't bear to think of him taking back my son."

Isaac crossed his arms. "I think the three of us need to stick together. Here in California."

Alden nodded. "I agree."

But Alden didn't mean it. One day he would meet a woman whom he'd want to marry. He wouldn't want to be burdened with her too. "In Victor's eyes—and others here—Isaac and I will always be slaves."

"I don't see a slave when I look at either of you," Alden said, glancing at both of them. "In Isaac, I see a boy who is smart and kind and funny. He's one of the hardest-working fellows I know and a faithful friend."

Her heart pounded as his gaze settled on her again. "When I look at you, Isabelle, I see a beautiful, genteel woman who is capable and strong. A woman I'd be deeply honored to have as my wife."

She drank in Alden's words, savoring every one, but she couldn't allow him to give up his future for her. "You don't have to be a martyr, Alden."

"A martyr?" His eyebrows climbed with his question, and then he left his chair, sitting on the bed beside her. "I don't think you understand."

"But I do—"

He turned back toward Isaac. "Do you mind if we have a moment?"

Isaac groaned. "You never let me stay around for the important things."

"I actually need your help." He leaned down beside him, whispering as if she couldn't hear. "Right now, I need a moment to convince your mother to marry me."

Isaac eyed Alden. Then he picked up his book.

"I suppose I can read a few more pages in the parlor, but don't take all night. She and I have a lot of catching up to do."

He closed the door behind him, and Alden took her hand.

"Isabelle." He knelt before her. "My love for you is stronger than the quartz threaded through these mountains, and it's as endless as the gold embedded in them. If you don't feel the same about me, I understand, but if you do, it would be the greatest privilege for me to be your husband."

"I have Negro blood running through me," she reminded him, as if he'd forgotten. She might be proud of her ancestry, but every child they had, if they had any children, could have Isaac's brown skin.

"I love you and every ounce of blood flowing through your veins." He took her hand. "I will care for Isaac as my son and any other children that God may bless us with."

As she pulled his hand close to her heart, she smiled. "Then I would be honored to be your wife as well."

Her face warmed as he leaned closer to her, whispering. "I don't want either of us to hide in the shadows anymore."

When he kissed her, the storm raging through her began to settle, her heart finding calm in the safety of his affection. Even the pain from her wounds was soothed in his love.

Isaac cleared his throat by the door. "Are you two done yet?"

"Not exactly." Alden stepped away, but his gaze was still locked on her.

"I'm hungry for oysters."

They all laughed. "I suppose we could find some in this town," Alden said.

Isaac's nose crinkled. "I sure hope you don't keep kissing like that."

Alden put his arm around Isaac's shoulders. Then he glanced back over his shoulder like a kid, conspiring with her in his wink.

She closed her eye again as she rested back against the pillows.

Mother. Wife. Guardian of truth and light. She would step boldly into this new life, embracing the love of her family and these beautiful new names.

No longer was she alone.

Epilogue

The steam from Isabelle's cup swelled as she added a spoonful of clover honey to her tea. Leaning back in her upholstered chair, she glanced over the empty dining room of the Golden Rose, the hotel renamed in memory of Uncle William and Aunt Emeline's daughter. After the rush of the breakfast meal, the room was at peace, the scent of summer flowers drifting over the new piano and the white-clothed tables.

So much had changed in the past three years since she and Alden married in the floral gardens outside town—with Sing Ye as her matron of honor, and Isaac standing proudly as Alden's best man.

Judah had waved good-bye to Victor and his brig as it departed San Francisco. Then he returned to Sacramento to preside over the Paynes' wedding ceremony on a Saturday afternoon. The following Monday, Alden joined his law practice.

At the end of 1854, Alden passed the bar exam before the Supreme Court and had since appeared before Judge Snyder with multiple cases for Fallow & Payne, many of them in his quest for abolition.

Alden had rescued her back in Columbia, and he'd asked nothing of her, patiently waiting as her wounds healed. And he was still patient as Isabelle embraced her role as a beloved wife and mother. Aunt Emeline would be so pleased. She had married a man who knew her fully and loved her for exactly who she was. And every day, she had the privilege of caring for her son.

It had taken six months for their family to restore the hotel, but Isaac enjoyed his job as steward, and she resumed her work as proprietor and maître d'. Alden had hidden the gold nugget he and Isaac discovered—waiting, he said, for its purpose to find them. She'd spent part of her savings on the court fines for harboring Persila; the rest had gone to the hotel restoration and buying finery like silk tablecloths, eggshell china, and gilded mirrors. But it was worth it. She'd once thought Sacramentans wouldn't frequent her doors when they found out she'd been a slave, but they continued to come. In droves. Even Mr. Walsh continued eating here every night when he wasn't in the mines.

Laws about fugitive slaves continued to change. Judah's safe house—where Stephan hid Micah—had burned down during the fire, but she and Alden continued to harbor runaway slaves in the room below her desk. Rodney had left the city a year ago to try his hand in the mines, and the new sheriff pretended to be inept when it came to searching for runaways.

Isaac was her companion every evening while Alden worked, helping her serve the many customers who frequented the dining room. During the day, he had achieved his dream of attending school. While colored children still weren't permitted in the common schools, a young woman from England had moved to Sacramento last year and started a school for Isaac and thirteen other black students. They were pioneers in their own way, planking a new road for the free blacks who continued coming to California in search of freedom.

The East Coast papers talked about a coming war between the Northern and Southern states, a fight to give liberty to those still enslaved. If that happened, Judah and Alden weren't sure what would happen in California, as it stretched from the southern tip of their country up to the territory of Oregon. Some talked of splitting their state in half—a free Northern state and a Southern state for slave owners—but she continued to pray that freedom would come to every man, woman, and child who lived in their country.

Persila had written several times from Vancouver Island, giving her regular updates about Micah, whom she and Stephan had adopted as their son. Each time Isabelle heard of more free blacks moving north, she thought about asking Alden if they could join them, but God seemed to bind the Payne family to Sacramento for now.

Still, she watched the paddle wheelers coming into the wharf with trepidation, beating back the fear that sometimes flared in her heart. If Victor attempted to take her again, he would be the one tried for kidnapping. Both her emancipation paper and the one he'd signed to free Isaac were stored safely away in Judah and Alden's office.

The door to their private rooms opened, and Alden stepped into the dining room. He'd stayed late at the office last night, preparing for a case.

"Good morning," he said, kissing her.

She smiled as she poured him a cup of green tea, savoring once again the realization that Alden Payne loved her as much as she loved him.

Then she offered him some sugar.

He took a sip of the sweet drink. "I saw Ross Kirtland when I was coming home last night."

"Indeed?"

"He wanted me to pass along his greetings."

She traced her finger around the handle of her cup. The last she heard, Fanny had returned east, and Ross was operating another boardinghouse someplace outside town. Turned out, he had also proposed marriage to a woman who operated a haberdashery in Marysville. Once Fanny was gone, the new Mrs. Kirtland moved to Sacramento.

"He also asked if I thought you would ever consider selling the hotel."

She shook her head. "I'm not selling anytime soon."

Her husband's smile renewed the joy in her heart. "I already told him."

She motioned toward the small stack of envelopes by the teapot. "Isaac retrieved the mail before school."

Alden picked up the top letter and looked at the address. She already knew who it was from —Rhody Payne, Alden's youngest sister. Her husband read the letter as she perused the headlines of the *Sacramento Union*.

"My father passed away," he said.

"I'm sorry." She reached forward to take his hand. "Are you sad that you didn't get to see him again?"

"I wish I missed him, but no." He tapped the letter on the table. "He left Rhody the plantation and all the slaves."

"Victor must be furious."

"Rhody said that she invited Victor and Eliza to live with her and Mother, but only Eliza came."

"Did she say anything about Naomi?"

He shook his head. "I will write her back today and ask."

"Perhaps Naomi would like to come to California."

He smiled again. "Perhaps."

"Look at this," Isabelle said, pointing at the advertisement in the paper. "A slave girl is being auctioned off this afternoon, outside the Southern Hotel. The owner is asking eight hundred dollars."

"That's the girl I'm defending this morning in court."

"I don't understand how Judge Snyder can justify auctioning off slaves in a free state."

"If we don't win this case . . ." Alden took a sip of his tea. "Perhaps it's time to sell our nugget and put eight hundred dollars of it to good use."

She smiled. "Isaac would approve."

"No matter what happens in court, we'll win today."

She touched her shoulder as he spoke. The rose used to remind her of death, but now it reminded her of the delicate blooming of renewal. New life.

And the beauty of freedom—the greatest gift of all.

Author's Note

I've been fascinated by stories of the Underground Railroad since I was a child growing up in a small Ohio town where residents once harbored runaway slaves. Until recently, I didn't realize that freed slaves—along with abolitionist lawyers who fought alongside them—organized a movement in California to help runaways find freedom as well.

Even though California technically became a free state in 1850, it's estimated that there were between five hundred and six hundred slaves working in the mines during the gold rush. Slavery was a hotly contested issue in California for the next decade, and I read multiple accounts of the Fugitive Slave Act being tested in the courts as judges and lawyers tried to interpret contradictory federal and state laws.

In 1854, for example, a former slave by the name of Stephen Hill was kidnapped from his home near Columbia. His deed of manumission had disappeared, and because Mr. Hill was not permitted by law to testify about his freedom, an agent sent by his former master won the court case that remanded Mr. Hill back to slavery. The agent took Mr. Hill to Stockton and held him in chains on a steamer while he gambled and drank. During the night, neighbors of Mr. Hill swept in and stole him away. There is no record of what happened to Mr. Hill after his rescue. I suspect his friends took him up to Vancouver Island.

Four years later, a runaway slave by the name of Archy Lee hid at the Hackett House in Sacramento, a hotel run by two African American men who were leaders in the free Negro movement. The wrangling in this case resulted in the arrest of both Lee and his owner, but on April 14, 1858, the courts declared Archy Lee free. He left for Vancouver Island as well.

The state of California and the entire West changed dramatically between the years of 849 and 1858, and I've tried to remain as historically accurate as possible to that era. This novel was inspired in part by the stories of Mary Ellen Pleasant, a light-skinned former slave and wealthy boardinghouse owner in San Francisco who helped fugitive slaves. Little is known about the Hackett House, but this safe haven inspired Isabelle's hotel.

While most of the mining towns in the Sierra foothills are gone, the historic town of Columbia is thriving as a state park, and many of the old brick buildings are still intact. The inspiration for the hidden room in the Golden Hotel came during a tour in Columbia when a child pointed out the crack in the outside wall between the bank and building next door. Our guide said it was a narrow room where the original owner could hide his gold and escape out a secret entrance in the back.

If you visit Old Sacramento today, you'll discover a labyrinth of abandoned rooms hidden under the street, left behind from the 1850s before the city began the immense task of elevating all the buildings to prevent flooding. Stepping under the brick archways, through these underground rooms, is like stepping back a hundred and fifty years.

I relied on a number of experts and resources as I researched this story—any errors are my fault. A special thank-you to:

The amazing librarians at the California State Library in Sacramento—Marianne Leach, Kathleen Correia, Karen Paige, and Elena Smith—and their support staff for helping me find old journals, newspaper articles, and other documents written during the gold rush era.

Shawn Turner at the Sacramento History Museum for escorting me through streets of Old Sacramento and down into the underground. Bob Holton, a history writer from Sonora, who shared stories about the freed slaves who lived around Columbia before the Civil War and educated me on the prejudices that people of different ethnic backgrounds faced. Thank you to Janet Lee Turner as well for connecting me with Bob.

Julie Thomas, the special collections librarian at California State University, Sacramento, for her gracious direction. CSU Sacramento's collection about California's Underground Railroad, a collaborative project directed by the late Joe Moore, inspired the heart of this story.

Dolores with California State Parks, the volunteers at the Columbia Museum, and Diane at the Tuolumne County Museum for answering my many questions. Pinn Crawford—my research partner—for once again helping me locate a mound of books. And my critique partners— Nicole Miller, Dawn Shipman, and Kelly Chang —for helping me stay on track and editing my work.

My dear sistas—Ann Menke, Jodi Stilp, Diane Comer, Julie Kohl, and Mary Kay Taylor—for your prayers and love. Michelle Heath—my amazing first reader—for the gift of your insight and encouragement.

My agent, Natasha Kern, and my editors, Erin Calligan Mooney and Jennifer Lawler, for all your support. It's such a joy to work with each of you!

My entire family, including my parents, Jim and Lyn Beroth, for your encouragement and prayers—and to Lyn, an amazing sleuth, for helping me hunt down information about the Hacketts.

My husband, Jon, and my daughters, Karlyn and

Kinzel, for venturing down to gold rush country with me the week before Christmas and for celebrating Christmas Eve on the way home in a snowstorm. I treasure each one of you and am so grateful to be on this adventure of life as a family.

And to our Creator God, who gives the gift of freedom to every man and woman. Psalm 57:1 says we can find refuge in the shadow of his wings.

With joy,
Melanie
www.melaniedobson.com

Book Club Questions

1. Each of the main characters in *Beneath a Golden Veil* valued freedom for themselves, though not all the characters valued freedom for men and women of African descent. How did those who supported slavery justify it as a necessary institution?

2. Isabelle referred to California as a haven for people to hide, but her own past eventually caught up with her. Do you think it's possible for someone to truly hide from the past?

3. Alden opposed slavery, but at the beginning of the novel, he felt as if there was nothing he could do to oppose or change it on his family's plantation. How did his anger and opposition to slavery impact his life and those around him?

4. While Isabelle wrestled with guilt and pain from her past, Emeline saw her as a beautiful, intelligent woman with hope for the future. What was the difference between Isabelle's core identity and how she perceived herself? How did a new name and clothing along with Emeline's love help Isabelle begin to see herself in a different way?

5. One of Isabelle's greatest struggles was keeping her past secret even as she helped other runaway slaves escape. If you were Isabelle, would you have kept your past a secret?

6. The issue of slavery divided the United| States of America in the 1800s. What moral issues today divide our communities? How do you fight for what you believe is right?

7. Victor had a warped perspective of admiration and love. How did his obsession with controlling Isaac and then Mallie lead to his demise?

8. The manumission paper was a simple document that had the power to change a slave's life and future. How have words—spoken or written—changed your life?

9. What is the significance of shadows and light in this story? How does Isabelle finally decide to embrace the light?

About the Author

Melanie Dobson has written fifteen historical, romance, and suspense novels—including *Chateau of Secrets* and *Shadows of Ladenbrooke Manor*—and three of her novels have won Carol Awards. Her first novel featuring the Underground Railroad, *Love Finds You in Liberty, Indiana*, won Best Novel of Indiana in 2010, and *The Black Cloister* was named *Foreword Reviews'* Religious Fiction Book of the Year in 2008.

"My desire," Melanie says, "is that the stories God has etched in my heart will give readers a glimpse of His love and grace, even when they don't understand His plan."

The former corporate publicity manager at Focus on the Family and owner of Dobson Media Group, Melanie now writes full time. She and her husband, Jon, and their two daughters live near Portland, Oregon, where they enjoy hiking and camping on the coast and in the mountains of the Pacific Northwest. When she isn't hiking, practicing yoga, or reading with her girls, Melanie loves to explore old cemeteries and ghost towns.

Center Point Large Print
600 Brooks Road / PO Box 1
Thorndike, ME 04986-0001 USA

(207) 568-3717

US & Canada:
1 800 929-9108
www.centerpointlargeprint.com